BLACK SUNRISE

Book 1 of the Day Zero Trilogy

by
Brett Tompkins

*To my beloved zombie assault warrior
wife Michelle*

CHAPTER ONE

The crisp, cool air made the perfect spring morning in the streets of Reykjavik when I woke from a late night at the pub with my co-workers. I wasn't much of a drinking man after my attempted college years and had no interest in losing control. I was all about controlling the situation. My name is David Sangora. I was born in a small town outside of Dallas, Texas. My parents and I kept what some would call a professional relationship, as they were people of business and that's all they really understood it seemed. They were in the Real Estate market, which benefited me a nice home outside the metroplex. I was supposed to follow in their footsteps after college, but adventure to me was more important than a paycheck. Right now Iceland was providing that adventure; and the paycheck wasn't bad either.

The weather had been very nice in the bay since we arrived a week ago and I enjoyed working without a hangover, unlike the others at times. I managed to sip on a single pour of Iceland's popular single malt scotch all night while my co-workers swore they were going to drink the friendly pubs dry. They were leather skinned oil rig workers that were as tough as they come. I enjoyed the excitement of working around such characters, and they were a positive change when I left my dead end job behind a desk in north Texas. I wasn't satisfied with settling down in the town I called home since birth. Aquafex Petroleum Innovations was hiring out of Galveston for travel available young men ambitious to earn money, could work long hours, and wanted to see the world. I kept my two bedroom house in a suburb of Dallas and went straight to work for Aquafex on a rig. The time spent out at sea meant a lot of solitude, but the extra pay was worth it. I'd been traveling with this charismatic bunch close to three years now, and had grown quite fond of my brothers on the rig. This trip to Iceland was the furthest we'd been from the usual drilling off the southern coast of Texas.

Aquafex worked with a sister company in Iceland for a surge of oil production to really put them ahead in the oil business.

The morning was mature enough to heat up the salty air and it felt good to feel the breeze as I stepped out the front door of my motel room. Aside from the occasional passing truck, the air was calm and peaceful as I leaned against the doorframe, sipping my coffee and analyzing the local town photos in the newspaper. I couldn't speak a word of the island's language other than 'hello'and 'please forgive my friends'. A slow creak of door hinges broke the tranquility as my good friend, a burly man named Jake grunted as the sun hit his face. Jake was a monster of a man with a big heart. He was hired on with me, and we were friends ever since. His light shaggy hair dangled in front of dark sunglasses as he scratched at his beard. I could really count on him when everything started hitting the fan.

"Why are you up so early? You know we have the day off right?" Jake groaned.

I grinned at my friend's subtle plea for relief.

"I'm just enjoying a cup of coffee, trying to understand this gibberish," motioning to the newspaper.

"Last night got a little crazy dude." Jake said a little more awake this time.

"You looked like you were having a blast Jake, flirting with that blonde all night."

Before I could finish a beautiful brunette dressed in last night's black cocktail dress stepped out of Jake's room, gave him a kiss on the cheek, said something in a sexy, sultry voice, and then walked to a red convertible parked nearby. We both watched her swagger back and forth as she approached the car door. I looked at Jake as he displayed an ear to ear grin of accomplishment to the previous night's conquest.

"You lucky bastard."

His grin grew even bigger as the mentioned blonde ran out of his room still putting her shirt on as she opened the passenger door to the red convertible and waved Jake goodbye.

"Want to grab some breakfast?" he said still grinning.

"Yeah I bet you're hungry. Get dressed and I'll get Tommy. We'll let the others sleep."

Tommy Durant was the third member to our clan. A tall, stout black man with curly hair and a friendly smile, he was always a hard worker but knew how to have a good time. I went back inside my room, tossed the newspaper on the counter and poured my mug of motel coffee down the drain. I picked up my favorite faded blue jeans off the floor and quickly slid into them. My faded John Deere shirt was waded up on the floor, but separate from the dirty clothes. *It's still good* I thought as I gave it a good sniff. I wrestled the shirt on and slipped into my boots, grabbed my keys and wallet and I was out the door. Just as I shut the door I remembered my cell phone on the bedside table.

Better not forget that.

On my way to Tommy's room I couldn't help but notice how busy the area had gotten by 8 a.m. on a Saturday morning. This was a major seaport city, but it was the weekend, and in the least the locals could sleep in another hour or two. After all, I didn't want to wait for breakfast. I knocked firmly on Tommy's door with authority. Inside I heard someone stumble, quietly cuss the noise at the door, then Tommy threw the door open. His face went from concerned to not amused quickly.

"Shit man knockin' like you the damn police. What's the matter with you?"   "Hey bud Jake and I are going out for breakfast, you wanna go?" trying to avoid his grumpiness.

"Yeah let me throw on some clothes. Did Jake go home with that blonde?"

"Yeah I'm sure he'll tell you all about it. C'mon I'm hungry."

Tommy threw on a collared gray shirt and jeans and made his way out the door. We walked to the white beat up Chevrolet truck they were issued by the company to drive around town

4

when we weren't out to sea on the derricks. Jake was standing by the driver's side door straightening his hair with his hands looking into the side mirror. He already had the truck running with the radio a little loud for the morning air.

"Hey look at you sunshine!" Jake bellowed out as Tommy walked up.

"You must have had a good night. I woke up and saw David's ugly mug this morning."

"Yeah, WE had a blast. I'll tell you all about it over some bacon and eggs."

As Tommy hopped in the backseat, I climbed into the passenger's seat and immediately turned the radio down.

"There's a little café right around the block that always smells good. Why don't we try it?"

Jake settled in behind the wheel, checked himself out in the rear view mirror, and started backing out.

"Ease up brother" Jake replied. "We're in a foreign country, and the women sure know how to party."

The streets were bustling with activity. Saturday morning shoppers were out with their families, going from shop to shop carrying little bags labeled with the stores' names on the sides. *What a pleasant community* I thought. The heritage of this country is displayed through the old world architecture. The little friendly shop keepers sweeping their entrance, greeting every passerby with a warm smile.

"This place is really relaxing."

With one hand on the steering wheel Jake gave me his pitch.

"You should cut loose with us sometime David. I mean really experience the place. Drink more than one drink, and talk to a stranger that's not serving you those drinks. Hell, take one of these pretty ladies home with you."

I took a minute to let Jake's comments really sink in, almost like it was permission to have fun.

"We always have tonight. I tell you what Jake, I'll have enough drinks to loosen up, if you can introduce me to one of your lady friends tonight."

Tommy got excited by the idea "Hell yeah! My boy's gonna get wrecked tonight!"

I gave him a half smile.

"Fuckin A dude" Jake smiled satisfied.

We pulled into the parking lot of the café and instantly the smell of eggs and pancakes filled our nostrils. Tommy gave a hum of delight as we parked. Walking to the door I noticed the smiles of satisfaction on the faces of the customers leaving the café. *It's going to be a good day.* A young waitress with a pretty smile greeted us at the door, she spoke decent English, immediately recognizing us as foreigners. She led us to a booth along the wall, I was quick to get a window seat to see the bay, but also so I could see everyone in the café. The waitress introduced herself as she passed out menus, I was somewhat regretful that I didn't catch her name. I probably couldn't have said it right anyway.

"Let's check out the strip today," Jake began.

"I need a new shirt, especially if I'm going to be a good wingman tonight," as he playfully elbowed me. He ordered an orange juice, and before the waitress could ask Tommy for his drink order he called out.

"A big glass of grape juice" licking his lips. I humored at his selection.

"Grape drink eh?" Tommy's smile straightened quickly.

"You honkies don't know anything about good taste. Get your boring water man." I chuckled, and ordered my water.

As Jake began telling Tommy about his bedroom fun after the pub, I peered out the window to admire the glistening blue waters of the bay. It seemed like every boat that was tied off yesterday was out in the water for a Saturday outing. There were boats of all styles and sizes. There were sailboats tipping back and forth, fast motorboats speeding past them, and even a few yachts. I interrupted Tommy's laughter.

6

"There sure are a lot of boats out today. Maybe we could go down to the cruiser and go out for a bit. It would be a good way to meet people."

Tommy gave me the straight look again.

"Nobody wants to see some good 'ol boys cruising around in a boat that takes them to work. That's not how you pick up women man. Besides, it's our day off. I don't want anything to do with that boat."

The waitress brought the drinks out and overheard the conversation.

"You have a boat?" she asked.

"As a matter of fact I do" Tommy stated with a grin. "It's a big ocean liner made to last."

The waitress showed slight amusement, then asked what they would like to order. Jake piped up excitedly about bacon and eggs, Tommy gave her a sweet smile ordering a stack of pancakes.

"I'll have what he's having" and pointed to Jake.

She smiled as she finished writing the order down and walked away.

"I thought the boat was a horrible idea" I smirked at Tommy. He was quick to reply.

"I don't think you will ever understand the game David."

We sipped on our drinks, discussing what to do for the day. Jake wanted to buy a new shirt, Tommy wanted to see the local attractions, but I went back to staring out the window. I spotted something dark on the horizon, heavily contrasted against the bright blue sky. Looking closer, it appeared to be smoke rising from a structure off the water. *Could that be a boat? Or worse, could it be an oil rig on fire?* The other crew was out today, and I'd never really met anybody on that shift, but what a horrible situation that would be. A few minutes passed as the structure just kept burning. I was trying to stay calm, but my mind was racing. The waitress broke my tension when she brought the food out. The aroma of fresh cooked eggs and bacon filled the air and I was now focused on the meal in front of me. *I'm sure if there was a real situation on the water the authorities would know what to do. It is a main seaport for this island.* The talking stopped and only the sounds of forks hitting plates could be heard at the table. Each of us was halfway through our meal when Jake's cell phone on his belt started to vibrate. He looked at the caller ID, hoping it was an acquaintance from the night before. His smile turned into disappointment.

"Work is calling. I wonder what they want?"

Now Tommy's phone was sounding off with a rowdy club song, his ring tone turned up. Jake looked at Tommy and his look confirmed it was also someone from the company calling. I suspected it, and sure enough my pocket began to vibrate. We gave each other the 'if you do it I'll do it' nod, and we answered our phones. Our jaws dropped at the same time.

"David, this is Sam. There's a raging fire on that abandoned oil derrick ten miles east of our site. We thought it was inactive, but apparently someone turned it into a laboratory of some sort and they sent out a distress signal early this morning. All available boats in the area are asked to assist with evacuation of the rig as soon as possible. Could you grab the guys and take the cruiser out there to help out?"

We looked at each other and silently agreed we must do it. We paid our checks, hustled to the truck and decided to drive straight to the docks. Once there, I realized why all the boats were out. It seemed as though every boat in the bay was going to rescue the workers on this rig. We met the rest of our crew at the boat, we boarded and untied. The boat picked up speed as we sped away to the smoke on the horizon.

After a thirty minute boat trip we arrived to the scene of the smoke. It was far from what we expected. There were dozens of boats circled around the rig, but they all appeared to be leaving. They weren't taking survivors back to the mainland, no two boats were going in the same direction. We gave each other the same confused look, but we were here to help. I wasn't sure how we were going to help. We didn't have the equipment to put out a large oil rig fire, and how could we get the boat close enough to dock and keep us safe from falling ash? It occurred to me now why things seemed so strange. There were no flames coming from the rig, just wisps of smoke. It stood tall out of the water, looming over us. The whole rig seemed black from charring, but not quite like fire damage. It was as if the fire burned hot as the sun for a few minutes and then put itself out. The rig was eerily still. There was no movement with the exception to a steel door that kept slamming in the wind. Tommy broke the silence.

"I thought we were here to help a burning rig. You need fire for a burning rig. There's nobody here, that's why the other boats left. Let's go back man."

The crew looked around at each other, halfway agreeing. Ted Johnson was the supervisor on board our boat, and although he didn't want too either, he said we must board the rig and look for survivors.
"I don't like it anymore than you Tommy. If it is an abandoned rig then it won't take us long to search it and get back on the boat. Everyone grab a flashlight."

We did as we were instructed, tied off to the rig, and one by one we collected on the scaffolding below the main deck. Now the rig took on a new level of eeriness. We were used to the bustling sounds of workers turning wrenches, and hammering out finicky pipeline. The rig was dead still. It swayed slightly from the waves, and the beams had a slight groan when a large wave would hit. We moved up the rickety stairs as we made our way to the main deck.
"Whose going to send a rescue for us when this damn thing falls apart?" Tommy asked, to anyone listening.

The crew circled up on the main deck beside a broken shipping container with bottled waters labeled *Genesis*, awaiting instructions from Ted who was reading the manifest of the crate.

"How ironic. This crate is addressed to go to FEMA."

There were a dozen of us, so we broke into groups of three and picked a direction to investigate and search for survivors. I took Jake and Tommy, we decided to move towards the cafeteria.

"Ted said this place used to be a floating laboratory?" Jake asked.

"Rumor has it" I replied, although not sure from the looks of things.

"If so maybe they left us some food" Jake said, hungry from not finishing breakfast.

We did a radio check with Ted to make sure they worked, and we opened the rusty outside doors to the dining hall. Tommy used a nearby broken section of pipe to prop the door open. As sunlight flooded the room, we could see the tables and chairs still out as if we came in during rush hour. There were trays on the table, some still had food on them. Everything looked as it should during a busy rush, except there were no people. We walked through the room, inspecting everything that could have been out of the ordinary. The food on the trays wasn't but a few hours old, and the beverage glasses weren't dusty or broken. It's as if we walked in and the people disappeared.

"What the hell is going on here?" Jake asked.

"Where are all the people? Why did they leave?"

We made our way back to the kitchen. To no surprise, everything looked to be in order. There were pans on the stove, trays in the oven. I flicked the power switch, but nothing came on.

"Looks like this whole wing doesn't have power."
I pulled the radio of my belt to call Ted.

"Ted do you have any electricity up there?"
I waited a moment, then the radio broke the silence of the empty room.

"No electricity here. I think the whole rig is out of power. I'm taking Darren and Vick with me down to the power station. We'll see if we can get some power up."

I called out for anyone who might still be on the rig, only to hear short echoes off the steel walls. We proceeded out of the kitchen down the empty halls to the medical facility. The only sounds heard were our boots clopping down the hallways. Turning a corner, Tommy's flashlight hit the walls of a medical room. Half of a red cross could be seen, but the rest of the wall was burned black as night. It was as if the paint was cooked off the walls.

"Oh Jesus." Tommy said.

"This place looks like it was cooked from the inside."
I found a closed door and wrapped my hand around the knob.

"It's still warm" I told the others.

The handle turned, but the door must have been dead bolted from the inside. Jake smiled with approval.

"Hehe, do it!"

I turned my shoulder down and threw it into the door, hearing the lock smash like fragile wood. The door opened easier than I thought, as I stumbled a bit tripping over myself. The room was charcoal black. There was a strong sulfur odor that burned our nostrils.

"It must have been a thousand degrees in here!" Jake said coughing.

Everything was ash, even the metal cabinets would crumble when touched. There was nothing in the room that could fuel a fire hot enough to do this. The radio crackled to life.

"Ted we need you on the third level. You need to see this." There was nothing left to see in the medical facility, so curiosity got the best of us and we decided to move up to the third level also. Ted came back on the radio.

"We've almost got the power back on, just a few more minutes. David can you take your team up there?"

I replied that we were already on our way. Everything we saw now was like the medical facility, black as could be and ashes everywhere. There were piles of ashes in the hallways, some in the rooms where the doors had been burned off the hinges. Maybe they were boxes, maybe they were some sort of equipment left laying around. We figured we were close to the center of the rig now, every hallway leading to a vertical shaft that was not an original installment on this platform. The steel was newer, kept in good shape, and very structurally sound. It must have been a part of some central hub, there were pipes in every hallway, in every room, coming from this shaft that were installed after the platform had been built.

"What do you think they were doing down here?" Tommy asked, a little hesitant wanting to know the truth.

"The medical facility was much bigger than anything we've ever used on a rig. Why would they need so much equipment?" Jake said, sifting through some of the ashes looking for clues.

"I'm not sure guys, but they found something up there so let's just get there, do what we gotta do and get the hell out. This place gives me the creeps."

A small shiver went down my spine as I said it. The stairwell was next to the central shaft, but had no pipes coming from it. It obviously hadn't been used often, the stairs were old and rusty, and made us a little uneasy to use them. Passing the second level we could see it looked just like the first. The walls were blackened, there were piles of ashes scattered about, and of course there were pipes coming from the central shaft. The third floor was no different as we met three other crew members standing outside a stainless steel door. Aside from a little soot on the door, no damage was taken from the blaze. One of them shone their flashlight on the door, to show me the last thing I wanted to see. There was a bright yellow biohazard sticker displayed on the door for easy recognition.

"Fuck me" Jake said turning away.

Not one of us really wanted to get into this, but we were still curious. Sarah, a tough as nails leatherneck, but the looks of a blonde beauty queen, asked me what I thought about it. I'd had a thing for her since she joined our shift.

"Sarah that's the last thing any of us want to see. We came here to help any survivors, let's just look around safely. The sooner we do, the sooner we leave."

She nodded in agreement, feeling a little better about the situation. A sudden loud crash on the other side of the door broke her long exhale, and startled us all.

"What the hell was that?" someone asked, after we'd all jumped.

The radio startled us once again as Ted's voice broke the silence.

"We found the problem, power should be coming on real soon."

After being so jumpy I was a little irritated.

"It took you that long to flip a switch?"

Ted was quick to reply to my outburst.

"Well it wasn't a damn switch Dave, we had to reboot the entire system. It's like the power was shut off when someone hit the fire alarm."

Weird, I thought, but maybe that was protocol when a large fire grew out of control to prevent any electrical fires. I'd heard of a back up system like that in large facilities in the States, but I thought it was still in the experimental phase. This door didn't have a turn knob. There was a large compression handle, much like that of a walk in freezer. I reached down and squeezed the handle. There was a loud hissing noise as the door popped open. Inside the lights were on, and there were no signs of charring. The six of us walked in and immediately noticed something else had happened here. There were computers thrown on the floor and papers everywhere, like a tornado went through this room. There was a soft beep that came from a single humming computer that hadn't been touched. It looked like it was booting up, but the screen read 'Fire Sale Operation in Effect' in the upper right hand in simple green letters.

"I had a computer like that when I was a kid" Jake stated, a little nostalgic.

"I'm sure this one's a little more advanced Jake" Sarah said matter-of-factly.

We all looked around and all at once noticed a pair of legs coming out from behind a desk. We hurried over to see a skinny pale man in a white lab coat. He had thick glasses, enlarging his eyes revealing a very bewildered look on his face. He repeated the same statement softly.

"The Holy Grail is poison. The Holy Grail is poison."

As strange as he was acting it wasn't his looks, or his ramblings that kept our eyes glued to him. It was the pistol in his lap. I read his name from his ID badge. Dr. Bronson Aldwick.

"What happened here Bronson?"

"The Holy Grail is poison" is all he would say.

"Somebody give me a hand with this guy" I said, hoping somebody strong would help. Before we could pick him up he grabbed the pistol with his right hand, shaking as he brought it up. We backed off him, hands held up like shields, as if they would have stopped the bullets.

"Take it easy man, we are here to help you" Tommy said begging for a compromise.

"You can't help me! You can't help yourselves!" The scientist yelled.

Behind us the computer started beeping very loudly. We turned to look as the screen began flashing two shades of red. I read out loud the message.

"Fire Sale Operation in Effect?" not knowing what it meant.

The scientist was the first to speak, as our mouths were wide open.

"Oh God it's begun! All the evidence is gone! That's not what I wanted! That's not what *we* wanted!"

We looked to him for answers to this chaos. I wanted to yell at him, but I slowed down.

"What has begun Bronson?"

His eyes glazed over. His stare went blank.

"The end. God forgive us. God save us all."

He turned the pistol to his right temple and with a sudden crack his brain sprayed the desk next to him, and his body slumped over. We stood there silent in shock as blood poured from his nose and mouth, collecting in a puddle at our feet. We backed away slowly, filled with a mix of shock and devastation. Nobody knew how to react. We had never seen anything like this. *What had we gotten ourselves into?* This time I was somewhat relieved the radio startled us. At least getting startled broke the awful silence we were experiencing.

"Everyone get back on the boat!" Ted screamed into the radio.

"Get down here now! The alarm is going off again!"

Like a starter pistol shooting next to our ears we sprang out of the lab and ran down the creaky stairs jumping two steps at a time. There was a deep rumble coming from the central silo, resembling the sounds just before a blowout of oil on a rig. In time to clear our misinterpretations, a loudspeaker announced in a calm, female voice.

"Sterilization in ten minutes."

"Oh that can't be good!" Tommy yelled from the back of our stampeding crew of six.

We exited the stairwell in a different hallway than we had come in, this time near the loading docks. We entered a large room, most likely for storage. There were piles of ash everywhere. Sarah stepped in a pile, tripping over what looked like a shoe. She slid a few feet as Tommy reached down to pick her up. I looked in horror at the shoe she tripped over with a

15

burnt ankle nub sticking out.

"Oh my god!" I gasped.

"We have to get out of here! Those ashes were people!"

I knew something awful happened here. It was clear now that the central shaft was a fire cleanser for the whole facility. The biohazard signs, the wrecked lab, the piles of ashes that used to be people. *What did that scientist mean by the holy grail is poison? What were they working on here?* We now reached the docks and were greeted by Ted and the others who motioned us onto the boat and helped us aboard. Ted signaled the boat captain that we had everybody and were ready to go.

"Ted get us out of here, this place is going to be an inferno!" I yelled.

Ted, looking a little confused, didn't hesitate to get the motors whining. Our boat pulled away from the rig as fast as we could, although it felt like we could have swam away faster. We gazed at the rig getting smaller in the distance. Once again it was the lifeless mass that towered against the horizon. There were no boats around. No Coast Guard. Our questions were answered as the dark rig lit up like a flare as fire shot out of every opening and doorway we had just been in. The fires were quick. Explosive. The fires were meant to destroy everything the lab had in it's belly. The flames withdrew, leaving a smoking steel carcass. *Sterilization complete.* As we put miles between us and the mysterious rig, the image of the scientist killing himself couldn't leave my mind. *We tried to save his life*, I kept repeating in my mind. It's over now. It's over now. I almost had the scene out of my head until something came back like a hot poker prodding me. *The end. God forgive us. God save us all.*

CHAPTER TWO
24 Hours Prior to Sealab sterilization:

Early into the 21st Century the world began experiencing economic and natural disasters in many of the countries that held importance to the global market. The need for remarkable medicine was in high demand. Phillipsbrand, an experimental pharmaceutical company with fresh scientists out of college, were equipped with plenty of funding and state of the art equipment. They specialized in viral medicine. Their goal was to create a virus that could work for the human body instead of against it. A theory that was based on the 'who has the stronger army' in the fight against cancer and decease. The experimental phase labeled Alpha Dog began with research off the coast of Iceland. The company bought an oil rig that was no longer in service. Being several miles off the coast and in international waters, they were not held to a nation's laws concerning experimentation. There was also a key element to their experiments deep beneath the ocean surface, along a fault line that produced hydrothermal vents. Nanoarchaeum Equitans is a species of microbe found in these vents. For years the Sealab sent robots down to bring collections of this organism back to the surface. They discovered the potential of this organism right away. The species has it's own DNA repair system, as well as everything necessary for DNA replication, transcription, and translation. It cannot produce it's own amino acids or protein, so it required a host that would be capable of consuming proteins and producing amino acids for tissue growth.
It became an elite ingredient of a cancer fighting agent. At least that's what the scientists thought when they began.

"So you really think you've found it this time doctor?"

A young, ambitious Adriana Jackson asks her mentor Dr. Bronson Aldwick. He never accepted the role as her mentor, but really had no choice. She looked to him for all her answers.

"Time will tell Adriana." Dr. Aldwick said, refusing to

take his eyes off the test tube he was drawing liquids from.

"Are you nervous about your presentation today?"

Adriana was persistent, trying to get him into a conversation. She was referring to the Board of Directors coming to the Sealab today. Bronson wasn't thrilled about unveiling his findings just yet, but to receive more funding he would need to play the part.

"I don't like to think about it Adriana. We have seen what this new medicine is capable of, but I think we need more time testing it before we let it hit the market."

Dr. Aldwick was referring to their latest findings in cellular growth. It was truly amazing he thought. With the help of this underwater microbe we can grow new cells in the body, and reanimate the dead cells so the host would experience minimal change from cell growth. This would be the Holy Grail of medicines. The human body would be able to fight of the effects of cancer by keeping the dead cancerous cells alive.

Below the rig, the boat crew was preparing for another launch.

"Where the hell is Gordon?" a mad captain yelled out.

"I'm tired of him thinking he can do whatever he wants around here. We were scheduled to launch thirty minutes ago!"

The crew had no answers, so they kept toiling away to prevent themselves from receiving the anger of the captain, although the boat was ready to go. This was another routine dive to the thermal vents for microbe collections. Just when the captain was ready to explode, an out of breath Gordon comes running down the stairs carrying a full gear bag.

"Where the hell have you been?!" The captain exclaimed.

"What's in the bag?"

"It's my gear boss. Sorry I'm late, I'm just getting back from R&R."

The captain paused, trying to refrain and keep his calm.

"We're only going to be out a couple hours…Whatever. Get your ass on the boat."
Gordon jumped into the boat and walked directly to his robot that would be underwater soon.

The boat was equipped with a large, four man submarine used for deep ocean diving. Gordon's robot was the detachment sub that could withstand the temperatures from the hydrothermal vents. The sub was about the size of a large SUV, with enough room for the scientists inside to move around to each of the bubble windows on the side. The three other scientists were already doing pre-mission checks on the sub when Gordon approached.

"Well look at you! I thought the Captain was going to rip you a new one!" Said a red headed, geeky scientist. Gordon didn't like working with him, they were two completely different people.

"How did your trip turn out?" The average sized dark haired scientist asked.

"You went to Italy didn't you?"

"No, I went to Spain." Gordon corrected him.

"It was a horrible trip though, they had a bad storm there that took out the power along the beaches so everything was shut down. FEMA was there providing bottled water to everybody. It was odd seeing beautiful women in bikinis in line for bottled water. That was about the best sightseeing I got to do. I went to Spain and all I got was this bottle of cheap mineral water."
He held up a half drank bottle of Genesis water he pulled out of his bag.

"We have containers here full of that you know." the red headed scientist said to dim the little excitement there was.

"Yeah I know William, but this one has a hot, sun kissed girl's phone number on it, but I bet you'd never recognize one of those."
The others chuckled a little under their breath as William walked away sulking.

Their seats vibrated as the ship's engines pushed them out to sea. The four scientists rode separately from the ship's crew. It wasn't for any reason other than the 'thinkers' and the 'tankers' didn't get along so well. Gordon was sitting beside Jonathan, the dark haired scientist he could tolerate the most. Gordon's lifestyle was a single man's fantasy, and for the others, it was all fantasy.

"Tell me some of your stories about Spain." Jonathan requested, in an attempt to live vicariously through him.

"It wasn't terrible, but it could have been better. Like I said the hottest clubs along the beach were closed, and almost nothing had power. I saw more girls waiting in line for the FEMA tent than I'd seen in days, so I tried my luck there. I stood behind this gorgeous dark blonde with a lime green bikini. She had these dark mysterious eyes, and lugs that went all the way up. We began talking about the storm and how it ruined our vacation, and blah blah blah. I told her I was in charge of the company that made the Genesis water, but she didn't seem too impressed. It occurred to me that making water couldn't be too interesting so I spiced it up a bit. I told her about how the water was originally designed for astronauts to prevent zero gravity sickness, and it was my idea to sell it in airports for pre-flight drinks to deter jet lag. She ate it up like a sandwich to a refugee. I spent a few minutes feeding her more BS about the minerals and stuff in it, and about that time we were at the front of the line. Some guy handed me a bottle and before I could twist the cap she was writing her phone number on the label for me. She kissed me on the cheek and trotted off to meet her friends. What a tease."

"It sounds like you just read off the brochure about the water to her. You make it that easy huh?"

"All you need is confidence. If I had another night there I would have been at her place turning down a wedding proposal and sleeping with her sister."

Jonathan laughed along with the idea, but he could never have the nerve to treat women the way Gordon does. Maybe that's what his weakness was, he thought.

"So was the water any good?"

"It's fucking water. I don't think it's even good water. We sell it for so cheap because it's full of junk. My stomach's been hurting since I drank it, and that was yesterday."

"That's no good. You're not going to be sick on the sub are you? We're almost there."

"No I'm not going to puke or anything."

"It's not the puking I'm concerned with. We can't just roll the windows down, if you know what I mean."

Gordon gave him look like 'oh grow up'.

"We're here, get your stuff together." William barked out.

God I hate that guy Gordon thought to himself.

His stomach was twisting in knots when they boarded the sub. Gordon was the last to buckle in, catching dirty looks from William. The sub jerked about as it was lifted and swung over the edge of the deck to be lowered in the water. They always said the crane portion of movement was the most dangerous, even though the sub was rated to handle several atmospheres underwater. It was something to do with the possibility of a cable snapping, but they had taken many precautions to avoid losing a $10 Million submarine.

Lowering into the water usually gave Gordon butterflies, but this time nothing could overpower the feeling of knots in his stomach. His stomach felt like it was hardening, and turning into beef jerky. Once the water cleared the windows and the sub was under, they each unbuckled to move about to their stations. The sub moved at such a slow and easy pace there were never any sudden movements when it idled through the ocean depths. Going from the surface to the ocean floor was always an interesting journey. No matter how many times they did it, the trip never became routine. The light ocean blue water at the surface would be filled with vibrant wildlife, then the deeper they traveled the darker and less populated it got. There was always a passing moment when it felt like they were sinking into nothingness, and then the fissures on the ocean floor could be seen. Sometimes they were very dull and hardly visible, sometimes they were fully illuminated from spewing lava and cast a warm red glow across the sea bottom. William was the first to see the fissures this time.

"There they are! Gordon get your robot ready."
I know the drill you little kiss-ass. Just stop talking to me.

Gordon sat in his command chair for the robot and placed his hands on the twin joysticks. The command chair always reminded him of a very large video game controller, with actual joysticks instead of thumb sticks and a lot more buttons to push.
Just hurry up and get what we need and so I can get to my room faster and download whatever's making me sick.

Everyone noticed the robot's acceleration from the sub was much too fast this time.

"Be gentle Gordon, if that robot goes down we'll be in a lot of hot water."

"We're already in hot water!" William joked in his nasal voice, referring to the hydrothermal vents beneath them but nobody laughed.

Gordon ignored their remarks and continued pushing the robot at full speed. His stomach hurt terribly now, and the pain was reaching into his chest like a severe case of heartburn.
Keep pushing, keep pushing.

They huddled around Gordon and watched the robot's camera feed from the main screen. The vents were fully flowing this time, spewing boiling acid up from the Earth's core. The camera rocked downward as the robot's base snagged on a taller vent sticking up. The gasped as he did his best to get control of the robot again.

"Gordon slow down!" William burst out.

"Slow down or I'll get you kicked of this project for

destroying company equipment!"

The pain in his chest spread throughout his veins now. His adrenaline only made it worse. Every inch of him burned like fire was snaking its way through his veins. Anger overwhelmed him, and he shot out of his chair and before he knew it his hands were around William's throat. Hatred flowed through his veins. All he could picture was ripping his face apart with his hands. Fear washed over William's face before Gordon sank his teeth into his neck just below his right ear. William's blood curdling scream was the last sound Gordon heard before his world went black from weakness, and he fell to the floor.

"Oh my God! Stop it! William are you okay?!" Jonathan screamed.
William stumbled backwards into the wall of the sub, then slid down the wall into a seated position as his warm blood flowed down his body. His gurgled pleas of yelp trailed off as his eyes rolled into the back of his head.

"Give him CPR! I'm taking us up!" Jonathan yelled to the other scientist.

"Vessel Sealab this is Sub 7, we are coming up for immediate first aid! We have two severely wounded, over!"

"Sub 7 what happened?" the radio crackled.

"Gordon went crazy, he, he bit William and he's in critical condition!"

"Roger Sub 7. We'll be waiting."

He jumped behind the controls and gave the sub full power to the surface. They would be safe from the bends inside the sub, and reaching first aid was his first concern. The other scientist knelt down beside William, applying pressure to his neck to stop the bleeding. Beside them a lifeless Gordon lay on his back, with a mouth full of William's blood and flesh. The scientist moved William sideways so he too could lay on his back for chest compressions. Each time he pushed down on William's chest, bright red blood spurted from his wound. *Shit it's arterial bleeding!* He slowed the compressions on his chest as they got closer to the surface. William was dead. Gordon was dead. When he looked down at his watch he didn't see Gordon's eyelids shoot open. Gordon sat upright, turned and looked at the scientist with cloudy, milky eyes. The scientist took a double take at Gordon, the second time seeing the color gone from his face and life taken from his eyes. Gordon let out an evil growl as his lips opened up, revealing blood soaked teeth with bits of flesh between them. The scientist froze in fear as his eyes stayed locked with Gordon's. He never saw William sit up with the same look of intensity until William's teeth were buried in his arm. The scientist screamed in pain, punching William with no effect.

The sub surfaced quickly, popping above the water like a balloon held under. Jonathan killed the engines and jumped out of his seat, freezing in horror at the crew behind him. William and Gordon were crouched over the scientist, eating and pulling his flesh from his abdomen. He wanted to yell but he couldn't the air wouldn't leave his lungs. When his lungs burned for oxygen he felt the need to escape after he snapped out of his daze. The hatch beyond the bloodthirsty crew, and there was no way around them. Jonathan darted between them, pushing them away as he leapt over the half eaten corpse. Gordon's head hit the wall but William spun and sank his teeth in Jonathan's shoulder just below the neck. He punched William again, cutting his knuckles oh his teeth. Gordon was quick to respond from the hit, and lunged after him once William slowed him down. Jonathan climbed the ladder while kicking at the lifeless faces below. He felt the warm blood travel down his body under his shirt, but it was nowhere near the flow he saw from William. Once outside the hatch he slammed it down, hitting Gordon in the face and smashing some fingers. He spun the wheel as hard as he could, ignoring the pain in his right arm. The ship already had the crane's hook lowered, and Jonathan was quick to get it attached. When the sub began to lift out of the water, he leaned against the taught cable with his arm laying in his lap, throbbing in pain and bleeding down the side of the sub.

The board members landed on top of the platform in a fancy company helicopter. They were always given the star treatment. As Dr. Aldwick was putting his last test tube on the rack for the presentation, his phone rang to notify him of the board's presence.

"Here we go Adriana" he said in a flat tone, just ready for this to be over with.

The phone rang again, Dr. Aldwick again greeted with his name.

"Doctor the board is going to have breakfast first. They will be in the dining facility if you would like to speak to them before the presentation."

"Ok thank you, I'll be down there soon."

He knew he told a little white lie. He wanted to put off the presentation by at least a week, and surely didn't want to sit around with the money bags and talk with them about something they would have no idea about. They just need to know if it works or not. The doctor did a final check on his equipment, grabbed his binders, and as he was walking to the door the phone rang again.

"This is Dr. Aldwick, yes I know the board is here."

"Oh, sorry doctor, this isn't about them. We've had a problem on Vessel Sealab. Gordon has bitten one of the workers, and Jonathan's in the aid station now. Apparently there was a huge fight on the sub."

Jesus Christ, Bronson thought to himself. This is all I need, of all the days it could happen on.

"Ok I'll be down there in a moment."

He put his binders back on the desk and left the lab. Down the hallway there were the other scientists going about their day, everyone smiling at the doctor as they passed.

The first aid station was empty when Dr. Aldwick arrived. There were open bandage wrappers scattered on the floor, and everything was tossed around. It looked as though a tornado came through here.

"Hello?" He called out, but just silence in return.

He decided to look in the makeshift operating room next door, maybe the bite was serious enough it required stitches. When he turned the corner he froze in place. There was a large puddle of blood on the floor, and arterial blood spray on the walls. The operating room looked like a crime scene. It wasn't just the blood that spooked him, he had seen blood so many times before during surgery. It was the severed hand laying on the floor that stunned him. It hadn't been surgically cut removed, the hand appeared to have been chewed off. There are no animals here that could have done that, he thought to himself. He stepped forward to pick up the hand, but checked himself when he realized this could actually be a crime scene. Looking around for clues, his eyes stumbled upon the camera in the upper corner of the room, above the cleaning sinks. He could view the footage in his office, and in one quick move he was out of the aid station and in the stairwell.

Both curious and apprehensive about what he would see from the security camera, he had to know what happened. He didn't want to alarm any of his coworkers by sprinting past them in the hallway, but strangely no one was around. In what seemed no longer than an instant he was in his office. He didn't think about it, but instinctually he locked the door behind him, locking himself in his office. The security screen reminded him again of the horrible images burned in his mind. He began rewinding the footage, with a number of possible scenarios running through his mind. Did somebody lose their mind being on the platform too long? Every scientist was thoroughly screened before getting the job here, and they all had to pass a mental evaluation. Dr. Aldwick just couldn't think of any possibilities that made sense. Unless.... Oh god no. There's no way.

After rewinding fifteen minutes back, he pressed play and the screen came to life. Everything was normal. He saw the nurse sitting at her desk in the first aid room, reading a book, alone. Dr. Aldwick had only talked to her on a few occasions, her name was Janice. She was a real friendly, short woman with curly grey hair, always eager to help. The nurse looked towards the door, stood up from her desk and moved to the door, the wounded worker must be coming in. The operating room filled with activity as Janice and another scientist helped the wounded man lay back on the operating table. He was gripping his neck tightly, and it appeared there was blood on his hand and dribbling down his shirt. Well that explains the crime scene look, Dr. Aldwick thought to himself. Janice frantically grabbed bandages, ripping the sterile packages off and throwing them on the floor. Everything was making sense so far, except for the severed hand. The patient began flopping violently on the operating table, his arms and legs flailing uncontrollably. The scientist that helped the wounded man lay down stood back in horror at the scene that was going on before her. Janice was using bandages to try to stop the bleeding, used some to mop up blood, while trying to hold the man still. She yelled at the able bodied scientist to help restrain the man. She snapped out of her daze and grabbed the patient's feet. Janice had one of the man's arms under control, reaching across him to grab the other. As if a switch was turned off, the man's limbs fell to the table as he laid lifeless. Janice and the female scientist looked at each other in stressed bewilderment.

"Is he...?" the scientist sputtered out.

Janice was covered in the man's blood, the wound near her. She reached across the man, attempting to find a pulse on the side of his throat not gushing blood. At this point it would be the only place she would be able to find a pulse after the man lost so much blood. There was a silent pause in the room, as Dr. Aldwick's eyes were glued to the screen, anticipating Janice's results, just the same as the female scientist in there with her. The stillness was broken when Janice looked up to the scientist and shook her head. Dr. Aldwick could see tears well up in her eyes. She turned away, using a hand to cover her face. Janice was still searching for a pulse, hoping maybe she was wrong, but she knew the patient was dead. Before Janice could sigh, the man sat up and sank his teeth into her wrist. She screamed as loud as she could as he lashed around, ripping and pulling her flesh away. He was trying to stand up now, hands gripped tightly on Janice's arm, her hand dangling from both her arm and his mouth. He pulled her hand off as his head jerked back, sending blood spatter all over the room. Janice was screaming as she fell to the floor, cradling her bloody arm. The scientist's jaw was dropped, she was frozen in horror. Her bottom lip quivered as she was trying to find the air to scream. She finally caught her breath and let out a bloodcurdling scream. This caught the man's attention, and he whipped around to face her. She acted instinctively, grabbing an I.V. stand and thrusting it into the man's abdomen. It sank deeper into his flesh than she could have thought. The man stopped moving towards her, and fell to his knees. The scientist took advantage of the moment and helped Janice up, running out of the operating room. Dr. Aldwick realized he hadn't taken a breath and gasped for air now that he had his answers. His chest hurt from the pain.

As he clutched his chest, eyes still glued to the screen, he saw this pronounced dead man rise off the floor and walk out. He had his answers. His nightmare was now a reality. The medicine worked, it reanimated dead cells. The gruesome corpse he just saw attack a woman answered the experiment's dilemma about the virus' need to find nutrition for itself.

Realizing the situation wasn't over with, he set the security system back to 'live' mode. The screens exploded with activity. There were scientist running down the hallways, chased by other scientist, but these scientists were smeared in blood. Their mouths were frothing, spewing blood as the lifeless creatures grabbed the nearest living person, ripping their flesh

28

apart, taking bites our of them as they screamed. Each scream would soon drown in a gurgling of one's own blood. Dr. Aldwick began hyperventilating. This was too much a nightmare for him. The board members lay in a bloody pile down a still hallway. Not before long movement came from the pile as the board members slowly stood up and began walking down the corridor. Their eyes were lifeless, their movements jerky. Dr. Aldwick knew all was lost. He turned to his computer to run a laboratory diagnostics. The computer beeped and began scanning. While the computer ran it's programs, the doctor pulled out a lock box from the bottom drawer in his desk. He fumbled getting the keys out of his pocket, his hands shaking they key chain. He found the small key and unlocked the box. Inside a pistol lay under some notepads with a full magazine next to it. The doctor pulled out the pistol and slid the magazine in, then chambered the first round. The computer was finished with the diagnostic and began to beep. The screen flashed red.

ACCESS DENIED. STERILIZATION IN EFFECT.

The color left his face. His gasps for air slowed to light breaths. He slowly sat down in his chair, staring at nothing. This was it. The beginning of the end. His quest for the miracle cure only brought something horrible. He was told he was doing something great for mankind and that there were no risks. Snapping back to the situation at hand, he typed in his final command on the keyboard, which had no affect on the computer's actions.

ACCESS DENIED. LAB STERILIZATION BEGINS IN: 10...9...8...7...

Dr. Aldwick slumped to the ground beside the desk with the pistol in his lap. *The wild lunch room theories about this miracle cure are true.* The floor started to rumble, soon the whole platform began to shake. The entryway made a hissing noise as the blast door closed. It sounded like a hurricane was making it's way from the center of the laboratories and down the hallways.

Moments later the hallways filled with flame, incinerating all that was inside. Dr. Aldwick's eyes began to sting, welling up with tears, as he stared down at the pistol in his lap.

———

CHAPTER THREE

It was a long boat ride back to the mainland. There were a few words spoken, but no real conversation. Someone would comment on a room they were in, trying to leave out the macabre nature of the horrors present. I was shocked by what I had seen. I told myself I wasn't devastated. I keep telling myself that people have been dying since the beginning of time. It was the nature of man that led these people to their end. No company would fund something like that with an end-all security system to protect the cure of cancer. They were building or designing something important at that lab. They were making progress.

Our boat batted against the dock when we arrived back in Reykjavik. There were fewer boats around the bay, and even less tied to the dock. The sky was still clear and the sun was out, but not for long. Ted made his first attempt to welcome us back.

"I understand today has been a little disturbing. We came out on a rescue mission, and there is no reason what happened should have happened. For those six of you that were in the lab when it happened, I would like to talk with you in my office when we leave here."

I stepped onto the dock behind Jake and Tommy, and I heard them joking.

"What do you think he wants to talk about?" Tommy smiled, "maybe he wants to give us a raise."

Their smiles couldn't hide how weird today had been. The six of us stepped into the white van ready to take us back to the office, the one place we didn't want to see today. Ted sat up front and said a few things to the driver before we pulled out. The office wasn't far away, perhaps ten minutes. I was thankful for that. The van pulled into the parking lot and we got out at the front door. Ted was the first one out of the van, and he moved to the front door to hold it open for us.

"Let's get this over with" Jake stated and we all silently

agreed.

I was the first to sit down in the conference room, of course so I could see the whole room. Sarah sat between Jake and Tommy across the table. The other two sat on my side, and I felt uncomfortable about it. I hadn't known them long, and to be honest I couldn't remember their names.

"I've talked to the company back in the states about what's happened today."

Ted started the meeting off with.

"We are offering you a week off and we'll fly you back to the states. This is optional, you don't have to take it. We want you to have time with your families if you would like. However, you will not be paid for that week."

Tommy was the first to opt out of the opportunity.

"I need the money man. There's no need for me to go back right now. I'll stay and finish out here."

The two strangers also opted out. I looked at Jake and Sarah. I knew the look Jake was giving me. I could see it in Sarah's eyes to. We decided we would take the week off.

It was nice to be back in my motel room. If I could sleep tonight, tomorrow I would be on a plane at sunrise flying home. I kicked off my boots, practically threw my clothes off, and was asleep by the time my head hit the pillow. The alarm clock came later than it felt like. I felt like I had just lied down. I put on a fresh pair of jeans, a new shirt, and threw the rest in my bag. I met Jake and Sarah outside, where they already had a taxi van waiting for us. We loaded our bags into the back of the van and Sarah was quick to get in. Jake leapt in and sat beside her in the rear seat. Jake and Sarah got along well since they were hired on. They never tried to date each other, I guess they figured they made better friends than lovers, and secretly I was happy about that. Sarah had always been a hard ass, and Jake loved his female conquests. I sat in the middle seat and instructed the driver to the airport using the best hand gestures I could, but luckily he spoke some English. Traffic was a little busier than I'd ever seen before.

There were cars running red lights, driving on the wrong side of the road, it was chaos. It seemed like every few blocks or so another police car would scream by with it's sirens on. I looked back at Jake and Sarah jokingly.

"I guess we're getting out of here just in time."

"Yeah, these people act like the sky is falling!" Jake chuckled.

The driver yelled something at another car that sounded like Icelandic cursing, and his actions brought on a bigger smile to our faces. Maybe this is what I need I thought. I just need to kick back and relax, cut loose.

"Jake what do you say we go out for a few beers when we get back stateside? I want to order a few this time."

"Well that's the plan buddy!" he exclaimed.

"We got a week off!" Sarah was also excited about the idea.

"David you are going to have a blast. I know a great place we can go and our drinks will be half off! I used to date a bartender there." She said, proud of herself.

"Well I'm ready to get away" I said, ready to forget today.

We arrived at the airport two hours before our flight, so we let the herds of people move through the crowded airport as we took our time.

"I'd hate to be security" Sarah said, watching the lines of people get longer and longer.

"That has to get so boring just watching people walk through metal detectors all day."

Jake nodded in agreement.

Our boarding area wasn't too crowded, apparently there were some people taken off our flight for health reasons, so I guess we just lucked out. After we sat down Sarah picked up a magazine similar to Home and Garden, but in another language. I guess she liked looking at the pictures like I do, for the language barrier reasons. Jake pulled out his phone and checked his fantasy football stats. An airline representative came by and in her best English tried to sell us on miracle water.

"Hi gentlemen. We have special mineral that will prevent jetlag. It's called Genesis. Just went on sale yesterday. It's guaranteed to work and only 5 US dollars. Would you like one?"

"No thanks ma'am."

The gimmicks people fall for these days. There were a few people I could tell were ready to get on the plane as soon as possible. I guess they'd had enough of Iceland I thought. A voice came over the loud speaker and I didn't know what it was saying, until the English translation came on.

"We would like to provide you a hospitable experience here at Northern Airways and get you on your flight as soon as we can. Please listen to the following options. If you are experiencing any kind of sickness please report to the nearest Northern Airways representative, as we have medical personal on site. If you notice anyone near you showing flu like symptoms, please notify a representative. We like to offer our customers a safe and healthy travel experience and with your help we can provide you the best experience possible. Thank you and have a safe and wonderful flight."

"The sooner we get out of here the better" Jake said to me as I was nodding in agreement.

"Hurry up and get me on that plane then" Sarah said to anybody listening.

The loud speaker came to life again, this time the stewardess announced we were ready to board. Once on the plane after I put my bag in the overhead compartment I got settled in to my window seat. I couldn't help but notice half the plane was empty and no more passengers were boarding. Quieter is better I guess, as I leaned my chair back and closed my eyes. I never had a problem falling asleep before the plane left the runway.

I woke up to the sound of the plane's tires screeching on the runway at the Dallas International Airport. Home never felt so good. Jake and Sarah were laughing with another passenger they'd apparently been joking with the whole time. I knew it wouldn't be long before I was in my house, on my couch relaxing watching TV, and we had a fun night ahead of us.

"How about we get home, clean up, and do y'all just want to meet at the bar or meet at somebody's house?" I asked.

"David your house is closest to the bar, we'll just meet you there and then leave. How does nine o'clock sound?"
Sarah must have had this figured out already.

"Nine o'clock it is. I'll see you here."
We each took a separate taxi and went three different directions.

Walking through my front door immediately put me at ease. This was a house my parents left me from a short attempt they had as renters. It was paid for, but in this neighborhood, only buyers wanted to settle in. It was kind of a gift to me for getting out of their house, and I think they wanted me to grow up faster and get settled down. Everything was exactly the way I left it. I sat in my big broken in leather recliner I'd bought with my first paycheck. I slid off my boots and leaned back in the chair as the ceiling fan hummed above me. I took a moment to attempt to erase the scene at the oil rig, and slowly I was forgetting the details that haunted me. I knew it would be a moment before Jake and Sarah got home, so I reached for the remote and turned on the television. The news was the first to come on. I watched long enough to hear about riots breaking out in the north eastern states for no apparent reason, and a few scattered disturbances around the nation. There was a tornado in the Midwest and a chain of them through the central plains and shelters were being set up. I had enough of that and looked through the guide. Nothing was on so now was a good a time as any to clean up. My bedroom was cool and shady when I walked in. I pulled my shirt off and tossed it into the dirty laundry hamper, followed with my jeans and got the water ready for my shower. The hot water felt incredible pouring over my dirty hair and face. I was finally home. I took a good, long hot shower and loved every minute of it. After I dried off I stepped into the closet to look for a nice shirt to wear out. I found a long sleeve I liked, not too heavy, but comfortable. Something caught my eye on the shelf above the shirt I'd forgotten about. My dad's old 1911 pistol he gave me when I graduated high school. His father gave it to him, and he gave it to me for tradition. I hadn't fired it much, and the two boxes of ammo that came with it were still pretty full.

"It's been a long time since high school" I said aloud to myself, reminiscing.

I finished getting dressed because the others would be here in about thirty minutes. I went back to my cozy recliner and began flipping through the channels again, just to pass time.

Sarah arrived a few minutes before Jake. Long enough for us to start a conversation, but short enough for us to not get too deep into it. Since the three of us planned on getting a little tipsy tonight, we decided it would be best to take a taxi. The bar was roughly ten miles away, I paid the driver when Jake said he'd get the first round because he didn't have any cash on him. The bar was like any other. The music was too loud, it smelled of smoke and old beer stains, and very crowded. Jake's idea of a first round was a cold beer and a shot of tequila for each of us. From there the night turned into a blur of neon lights and strange faces.

I got a little more drunk than I wanted to at the bar tonight. Jake was used to it and offered to give Sarah a ride home. Now I'm in my quiet house and the room is slightly spinning. It's been a long time since I had tequila shots. Jake sure does have a convincing way of selling me on the idea though. I decided before I pass out I'm going to need to sober up a little bit, so I start running the water for another shower. I put my cell phone and my wallet on the bedside table as usual, so I always know where to find it. I turn the radio up in the bathroom and drunkenly do a little dance in front of the mirror. Tonight was exactly what I needed. I carefully stepped in the shower, trying not to slide on the slick tiles. I feel the warm water run down my body, and it feels amazing. I begin to sing along to the song playing, and lather up. A crash of breaking glass breaks my trance and I frantically try to wash the soap out of my eyes. I look at the window and my heart leaps out of my chest. There's a pale arm and face coming in through the bathroom window! Someone is breaking into my house while I'm here! The arm had cuts all over it from the broken glass, but strangely no blood. When I looked the intruder in the eyes I almost froze in fear. They were set in deep, with dark circles all around them. His pupils were bloody and had no depth at all, like there was no soul to this man. There was blood dripping from his mouth. I don't know how, but it must have been from the glass.

"Get out of my house! I'll fucking kill you!" but he didn't hesitate at all.

He now had his whole torso in the window and wasn't making an attempt to escape. He wasn't looking at anything else but me. I hit him with anything I could find, the biggest being a toilet plunger that made no stops at his advances. My heart racing now, I ran to the closet and grabbed my 1911. I chambered a round and pointed it at his chest, and threatened him one last time.

"If you come any closer I'll display your insides for the world to see."

The man made a sound similar to a yell and groan, and slid his body into my bathroom now. I closed my left eye and squeezed the trigger. The gun gave a deep boom as his torso flinched backwards from the impact, but he kept moving towards me. *No way* I thought. I put that .45 in his chest, he should be down. I squeezed off another round, this time aimed at his forehead. The deep boom echoed off the bathroom walls as his brains sprayed the wall behind him, leaving chunks of his skull in the sink. He dropped like a bag of sand and didn't move after that. I stood there mortified, watching the intruder carefully. Strangely no blood collected underneath him.

I heard a scream outside the window that sounded like it came from the neighbor's house. I looked out to see my neighbor's wife, in a pink bathrobe getting attacked by three men and a woman. They weren't beating her, or trying to rob her, they were ripping her apart! Biting her where she had exposed skin, pulling away her flesh as she lay there screaming. The screams soon became whimpers, and then nothing at all. She lay there lifeless as these....monsters kept pulling her flesh from her bones. I stood there shaking at what I had just seen. One of them looked at me and made what sounded like a growling noise. They began walking towards me very stiffly. I realized they hadn't seen me, but they heard my radio, which was still blaring rock music. I turned the radio off and threatened them to leave me alone as they got closer. I raised my .45 to the nearest one and screamed "Stop!" but they kept coming with no fear. Behind them the shredded woman in the pink bathrobe began to move. Impossible I thought. I saw her die. When she stood I realized I was right, but how could I be? She was dead, but she was walking towards me. I remembered what the corpse on my bathroom floor taught me. Aim for the head. I aimed at the nearest one's face and squeezed a shot. His brains sprayed the face of the man behind him after the boom. I did the same for the next three, all their faces exploded when I hit them, dropping them instantly. The woman in the bathrobe was getting closer, so I took aim and missed. With a deep, focused breath the next round hit her square in the forehead and the top half of her head disappeared, matching the rest of her flesh torn body. This couldn't be real. I just killed six people, but I swear they were already dead. This is the stuff in movies I thought, this is real life and this can't happen. While I was arguing with myself I was still going along with idea that the dead were walking. I unplugged the radio. I turned off the lights in the house. I went into my closet and closed the door. I put on my jeans and grabbed a shirt in the dark. I sat there on the floor as quiet as I could while loading rounds carefully into the magazine without making a sound. With no sounds coming from inside my house, I could hear what was going on outside now. There were sirens from all directions.

Every few minutes there were screams of pain that slowly died out and turned into moans. I heard cars crash into other cars. I heard gunshots ring out. Some gunshots ended in screaming. As long as I stayed quiet I could be okay. *Oh god what about Jake and Sarah?* Just as I thought about my friends a loud noise came from my bedroom. My cell phone was vibrating and ringing on my bedside table. I scrambled out of the closet to reach the phone before anyone heard it.

"Jake! Holy shit are you guys okay?!"

"David what the hell is going on?!" He replied.

"Sarah and I just saw the cops put bullet holes in a guy and he stood back up and attacked one of them!"
I stammered trying to say what I had just done here.

"Jake I just shot six people trying to attack me. One of them broke in, four of them killed a woman and then all five of them came after me."
There was a brief pause so both of us could absorb what the other just said.

"David you have a gun? Sarah and I are coming over." Jake demanded.

"Okay listen Jake, when you get close to my house turn your headlights off. I'll be by the front door to let you in. Don't slam your car doors, be as quiet as you can. From here we'll figure out a plan."

Jake hung up, so I closed the bathroom door, set my phone to vibrate, grabbed the pistol and waited by the front door. I thought about turning on the TV to see what the news was saying, but this was happening regardless of what was being broadcasted. I didn't need to attract the attention anyway. Outside I could see those infected were walking up and down the street. Our plan so far was getting them in the house, but what about afterwards? I've seen them attracted to sound and movement, and the walkers in the street are sure to see them approach. I called

Jake back.

"When you get here, kill the headlights and the motor, and shift it to neutral. Let the car roll into the front lawn, and once it's stopped, take a look at any walkers nearby. If they are looking, just stay in the car and don't move. Leave the radio off. They should continue walking if they think there's nothing worth going after in your car. Once they walk past, you can slowly make your way to the front door. Keep your heads low, and move as quietly as you can."

Jake took a moment to memorize the plan.

"Okay David sounds good. We are about a mile away, we'll see you soon."

When Jake hung up, I continued scanning for more walkers. A few minutes later I saw headlights blaze across the house on the corner. The headlights turned the corner and shut off. It has to be them I thought. Just as planned, the car gradually slowed down, as if nobody was driving it. The walkers stopped and watched it roll by. Jake hit the driveway next to mine and part of the curb, bouncing to a stop in the front yard.

"Perfect" I whispered to myself.

The car sat silent as the walkers stood still and watched, ready to move in. A few minutes went by, and there was no movement in the car. The walkers one by one continued to move down the street. Once the area looked clear, Jake and Sarah slowly opened the doors. I noticed the dome light didn't come on, Jake must have disabled it. Crouched low, they slowly made their way to the front door, as quiet as possible. I gripped the knob with white knuckles, trying to ease it open without a squeak. David opened the door just wide enough to squeeze through. Jake sent Sarah in first, while he watched behind them.

"Is this really happening?" Sarah whispered.

"I don't know what to think" was all I could say.

I killed six people tonight. We came into the living room and sat together on the floor. We pretended as though it would be quieter, but secretly none of us wanted to see out the windows.

"Turn on the TV, there has to be something on the news about what's going on" Sarah whispered, eager for answers.

As I reached towards the television Jake grabbed my arm.

"Don't turn it on! The light could attract them."

I hesitated for a moment, letting his warning sink in.

"Let's talk about what we *do* know about these....creatures. The first one broke through my window to get into the only room in the house making noise. The group of them attacked that woman after she screamed, and they weren't aware of me until I spoke up and got their attention. They move slowly and stiffly until they get near their target, then they lunge with force, like a surge of adrenaline an animal gets when it goes in for a kill. They act like primitive animals. They hunt by sound, and they are attracted to electric activity and movement. Anything that provides stimulation."

Sarah was nodding in agreement before she looked away, like she thought of a plan.

"David do you have any blankets? Put one over the television and stretch it out. We can watch from underneath it."

"Sarah that's brilliant!"

I was impressed. Jake's eyes lit up also.

"Even better, set up your high back dining room chairs facing outward and in a semicircle. We drape the blankets over them, use couch cushions to hold them down, and we'll have a place we can all watch and not attract any attention!"

Here we were, three adults talking about using chairs, blankets, and couch cushions to build a fort in my living room. However this time we weren't playing games and we weren't 5 years old, we needed this for survival. As ridiculous as it sounded, it wasn't as crazy sounding as dead people walking, but I knew what I'd seen. I grabbed the blankets out of the closet, Jake brought the chairs in from the dining room, and Sarah pulled the couch cushions up, all under the cover of darkness. A few times somebody would bump into a table, and everyone would freeze, awaiting any recognition from outside. After a moment when nothing happened, we would continue building. We finished in about ten minutes. Jake and I were under the blanket, my finger on the TV's power switch and Jake's on the volume. Sarah stayed outside to check for any light leaking from our youthful tent. Before I pressed the On switch I couldn't help but comment to Jake.

"The first time I get really drunk in a long time and the whole world turns upside down."

He faked a smile. I turned the TV on, Jake was already holding the volume button down. The screen flickered to life, and I saw a few corners getting pulled down, or more pillows being put against the chairs. There was a pause, and then Sarah crept in under a corner by the TV. I stopped channel flipping at the first news program I saw. Moments into it our suspicions were confirmed. There were reports all over the nation that the dead were walking. There was a reporter in New York in the streets getting first hand images of the carnage, only to be consumed by the dead herself as the nation watched. For once the desk reporters were speechless. A camera crew was filming from what looked the be the third floor of a downtown high rise, showing streets flooded with slow moving, stiff corpses wandering aimlessly for their next meal. A few times an unlucky person would be seen walking out of a building getting attacked by a crowd of walkers. It took them just seconds to rip apart a single person, leaving gnawed bones and puddles of blood. In one case nearby in downtown Dallas a group of people were seen attacked and killed, only to stand and join the dead army moments after. The news warned to stay away from any person showing flu like symptoms. We were frozen to the carnage on the screen. Homes and businesses were on fire. Cars were overturned in the streets. Some intersections were filled with crashed cars and trucks, all with broken glass and blood splatter on the windshields. The screen turned still, buzzed again with static, followed by the message 'Please Stand By'. I skimmed through more channels that showed the same message until I stumbled upon another news agency. Soon it would go off the air, followed by the same message. One by one each channel was going off air. Sarah was the first to fall asleep under the blanket canopy. Because I was sitting upright with my attention to the television Jake followed her soon after. If it wasn't for the alcohol I don't think I would have ever fallen asleep.

I woke up first to see the last channel I was on also displaying the 'Please Stand By' message. I gave a slight yawn and began flipping through the channels. Nothing. I turned the television off, making it completely dark under the blankets. *Surely the night is over with.* I thought, hoping it was all a nightmare. I hoped the blanket fort was for a few friends that got too drunk and relived childhood memories. I hoped I only dreamt of shooting those people. I crawled out of the makeshift fort and saw the sunlight pouring in through the window shades. I looked at the pistol laying next to the TV. *I won't pick it up because last night was just a dream. I won't need that pistol for anything.* I felt a slight pinch in my stomach, realizing I hadn't gone to the bathroom for several hours. Opening the door to the bathroom I was hit it the face by the stench of death that almost brought me to my knees. The headless corpse laying on my bathroom floor reminded me of the hell I was in. I forced myself to empty my bladder, trying to hold my breath the whole time. I quickly shut the door behind me, and after it slammed I remembered why we had to be so quiet when I heard a moan outside. I froze in place, listening for any sounds of movement. There was no breaking glass, or screaming, so I walked lightly to the living room. No screams. That observation frightened me some. There were no screams outside, no tires squealing on the pavement, no cars crashing into others, and no sirens outside. The outside world was eerily quiet. I crept to my living room window and slowly pulled the blinds open. The world I knew before was gone. The houses across the street were empty, the front doors swinging in the wind. I could tell where my neighbors made a last stand. The windows were stained with bloody handprints.

My neighbors across the street, whom I'd met just once, always took pride in the way their property looked. Grass was always green, the windows were always spotless. They proudly displayed two SUV's in the driveway. The only SUV now had it's driver's door hanging wide open with a blood trail staining the driveway down to the sidewalk. The windows marred by bloody hands, and the door banging against what looked like an arm draped across the threshold. I wondered if there was a body attached to that arm. Flames rose high enough off the horizon to kiss a blackened smoke filled sky. I prayed there were others that locked themselves in a safe place through the night. I heard the crack of gunshots a few streets over. Normally that's not something I wanted to hear in my neighborhood, but now I actually felt good about it. Those shots gave me hope that there were more survivors outside. My hope was quickly discouraged when I noticed the walkers on my street quickly snapped their heads to the sound of the shots, and began staggering in that direction. *Sound is a key element to their hunting instincts.* I heard rustling under the blankets and was relieved either Jake or Sarah was awake. This new world was becoming overwhelming. Jake crawled out from the covers in my direction.

"Brother tell me last night didn't actually happen."
My solemn look wasn't comforting him.

"I wanted to believe the same Jake. There's no denying it, Hell has opened up on Earth."
He gave a short peek through the blinds, then sat with his back against the wall.

"What the hell is happening David? What did we do to deserve this? How could this have happened?"
His questioning reminded me of a thought that kept me awake last night.

"Do you remember going to that oil rig laboratory? Remember by the time we got there all the other rescue boats were gone? I think that might have something to do with this. If

44

just a few of those boats docked on the mainland….. And remember all the passengers at the airport that were getting sick? They said on the news to stay away from anybody showing flu like symptoms. Whatever they made in that lab they were willing to kill everything to protect it."

Jake didn't move.

He thought about the possibilities, still staring at the floor.

"Or to protect us" he answered.

We sat for a moment, letting it sink in.

"What do we do now?" he asked, wanting assurance to go into complete survival mode.

"I don't know what resources we have left Jake. There are reports of these walkers all over the nation, so we could be at a total loss. We'll have to start off with the basics, food, water, and shelter."

They both looked around the living room, then back at each other.

"Hiding under a blanket fort in the living room is no shelter. How much food do you have here?"

I was never here, so I knew what little rations I did have wouldn't go far, especially with three people. I opened the pantry, and aside from a few random cans of vegetables and an opened bag of pasta, five beers in the fridge, there was nothing. I did however, have four gallon sized jugs in the pantry I could fill with water. I peeked through the kitchen window for any nearby walkers. Once the area looked clear I checked the faucet for running water. There was plenty of water coming out, with good pressure to. *Thank God.* I filled the four jugs with water and set them on the kitchen counter. Going back to the living room I noticed Sarah was awake now, sitting next to Jake. She had her head on his shoulder, her arm around his. Her hair was a little messy, but she looked fine for sleeping a hangover off and on a floor all night.

"We have four cans of vegetables, and some spaghetti noodles. That won't last us past today. If things stay quiet outside, we can go through these nearby houses and look for food, and maybe survivors."

Jake and Sarah looked at each other. They weren't too thrilled about the idea, but we didn't have many options. Then Jake reminded me

"What about shelter? There's a broken window in the bathroom, not to mention a corpse on the floor, and a number of other windows that could get broken." I thought for a moment, scratching my head.

"Jake you and I could get that body out through the window. Between towels and sheets I should have enough to cover the windows around the house. If we stay quiet inside the house we shouldn't attract attention, and we won't need to board up the windows just yet. We can fortify this place just long enough until we get a real plan."

Jake pondered on the idea, his slow nod turned into a full agreement.

"I like it, but you're forgetting something David."

"What's that?"

Jake grinned.

"We're going to need more guns."

CHAPTER FOUR

Fort Benning, Georgia
    The cool morning air always gives a spooky haze of light fog throughout the majestic pine trees of the natural, raw Georgia. Sergeant First Class Eric Mason was one of the twenty four out of forty remaining soldiers that were soon to graduate the Army's tough Sniper School in two days. Today they were at the range early in the morning testing their accuracy with the Barrett M107 .50 caliber sniper rifle.

    "Spotter ready."
    "Shooter ready."
    "Send it."
Breathe in, breathe out, breathe in, breathe out…hold.
    BOOM!
    As fire erupted from the barrel and smoke filled the air, Eric Mason followed the round through his spotting scope as it arched over half a mile of land, striking a steel silhouette target in the chest.
    "Hit."

    Mason followed his shooter, Specialist Pearson into the classroom after the morning practice at the range.
    "Good shooting today Pearson."
    "Thanks Sarge. My ears are still ringing from that damn gun."
    "Yeah no shit. Just make sure you can hear everything in class today. We're almost finished here."

    They took their seats in the fourth row, the left side of the classroom, with the Barrett standing on bipod legs between their chairs. There were two large dry erase boards at the front of the room, but mostly used for slides from the projector. The walls were lined with posters of history's greatest sniper rifles, along with motivational posters of a barely visible man in a gillie suit behind the scope of a high powered rifle. Mason thought it was strange to work with such a young soldier in the same class, but he respected Pearson's ability to act mature for his age most of the time. As the last of the students entered the classroom, the instructor began with the day's training.

"Listen up Snipers. In two days you will be ready to return to your units as a more professional, disciplined, and trained soldier above your peers. They will look to you for excellence. You will be proficient in your job and ready to train them with what you have learned here. Remember, sniping isn't about getting a 'glory shot' or single handedly winning a war. You will most likely not be recognized for the challenges you have overcome. Only those fighting with you will appreciate what you do and the sacrifices you have made. Having said that, we'll move into today's class on Recognizing the Threat."

The class was released just after 5 pm for the night. The soldiers were encouraged to eat a rib sticking meal, because tomorrow was the Top Shooter contest, in which the remaining candidates tried to earn the coveted Top Shooter award for their class. The barracks consisted of an open room, with metal bunk beds and lockers spread throughout with enough space so each soldier had enough room to change and sleep with little privacy. There were three orange couches arrayed around an old television, with a few VHS movies that had been collected over the years. A few soldiers were circled around the television, watching the latest news, hoping to hear something new about the war overseas. Instead, the news was focused on a large oil rig fire off the coast of Iceland, sparing few details to keep the soldiers entertained.

"We are unclear how the fire was started, but early this morning rescue crews and nearby boaters were asked to help the local fire department with evacuation efforts as the local civilian agencies were overwhelmed by the number of injured in the fire. As many as fifty workers were taken to Iceland's medical facilities, while an estimated two hundred more were quickly

transported to nearby Canadian and American facilities due to the extremities of their wounds. The death toll is estimated to be sixty three at this time, but we are getting reports that the toll will have risen by morning. Mark back to you."

"We have shocking footage of the evacuation efforts taking place on the rig, as a group of survivors are seen savagely attacking the crew of a rescue boat. I must warn you, this footage may be unsettling to young viewers."

The soldiers watched as a rescue boat tied to the rig could be seen from an aerial view, most likely from a helicopter, with people screaming and running frantically onto the boat, and what appeared to be burned victims following, or maybe chasing them into the hull of the boat. As two of the charred victims grabbed a woman in a blue jumpsuit and pulled her to the ground, the camera shut off and went back to the reporter sitting at the desk in awe.

"Awe c'mon! They left out the best part!" a soldier heckled from the middle couch.

"Ladies and Gentlemen we apologize for the horrible footage you've just seen, but reports coming from the incident has left authorities with anything but answers. We'll come back to this story when we've been given more information. In other news, the President has initiated talks with Russia about disarming the 'Stand Ready' nuclear missiles still waiting in missile silos around both countries...."

"Let's go to Olive Garden tonight." a soldier piped up as soon as the news went to commercial.

The idea was shared by six others, including Mason and Pearson. In an hour they were showered and ready to take a soldier named Jim Bowtoski's, or Jimbo for short, suburban to the city for a plates of pasta that would carb load them for the next day. The conversation was typical on the way to the restaurant, discussing tips they'd each heard about how to excel at the separate events for the next day, but Mason knew the challenge would require brains and stamina to complete, aside from the makeshift solution tips the others were considering.

The restaurant smelled of fresh garlic and uncorked wine, leaving the palates of the soldier's mouths salivating with excitement of the meal to come. The young, cute hostess sat them at a large round table, and smiled flirtatiously at the younger soldiers there. Once the discussion of who was getting which appetizer and who to share with finished, a young anxious soldier asked the group about what they'd seen on the news.

"So the president wants to decommission all our nukes huh? Could you imagine if the world launched them at each other and we were in World War III? I bet we could kick their asses!"

"No dumbass, there wouldn't be anybody left if we launched all our nukes!" another soldier replied.

"What do you think Sergeant?" they asked Mason.

"I don't get paid enough to make those decisions, but I think it would be stupid. The world would have to start at the beginning all over again. You wouldn't get to talk to your girlfriends on Facebook, you wouldn't get to drive your overpriced piece of shit muscle cars. How about you worry about finishing the competition tomorrow?"

"Ha ha roger sarge!"

"Besides, the world's going to shit anyway, why nuke when everybody's going to start fighting each other someday anyway?" Mason finished.

He was glad to see the waitress bring the drinks and Sergeant out. Her timing ended the conversation at the perfect time, Mason didn't want to discuss the possibilities of world war and how unprepared the average person was when it would come to survival.

The dinner went well and everyone ate all they could, setting themselves up for a food coma when they returned back to the barracks. Mason lay in his bed as the lights went out, thinking about what the young soldier had said about global nuclear war. *It would erase a majority of the dependencies most people rely on every day. Only a handful of people here and there would know how to survive in a catastrophic situation. A world like that could only mean God was willing to cleanse the Earth and start over with a new, beautiful creation. Only the strong would survive.* His thoughts trailed off as he slipped into a deep sleep, unfortunately filled with dreams of evils he'd only seen in combat.

"Wake up snipers! It's time to get hooah!" someone yelled as the bright fluorescent lights flooded the darkness. There were groans coming from around the room, they were used to waking up at 5 am, but it never becomes easy. Mason did a last minute check of his rucksack, to make sure everything on the packing list from gillie suit to extra boots were in, so he wouldn't face disqualification. He made sure Pearson also had the right gear, because they were a spotter/shooter team and qualified as one. Once his boots were tied tight, he slung his rucksack and they moved to the secondary classroom at the school, a block away.

The secondary classroom had bare concrete floors, with rows of large wooden tables large enough to spread gear out and work on crafting a gillie suit. They were given a brief on the day's events, and soon would move to the arms room to sign out the heavy thirty pound Barrett rifles and a smaller bolt action rifle. As soon as the sun would come up the matches would begin.

The first challenge was a push up/sit up challenge, where both members had to do as many as possible. Together, Mason and Pearson scored 140 pushups and 147 sit ups in the two minutes they had for each exercise. From there they put their rucksacks on, and began the 5 mile road march to the range. They exchanged turns carrying the heavy rifle every eight minutes, because carrying the awkward rifle would bring fatigue so soon. Sweat was pouring down their necks when they reached the range, where they quickly put down their gear to be tested on target detection in the woods. Next came the shooting phase, which required the two to work as a team engaging targets at various distances within a set time limit. Mason hit each of his targets in the time allotted, but Pearson missed one, which could cost them the challenge. They barely made it through the handgun range; even the advanced shooters questioned the accuracy of the small 9mm round. The long range with the Barrett was the last event, and Mason was up to shoot first. They had perfected their simple dialogue between spotter and shooter, but the winds from different directions proved difficult. Mason missed his target at fifteen hundred meters, and Pearson missed two targets at distances ranging almost two thousand meters. The day was full of dirt and sweat but they were finally finished, each team waiting for the results of the challenge. Mason and Pearson came in third place, but there was no award besides first. The class took a group photo and traveled by truck back to the classrooms to close out the day.

That night Mason lay in bed, staring at the ceiling. He felt accomplished by what they had done today, regardless of coming in third place. They had finished a challenge many soldiers will never get a chance to attempt, and everyone was proud of the work they'd done. Three soldiers were gathered around the television, attempting to keep it quiet but Mason could still hear it in the background. He heard from the reporter that civilians feeling flu symptoms were to report to the nearest hospital for diagnosis, because apparently an epidemic was breaking out in New York City. *Great, that's all we need now, is for everybody to wear those stupid masks around town like the Chinese during the bird flu scare. They can keep that shit in New York for all I care.* Tomorrow he would graduate the school and he and Pearson would be on the road back to their unit in Texas. His dreams gave him no relief, tonight they were filled with a world of devastation.

Mason's muscles ached from head to toe when he sat up in bed. The lights burned his eyes as he looked around for the off button of his buzzing alarm clock. Slipping into his boots he was reminded of the blisters of yesterday's conquests, as he felt the skin tear apart on his heel as his foot settled in. Today was graduation day, and he just wanted to get it over with and go home, although, he didn't have a family to go back to. He was always too busy with training and deploying to start a relationship.

The classroom was filled with high ranking officials, none of which he knew but they came from the local units to congratulate the soldiers. He and Pearson received their Certificates of Achievement, then hung around for a few minutes saying their last goodbyes to the friends they'd made at the school. While Pearson was smoking a cigarette with another soldier, Mason sat behind the steering wheel of their already packed truck dialing his First Sergeant to notify him they were leaving.

"Hey First Sergeant this is Mason, we are done here, about to hit the road back."

"Roger Mason, sounds good. The sooner you get here the better, we are on QRF for the post, and this epidemic keeps spreading across the nation, so it's likely we'll get called up if the infection reaches central Texas."

Great. All I want is a weekend off and there's no chance of getting it now. Quick Reaction Force always gets called up on a Saturday while you're doing something fun.

"Ok that sounds good, we can be in tomorrow just after midnight. We'll have to stop at a hotel on the way. What's the next hard time?"

"Mason I need you and Pearson to come in at zero five, with your gear."

Fuck my life.

"Roger that First Sergeant."

CHAPTER FIVE

Jake and I used a superstore's plastic bags I had under the sink to cover our hands when lifting the body up through the window. It made a nasty thud when it hit the ground outside, like dropping a large sack of sand. It wasn't terribly difficult, seeing as how there was no blood or head. Sarah used thumbtacks to hold up the towels and sheets over the windows. It didn't take long before we had an amateur fortress. Luckily the power grid was still on, at least for the meantime. I opened a couple cans of green beans and a can of corn, heated them on the stove and served each with a potholder and a fork. I felt like I was squatting in my own home. None of our cell phones worked, the same monotone beeping was all we could hear when we tried to call out. If this was indeed a mega disaster, we were going to need more necessities to survive. Sarah agreed to stay in the house and make it a little more 'homely' as she called it while Jake and I would go around looking for more supplies.

"I saw a jacked up four wheel drive a few houses down," Jake said.

"There was mud on the tires so maybe they hunt. There could be some packing jars and maybe some rifles there." I was impressed with his observation.

"I like where your head is at Jake, let's go there first."

I checked the pistol for a full magazine with one in the chamber and loaded the other magazine to capacity. Before we left the house I stopped at the front closet and dug out two leather coats. Despite the mildly warm weather I handed Jake a coat and he gave me a confused look.

"Bite proof" I explained.

We donned the coats and I looked out the front window for walkers.

"The street looks clear. For now at least."

I remembered the reaction the nearby gunshots got from

the walkers, and the last thing I wanted here was a last stand. With that in mind, I tucked the .45 into my waistband and retrieved a baseball bat and a golf club out of the closet also.

"We'll give them the silent treatment."

"You're just full of ideas today aren't you David?"

I opened the door slowly and we stepped onto the porch.

The streets were strangely quiet. *This was going to take some getting used to.* We moved like a pair of daytime bandits to the house with the 4x4. Luckily for us the front door was open, not so lucky for the previous occupants. Immediately I noticed a puddle of blood in the entryway, with bloody hand prints on the walls. There was no corpse though, hopefully that was a good thing.

"Make sure nobody's around" I whispered.

Jake nodded silently and kept his head on a swivel. On the living room floor lay a tactical home defense shotgun with a few unspent shells laying next to it. *God bless rednecks* I thought. Jake slung the shotgun and we moved into the bedroom. Nothing was out of place, it's like the people just disappeared. The closet had French style doors, we both opened at the same time, our weapons held up in a batter's stance. We found just what we were looking for. On the top shelf there were a few boxes of shells for the shotgun, and a medium sized suitcase on the floor. I dumped the leftover items out of the suitcase, but then replaced a few of the hotel sized shampoo bottles and bars of soap, remembering how nice my last hot shower was. The house was well equipped. They had lived here for some time it seemed, which led me to believe they should have a full pantry. I took the suitcase to the kitchen, as Jake picked up security watching my back. Opening the pantry door was like finding a lost treasure. There were rows of canned food, bags of instant rice, potatoes, and a box of saltine crackers. I stuffed the suitcase as tight as I could get it, and squeezed a few boxes of snacks under my shirt. *Not bad for our first score.* Jake draped a few blankets around his neck and each of us had about all we could carry.

55

We moved to the entryway again, and slowly peered out into the street. Our safe house was a hundred yards away, but between us and the house stood four walkers looking around for their next meal. We looked at each other, looked at our primitive swinging weapons, and decided to do it. I pulled the handle out on the suitcase, Jake wrapped the blankets around his neck one more time for good measure. He moved into the front yard first. I followed with my left hand pulling the suitcase, my right hand armed with a 9 iron. The walkers immediately saw us and moved towards us almost synchronized. Jake swung for the fences at the first walker, a middle aged male still wearing pajamas. When his bat hit the creature's skull it sounded like a watermelon hitting the pavement. Dry blood spattered the bat and Jake's face. I was now five feet from a young woman in jogging sweats, and I swung the 9 iron as hard as I could with one arm. It dented her skull in, and she went down, but it wasn't near as effective as the Louisville Slugger. Jake swung his bat down on the second walker like an ax, plunging it's skull down into its torso. I was beginning to think he was somewhat enjoying this. I used a wide arm swing on the chubby corpse in front of me, putting a deep gash in the side of his head, breaking the club head off and flying down the street. It barely fazed the fat son of a bitch so Jake had to take care of this one to. Sarah saw us running up to the front door and she had it opened by the time we got there. As soon as the suitcase crossed the threshold she closed the door without slamming it, still looking through the glass to make sure none of them followed us. We were safe for now. I rolled the suitcase into the kitchen, and we decided to unload it on the counter so if we had to leave in a hurry we could dump everything in the suitcase quickly. We both felt very proud of our first 'mission' so we each opened a beer in celebration. One sack of potatoes, a week's worth of canned food, one box of crackers, and two beers. We were off to a good start, but this could never be permanent. That night there were only a few walkers in front of the house. That wasn't what stopped us from going to more houses. It was the loud stomach turning moans we heard from nearby Dallas that didn't settle well with us. Just miles away, there must have been a horde of several hundred walkers, if not thousands. Sleep can be difficult with that kind of fear always in the back of your mind.

That morning the three of us sat down to come up with a 'grocery list' of things we needed. Food was always a plus, but we needed to start looking into ways to reinforce the windows, get more firepower, and some time to fight the boredom. *Thousands of people out there trying to kill us, and we are getting bored in this house.* That was the hardest part, filling time. We would hear military helicopters flying overhead every now and then, wondering how we could get their attention. *If they were taking survivors, where were they picking them up from? Where were they taking them?* We hadn't seen any survivors yet. It hadn't been long enough to start losing hope, but the absence of humanity was getting depressing. The conveniences we had gotten so used to were no longer there. Aside from being able to get food and water at our request, there was no internet connection, going to the movies or to a club. Recreation took a backseat to survival.

I remembered a house on the street behind us that the man was building a deck in his backyard, for a hot tub I think. There should be wood and building materials there we could use to bulk up the windows. Jake and I decided that should be our goal today. Sarah was tired of sitting in the house, and we could use the extra hand carrying the lumber, so we were quick to let her come with us. I had my pistol in my belt, Jake slung the shotgun and carried his slugger. I opted for the 3 wood this time, hoping for a little more skull smashing power. Sarah found an aluminum bat in the garage I forgot all about. I was a little jealous seeing her with that. We put on our coats and got ready by the front door.

"Do we need to lock the door?" Sarah asked.

I laughed at her question

"What, you think somebody is going to break in? They're all dead!"

She was quick to reply.

"Umm, what have you two been doing?"

Hmmm. Sharp as a tack she was. I didn't want to lock the door in case we needed to get in fast, but I didn't want anybody breaking in either.

"Oh stop it you two. David do you have any paint? Why not paint 'Alive Inside' on the door so people know we're here. It's not like the walkers read."

"Jake you're brilliant!" I exclaimed.

I didn't have paint, yet, but I had a sheet of paper and a marker. I wrote a note, put some tape on it and posted it on the front door. Jake poked his head through the entry, gave us the thumbs up, and the three of us stepped out.

We didn't see any walkers down the street as we continued to the first stop sign. Standing at the intersection seeing the devastation now first hand, it all sank it at once. Every house as far as we could see was still. It wasn't like 'nobody's home' still, but the 'lights are still on' still, dead still. I could hear the wind whistling through broken windows and pushed in front doors. There were no sounds of kids playing in the backyards. There were no people coming home from work. All that was around of any evidence that life once existed here was an occasional crashed car still burning, or the sporadic puddles of blood in the streets, in the yards, in the doorways. There were no corpses though. They had literally gotten up and walked away. I felt hopelessness. I felt suddenly alone. I wanted to see my family. I wanted to know everyone was okay. I realized now that we had been standing here for a few minutes, and I'm pretty sure the same thoughts were running through each one of our heads. Jake and Sarah both had the mouth open, statuesque face. The face not of horror, but devastation. Devastation was the only feeling we could feel. This was real, and there was no hope looming on the horizon. After the brutal mental anguish we had just absorbed, like the snap of a finger we were back on the move to the next street over. I could see the truck filled with construction material about a football field away.

"There it is. That's the house."

I pointed to the grey house in the middle of the block. A loud crash of glass shattering came from across the street. A man was yelling for anyone to help. Without hesitation we dashed across the pavement and turned the corner of the garage, hoping it wasn't too late. I was first to turn the corner, and the instant I did three quick gunshots rang in the still air, stopping me in my tracks. I could see two walkers trying to squeeze into a window of this house, with bullets ripping through their soft flesh. The man inside was screaming at them.

"Die you lifeless sons a bitches!" as he squeezed off three more rounds.

Each round hit a walker in the chest, leaving holes in their backside I could put a baseball in. I pulled my .45 and put the first round in the nearest dead skull, spraying the wall with clumps of brains and dried blood. The second walker turned his head towards me as I saw the next round impact his forehead, taking the top half of his skull off.

"Sir we are alive and we are coming to the window. Don't shoot." I said to the man, now seeing him frozen in place as I peeked around the broken bloodstained glass.

The revolver in his hand was empty, but he kept pulling the trigger, blank firing into nothing.

"Oh my god thank you!" He said loudly as he brought his pistol down to his side.

"Please come to the front door, I'll let you in, it's not safe out there!" He couldn't stop speaking to breathe.

Jake and Sarah were already on the move as I turned around and sprinted to catch up to them. The man had the front door unlocked when we got there and hurried us inside. He slammed the door behind us and locked the deadbolt in one swift move.

"Thank God you were here to help, those things weren't

going down!"

"Have you been bitten mister?" Jake asked, still uneasy about standing so close to him.

"No, no. They didn't get that close. My daughter was in her room crying and I guess they heard her. She screamed so I ran in there and saw those things pressing their faces against the window. I just wanted them to go away but when they broke the glass I had to shoot them."

I could tell the man did not want to shoot another human being, and it bothered him that he had just shot two people. He was a middle aged slender man, probably in his early forties. His simple glasses gave him the appearance of an average office working man. His collared short sleeve half button up all but confirmed it.

"Where is your daughter sir?" Sarah asked him without hesitation.

He pointed to the hallway

"Her name is Hailey."

Sarah quickly moved down the hall and into a room, seeing a young girl about nine years old sitting on the floor beside her bed, her hands covering her face. She had straight brown hair that covered her shoulders, a long sleeve pink shirt, and faded blue jeans. Sarah slowly approached her, not only to not startle her, but also in case she had been bitten or scratched.

"Hailey my name is Sarah, I'm here to help. Did those things hurt you?"

Hailey felt relieved to hear another woman's voice. She lifted her face out of her hands, revealing he bright red face and swollen eyes, soaked from weeping.

"They killed my mom!" she cried.

"I saw those monsters bite her all over! And then she laid there bleeding! She stood up and looked just like those things!" her tears came back again.

Sarah reached down and hugged the poor girl. *No child should ever have to see what this child has witnessed* she said to herself. Hailey cried into Sarah's shoulder, and Sarah began to cry also.

Jake and I stood there with the man, now in the living room. The couch had been pushed against a mattress on the wall, probably covering windows. There was a blanket in the middle of the floor with some empty food cans around it. In the corner were some pillows and blankets, with a stack of young adult books beside them. *He's been reading to his daughter to keep her mind off the world outside. This is a good man.* He offered his right hand out after putting the empty gun in his pocket.

"My name is Ben. I can't thank you enough for what you've done."

"David."

"Jake."

It was nice to experience something as formal as a handshake.

"I didn't think there were any survivors around." I stated, hoping he would know something. It turns out he had heard rumors.

"There were a few military helicopters flying survivors to a nearby post" Ben told us.

"The Army set up a medical facility in a nearby college football stadium, but I haven't seen any helicopters flying today. I put a ladder up in my backyard so I could paint the roof telling them we are alive, but before I climbed up I heard Hailey scream."

He must have been talking about the Fighting Eagles stadium about ten miles away. It makes sense, fenced in from all directions, plenty of room, some shelter, and easily controllable. Ben shook his head and turned away.

"It's probably a good thing I didn't climb on the roof, more of those things might have seen me."

He stopped in his tracks. I looked at him as he turned around to face us and I saw in his eyes what I just realized. Sarah and Hailey came in the living room to join us.

"Do you think they heard the gunshots?" Ben asked, slightly startled.

There was a moment of silence, and we each went to a

61

window to peek through the blinds. I saw nothing outside but the house next to us. Jake was the first to speak.

"Sure enough. There's about ten of them walking down the street looking around."

Ben and I both moved to his window and confirmed it when we looked through. Sarah brought her voice down to a whisper

"There are a whole lot of them coming down the street this way. I mean a lot."

Hailey pressed her hand against her mouth to prevent the scream from coming out.

"They aren't looking around, they are coming right for this house."

Sarah hugged Hailey to comfort her. She looked at me when she couldn't think of anything to say. I didn't blame her. *How are we going to get out of this? Maybe if we are quiet they won't try to come in.* We each backed away from the window towards the center of the room. I put two more rounds into the magazine.

"Do you have more bullets?" I whispered to Ben, motioning to the pistol in his pocket.
He nodded
"In the kitchen, half a box."
He crept to the counter and I heard the box rattle as he brought it back in. I noticed he was using a .357 magnum while he was putting the rounds in the cylinder. I gave him the thumbs up.
"Good choice."

Time seemed to have stopped. We sat together against each other's backs in the center of the living room, waiting for what might happen next. The moans outside grew louder. Sarah was right; there were a lot of them outside. They had numbers we hadn't seen yet. The moans filled every room in the house. We knew the house was surrounded. All I wanted to do was be back home in our fortress, but they would just follow us there. We all jumped when the first hand hit the glass and slid down. The glass didn't break, but the sound of that clammy hand running down the window pane made my skin crawl. They knew we were here, and it was just a matter of time before they were coming in.

"We don't have enough bullets David!" Jake excitedly whispered to me.

"We can't shoot our way out of this, let alone smash enough heads with baseball bats and a golf club!" As he finished it hit me.

We could get on the roof! but I shot that idea down quickly, because then we are just trapped somewhere else with an inevitable end. This was still the only progress I had made towards an idea so I moved to the rear of the house anyway to look at the ladder, and anything else he might have had in the backyard.

"David where are you going?" Sarah said worriedly.

"Please tell me you have an idea!"

I shrugged my shoulders and cocked my head to the side. I didn't want to say no, but I didn't want to say yes either. I looked in the backyard and immediately saw the ladder. There was also a swing set, a barbecue grill, and a lawnmower placed so appropriately for a family in the privacy fenced backyard. What I didn't see were zombies. *That's it! They can't climb over the fences!* The thought couldn't have hit me any harder. I knew exactly how to get home. We would move through the backyards to get back to my house, and as long as the walkers didn't see us we could lose them! I was so excited it was hard to whisper.

"I've got a plan!"

The front window shattered inward with bodies leaning over the ledge behind it. Pale arms reached out grasping at anything. The moans turned to throaty growls as the walkers saw us.

"Get in the backyard now!" I screamed.

"We'll go through the backyards to get home. The walkers won't even see us!" Sarah grabbed Hailey's hand and ran beside her towards me at the back door.

"David you're a genius!"

We collected in the backyard and Jake looked over the right side fence for activity.

"This side's all clear."

He used the horizontal slats to crawl over the top, landing in the soft grass on the other side. Sarah and I helped Hailey over so Ben and Jake could grab her. I was the last over, but before I climbed up I looked back at the house. The walkers had filled like water in a cup. They flooded in from all the windows and were making their way through the back door. I scrambled over the fence to join the others as two of them got just feet away from me. This yard had an inflatable pool in the center, with a garden hose running to the top of it. Ben sprinted to catch up to Sarah and Hailey, not seeing the hose. I stopped running, sliding over the wet grass as Ben tripped over the hose planting his face in the dirt. The fence groaned behind us as more bodies piled up against it. The fence would slow them down, but once enough of them pushed, that fence was coming down. I helped Ben to his feet and we both met the others at the far end of the yard. Jake was already over the fence, helping Hailey over. Sarah crawled to the top, and Ben and I soon joined her at the top. I had one leg straddling the fence when I saw the one before come crashing down as decaying bodies came pushing towards us. We moved across another yard and we were slowly putting distance between us and the horde. After the third yard the group was stopped, panting heavily with their hands on their knees.

"David the house is still on the other side of the street." Jake reminded me.

"Let's go one more yard over and then we'll check the street. I want them to collect in the backyards so they won't see us crossing the street."

"Sounds good" Ben nodded to me approvingly.

We leapt over the last fence into a backyard of the corner house. It's not exactly what I wanted, now we had to make sure there were no walkers on the front *and* sides of the house. Ben checked the side as Jake and I slowly lifted our heads over the front. I saw only a few walkers down the street moving towards the house the zombies followed us into. We heard the fence a few houses down crash to the ground and the moaning came closer. I looked at Ben, he nodded the street was clear on his side, so we met at the gate on the side of the corner house. Our lungs burned from hurdling the last fences, but we had to keep going.

"We have to sprint across the street. The house across from us has a gate on the left side, we'll go in through there. Stay quiet, and we should go unnoticed."

I felt like I couldn't move another step, but we couldn't stop now. The walkers were not forgiving. Like a plague they would destroy all in their path, and we would become one of them. The gate creaked open, and we moved to the corner of the house. I peeked around the corner for a last minute check. *Here we go.* I gave a nod and we were running as fast as we could across the street. My legs ached. My chest felt like it was going to burst. We slowed down just before we reached the gate on the other side. Jake gripped the latch and squeezed hard but slow to prevent it from making a sound. The gate swung wide open, and we poured through. Jake closed it behind us, making sure the latch closed. We paused for a moment to get our bearings. Across the street another fence smashed to the ground. The sound of cracking wood and snapping post followed by the *whoomp!* of fence sections hitting the ground sent chills down my spine each time. There was a destructive force the horde possessed that seemed unstoppable. I knew it was only a matter of time before we would have to leave this neighborhood for a structure that could protect us. We let our lungs catch up, turning our heavy pants into quick little breaths.

"I think the chase is over" Ben said, hoping to convince us to slow down.

"All we need now is to stay quiet so they can't track us right?"

I could see Sarah agreeing with him, probably for

Hailey's sake as well. I figured we had about seven yards to cross before reaching our backyard, and we had to do so without *any* attention. The slightest sound could direct them to us, and that meant we no longer had a place to hide nearby equipped with food and water. The five of us gradually made our way across each fence, taking notice of the yards in between. Some had an outdoor patio setup, some houses had laundry hanging out to dry. One house had hot tub with the cover off. Birds were using it as a place to drink water. Every yard had one thing in common. They were occupied a few days prior by a living, breathing family that had birthday parties, barbecues, pool parties, and other outings in the warm sun beneath a clear blue sky. Now there was nothing. Ghost town doesn't begin to describe it. There was no activity. Everything for miles was dead. Movement was done by the walkers. If someone attracted attention, it brought the dead. The army of dead, and silence, were the only elements that grew when the horde left. We finally made it to our yard, all five of us feeling dead on our feet. I was first to the back door. I grabbed the handle and turned. The door wouldn't open. *Oh Jesus it's locked. We secured the doors before we left. I pray Sarah still has....*

"Did you forget something?" she smiled over exhausting breaths, holding the key out in her hand.

"God bless you Sarah"

I took the key and turned the lock. The door swung open, letting light into the dark house.

CHAPTER SIX

Driving down a dark highway on their trip back from Georgia, Pearson is asleep in the truck while Mason is trying to drive all night until he gets them home. Mason figures they should be back at home by 2 am, with enough time to get a couple hours of sleep before they have to report in. He looks at his speedometer, reading almost 90mph. He doesn't feel the bumps in the road, he's simply focused on staying awake as he attempts to sip his coffee without spilling any in his lap.

Pearson woke up in an awkward position in the passenger's seat of Mason's truck with a mild cramp in his neck. Remembering what Mason had told him about their QRF, he realized he knew none of the details.

"Why do they need us back so soon Sarge?"
Mason carefully set his coffee in the cup holder without spilling it.

"Remember that infection we heard about in New York? Apparently it's popping up in cities around the nation. The news over the radio is saying it could be tied to the victims of that Iceland oil rig. They might have brought over some new bird flu or something."

"Those bastards. We offer them aide and they give us crazy bird flu. What a shitty deal Sarge."

"Something like that. The CDC is estimating Dallas and Houston will have an outbreak, because some of the victims went to each one of those places for burn treatment. If there's an outbreak, we'll have to respond QRF for quarantine because we're the nearest installation."

"Lame. Are we getting close to home?"

"About an hour and a half and I'll be dropping you off at the barracks."

"Sounds good Sarge." he said getting comfortable again, then falling asleep instantly.

The yellow center line in the road seemed to go on forever. Mason couldn't remember anything he passed after it went by, he was focused on the hundred meters in front of him and staying in his lane. He tried using range estimation from the school to keep him awake, but that only kept him entertained for a few miles. This late at night there was only talk on the radio, mostly about the outbreaks reaching new cities. They'd been on desolate roads for a majority of the trip, ever so often coming across a gas station. Mason wanted to avoid the large cities in part because the infections, but mostly because he like to keep his speed up. After what seemed like forever, he saw his exit sign and soon he was at the front gate of the Army post. The truck rumbled into the security gate, but now there were more guards than usual checking ID's.

"Sir, you and your passenger please step out of the vehicle."

"Roger. Pearson, wake up! Step out and have your ID ready."

Pearson jumped at Mason's command by habit.

The guard pulled them aside as another briefly looked over the inside of the truck.

"Where are you coming from tonight Sergeant?" The guard asked, looking at his ID card.

"We're driving back from Georgia. Went there for training."

"Did you stop anywhere? Did you have any interactions with anyone showing flu symptoms or general sickness?"

"Negative. We just stopped to get gas, and stayed in separate rooms at a hotel for a few hours last night."

"Okay that sounds fine Sergeant. This officer is going to check your body temperature, please leave the thermometer under your tongue until the told to remove it."

Mason and Pearson were both checked by the officer with the body temperature sensor, and were relieved when the officer gave a thumbs up to the other officer.

"You are free to enter post Sergeant. Please get some sleep and drive safely."

"Yeah roger" he said groggily.

It looked as though every light in the barracks was on, and a few soldiers still stumbling around holding a beer bottle. *They act like we're going to invade Dallas tomorrow and they want to drink every beer the post has before they leave. They've got a lot of disappointment ahead of them.* After dropping Pearson off, Mason could almost feel his soft cotton bed sheets against his skin as he struggled not to break the 30 mph speed limit. He lived in a neighborhood a few miles away from the barracks, but the drive seemed to take hours before he pulled into his familiar driveway. When he shut his engine off his ears rang from the silence in the empty street. *I'm way too tired to get up early.* The house was dark when he walked in, but he didn't bother turning any lights on. His confidence rattled when his shin crashed into his heavy wooden coffee table. *Ouch! Shit!* Rubbing his shin and stumbling down the hallway he found his bed was as soft as he remembered. *I'm just going to rest and then I'll take my shoes off.*

Mason's alarm sounded off, sending unwanted motivation through his body and springing him out of bed. He silently thanked himself for leaving a clean uniform hung in his closet instead of taking it to the school. He was dressed in minutes, but his momentum slowed when he felt the stubble on his cheeks. *No time for shaving cream.* The dry razor burned but it was fast. Twenty minutes after his alarm went off he was in the big truck and leaving the house.

The company was bustling with activity when Mason pulled into his designated parking spot. Rucksack on his back and body armor over his shoulder, he made his way into the building. A specialist greeted him at the door, with the instructions that the company commander wanted to see all platoon sergeants in his office for a mission brief as soon as possible. He threw his gear in his office and grabbed his notebook. Once inside the Captain's office, Mason could see they were waiting on him. The First Sergeant was the first to notice his late arrival.

"Glad you could make it Mason. Now we can begin. Sir?" The commander passed out road maps to each Sergeant, then began the brief.

"This is your brief for mission Cat Scratch Fever, please hold your questions until the end. We have been called up for QRF in an attempt to quarantine the spreading of some radical flu strain that's spreading in the larger cities around the nation. Much of these operations are a modified plan of Operation Garden Plot[1]. Dallas has reported an outbreak that is beyond civilian law enforcement and CDC capabilities to quarantine. Our mission is to establish a large quarantine zone so that we may contain the spread of the virus and provide medical assistance to those that require it. We will have the gun trucks staged by 1300 hours and will step off at 1400 hours in route to a college football stadium located in Dallas. From there we will establish traffic control points at every nearby intersection, and provide security at all entrances. We will also be helping out a nearby clinic by sending a platoon there to provide order and authority, but for the most part you will not be dealing with the sick. Stay out of the medics' way; you are just there for security. We will be accompanied with an attachment from a medical unit, along with trucks equipped with sections of chain link fence to cordon off sectors of the playing field for people showing different stages of symptoms. Yes we will have civilians from FEMA there helping out. Stay out of their way and don't interact with them. You know your call signs, and radio frequencies have been programmed by your RTOs[2]. The code word for infection will be 'Snowball'. There have been reports that those that are infected sometimes grow hostile and attack others, so be prepared for any hostile intent.

---

[1] Army procedure for conducting martial law
[2] Radio Transmitter Operator

You are authorized to use deadly force, but follow the rules of engagement. I say again, deadly force is a last resort. If by some chance we lose control of the facility and are being overrun, the code word is 'Avalanche'. According to our Intel that scenario is unlikely. We do not have much ammo so each soldier will be given two full thirty round magazines. Only the gun trucks will have a full combat load. Please ask your questions now."

Nobody had any immediate questions. They couldn't believe what they were hearing. *This is unreal.*

"Okay if there are no questions, you may return to your platoon and brief your soldiers. Release them for chow, but make sure those trucks are ready to roll by 1400."

There's not much room in a Humvee, especially for a soldier wearing armor. Mason looked at his watch as he wiggled around, trying to free up room. *13:55.* Last minute radio checks were filling up the headsets. The trucks called the commander in order of movement, giving him the 'ready' command. Mason stared at the MRAP in front of him. It is twice the size of his Humvee, with more room inside and equipped with a better air conditioner. It would take almost three hours to arrive in Dallas, but the commander wanted to set up the stadium under the cover of darkness. Reports were coming in that the main highways to Dallas were clogged with congestion and multiple car wrecks. Last minute adjustments were made to the route so as to avoid the congestion. The brake lights on the MRAP let off and the trucks were moving. Mason motioned to his driver to follow, and the mission began.

Even the back roads were clogged with car wrecks, although not near as bad as the highways. The commander wanted to stop and assist paramedics along the highway, but the orders remained to establish the quarantine zone as top priority. The convoy traveled at 50mph, avoiding clogged traffic zones where possible. *This can't be a coincidence. This many wrecks is not typical of the traffic flow in the area.* From his experiences overseas, Mason felt nervous anytime a car would speed past the convoy. A car speeding by meant there was reason to panic, and reason to panic usually involved a loud boom.

As the convoy approached the city, the front of the convoy noticed a bus on the opposite side of the road driving erratically, swerving between lanes. Just before the bus passed Mason's Humvee, it swerved into the ditch towards the convoy, plowing into the concrete barrier then rolling onto it's side. Before the chatter about stopping to help could come over the radio, the commander was broadcasting to all trucks to continue mission, they couldn't stop. Mason imagined the soldiers in every truck felt like he did as they passed, regretful and helpless.

As the convoy rolled into the city, they did not receive the welcome they were expecting. Civilians usually moved out of the way when large military vehicles armed with machine guns drove down the streets, but not this time. Cars were speeding past the convoy, not slowing down when they turned through the trucks. The MRAP narrowly avoided crushing a small hatchback that cut the driver of the truck off, cutting the wheel hard left and bouncing his gunner around inside the turret.

A call over the radio from the front truck reported a car burning on the side of the road. That report was soon followed from the rear truck about a truck crashing through the front window of a business, tearing a wall down with it. *It's like a damn war zone here.* The grizzly scenes followed the convoy to the stadium, displaying mayhem around every block. The convoy drove into the stadium, and immediately staged the trucks for security. The commander ordered the tanks to guard the street entrances to the stadium, accompanied by one or two Humvees for quick reaction to traffic changes. Machine gun posts were built up by sandbags at every available, but controllable entrance to the stadium. All other entrances or possible escape exits were blocked by fence sections. A small team of soldiers began building large, tan tents along the edges of the field, followed by medics setting up aide stations inside. The Commander's private security detail put together the HQ tent away from the others and closer to the helipad, then ran razor wire around it to prevent anyone from getting close enough to listen to voices inside.

Within an hour the fences were linked together, forming two small quarantine zones and a large 'cattle lot' for the infected masses. Medical tents and Command tents were positioned to control the flow of civilians coming in. FEMA established a tent inside the entrance so those coming in could get a bottle of water. People were already lining up at the security gates, begging for help. The soldiers began their duties at their assigned stations, while the platoon leaders came together in the command tent to prepare for the next movement. Each lieutenant was given orders for their rotation to assist the nearby clinics, then released to brief their platoon for the times and procedures for leaving Outpost 72, the football stadium.

"Sergeant Mason could you come to the back of the MRAP?"

"I'm following you sir."

Mason had known this fresh lieutenant for six months now, and while he understood Lieutenant Davis was smart, Mason questioned his decisions at times. The rear hatch of the MRAP was open, with a medic inside sitting under the air conditioner vents.

"Hey Doc can you step out for a moment?"

"Oh, yeah, roger sir. Just cooling off."

Lieutenant Davis stepped up the rungs into the truck first, and once he was in Mason followed.

"Sergeant we've got our orders from the Commander. Our platoon is to be the first in rotation for aide and assist at the Main Street Clinic, approximately eight miles from here. We will be there a week, then third platoon will relieve us. We are to take two Humvees and this MRAP, loaded with medical supplies and quick tents for overflow from the clinic."

"What time do we leave sir?"

"Sunrise tomorrow morning. The Commander wants us to be seen going to another clinic so hopefully it will draw some of the traffic from here over to the other clinic to spread out the patient flow. We've been in contact with a Dr. Benson, he's going to instruct us how he wants the stations set up."

"Roger sir. Where do our soldiers sleep tonight?"

"They'll have to sleep beside the Humvees tonight, rotating guard shifts. We can't afford any surprises."

Mason thought for a moment, working the plan out in his head and how to instruct his squad leaders.

"Alright sir, I'll brief the platoon."

The soldiers weren't happy about sleeping beside the trucks, but it wasn't like the stadium had condos built in. The fenced in areas quickly filled with people. Mason lost count after 300 'Snowball' codes had been called by the security gates. The stadium looked like a concentration camp filled with the sick and dying. The First Sergeant ordered everyone to put on their gas masks with no permission to remove them. The people were crying, screaming, coughing. The sound was deafening. Nobody in the platoon could sleep that night, as hard as they tried. Soldiers lay shoulder to shoulder beside the trucks, wearing a gas mask and ear plugs to block out the outside world, but it didn't work. Some of them begged Mason to begin the truck movement early, but they were on a strict schedule. Most of them wrestled around under their blankets trying to get comfortable but couldn't.

Several soldiers showed signs of relief when the sun broke the horizon, because they would be leaving soon, and hopefully get a few hours to nap once they got to the clinic. Mason called out to load the trucks and all at once each soldier sat upright and packed their assault bags before getting on the trucks. The trucks were idling, they were just waiting on Lieutenant Davis to finish his final brief so they could roll out. Mason could tell the soldiers were getting impatient, until the fresh looey ran to the open door and jumped inside the truck. 07:15 the trucks left the stadium.

The chaos in the stadium was nothing compared to the city just blocks away. There were no reports of rioters, but something happened to society overnight. Buildings were left to burned out rubble heaps, cars smoldered alongside the roads. *The quicker we get off these streets the better.* It didn't take long for the platoon to arrive at the clinic. There were people outside waiting for the clinic to open. Apparently the staff inside had been waiting for the Army to show up, as soon as the last Humvee pulled into the parking lot the doors opened and gray haired man began filing the people in a single line. Quickly dismounting, Mason began barking orders to the soldiers to get tents set up and put a machine gun nest near the entrance. Razor wire was run around the front of the clinic to direct the sick to the entrance. The medic zone and security were established thirty minutes after Mason's platoon arrived, soon offering medical attention to those in line. Dr. Benson spoke with Lieutenant Davis about bringing certain people inside, mostly those with early or weak symptoms to avoid any hostility inside the clinic. Lieutenant Davis was mid sentence with Dr. Benson when Private Cretes yelled for him from the truck.

"Sir you better come listen to this!"
Mad that the soldier interrupted him while he was talking with the Doctor, the lieutenant stormed across the lot to the Humvee, ready to scold the soldier.

"There better be a good reason for this private."

"Uh, roger sir. It's Command. Something's happened at the stadium, listen" as he hands the radio microphone to Lt. Davis.

"Command we have a riot at gate three!"

"Command this is gate two, a large hostile crowd is approaching us and refusing our commands to stop."

"Command, gate one, same scenario here. They aren't stopping sir! What are our rules of engagement?"

"All stations this is Command, are the rioters armed?"

"Gate 1, negative."

"Gate 2, negative."

"Gate 3, negative."

"You are not authorized deadly force on unarmed civilians, I repeat, you are NOT authorized deadly force on unarmed civilians!"

Gunshots sounded off at gate 2, creating buzz in the Command tent like a shook hornet's nest.

"Gate 2 status report!"

"They're attacking us sir! We have three KIA and are being overrun! There are too many of them!"

"All stations, this is Command, we are on full alert! Report to gate 2 immediately!"

Machine gun burst began rattling off at every gate. Every soldier in the stadium was running to the nearest gate to support their brothers. The fences inside were no longer guarded and the people inside burst into a frenzy, shaking the fences trying to tear them down.

"Command this is Medic 9 we have lost control of the quarantine zone. Be advised these people will have the fences torn down momentarily."

"Gate 2 this is Command!"

"Gate 2 this is Command, respond!"

"Command this is gate 3, we have lost control, we have taken mass casualties, we need backup immedia…"

"Gate 3, Command, say again last transmission!"

"Gate 3, Command!"

Silence.

"Any station this net, this is Command, we need a status report!"

Silence.

"Any station this net, Command, report!"

Silence.

"All stations this net, this is Command. Avalanche! Avalanche! Avala…."

The lieutenant dropped the hand mic and ran towards Mason.

"Mason we need to get these people out of the clinic now! The stadium has been over run, the last transmission was code Avalanche."

Mason's eyes grew wide before he forced his composure back. He ran inside the clinic and began spreading the word to his soldiers about code Avalanche. Dr. Benson was confused by the soldier's actions, then found Mason amidst the chaos.

"Sergeant what are your soldiers doing? These people need medical treatment immediately!"

"Sir we have been given the code word for emergency from our chain of command. We need to get these people out of here until we can secure and fortify this building. If we get word that the threat has been neutralized we will allow the sick to come back but until then please just stand back."

The doctor was furious but he knew there was nothing he could do against the armed soldiers. He apologized to the people as the soldiers escorted them out, some of them forcibly. The crowd was growing angry that they were being denied medical attention. Mason grabbed a bullhorn out of the truck and stood on top to broadcast to the crowd.

"At this time we apologize for turning you away. There has been reports of rapid infection spreading throughout the city and we must gain order. You will be admitted again once we have established order. Please get into a single file line before the sandbags over there and we will begin letting people in once we have gained positive control of the situation. Thank you for your patience and we apologize for the inconvenience."

The crowd grew angry and began throwing handfuls of trash, rocks, water bottles, anything they could throw at the soldiers. Following the rules of engagement, the soldiers pointed their weapons at the angry mob and told them to leave. One of the mob's members spoke out.

"There's a medical zone at the football stadium not too far

from here! Let's go there and forget these assholes!"

Mason wanted to tell them it was suicide to go there, but he couldn't for violation of OPSEC[3]. The crowd followed the man just like a herd of cattle and they left the scene. It instantly struck Mason as odd that they didn't take their cars, they just walked away. As the mob walked away, Mason followed the Lieutenant inside to try to get communications with Outpost 72.

Once inside, the RTO and Lieutenant Davis were already around the radio calling out when Mason approached.
"Anything from higher sir?"
"Nothing. The radios are working, we were just talking to them. After the Avalanche call it's like all communications stopped."

Mason didn't want to say what he thought, but he knew what it usually meant when the distress signal was called and line goes dead. It happened once overseas, and they lost a lot of good men when they received a similar transmission from a small outpost in the mountains.
"I'm going to try the radios in the trucks. They'll have a stronger signal. Mason stay here with the radio and keep trying."

Lt. Davis and the radio operator went to the nearest Humvee to try the radio inside. Again no response. Mason stepped out of the building just far enough to use his foot to keep the door propped open. He wanted to make sure nobody was going to do anything crazy inside, and security is always a soldier's number one mission. Everyone by the concertina wire stood up with weapons shouldered, and a soldier named Palmer yelled out.
"Here they come Sarge!"

---

[3] Operations Security

CHAPTER SEVEN

Ben, Hailey, and Sarah sat on the living room floor whispering about stories of their lives before the world turned upside down. Jake and I peered through the blinds to see stragglers from the horde that pursued us. They looked like hunters who had lost their prey. I wondered when they decided to disperse after they lost sight of us and how long it took them to lose interest. Thankfully none of them traced us back here. The roaring moans of the mob were dying down, and one by one they moved to another part of the neighborhood. *Where do they go when there's nothing left in the area to chase? Do they walk to the next neighborhood in search of more victims?* I kept thinking back to Ben's statement that there was a military force not too far away that could provide food and protection. There certainly was hope, something we hadn't felt in a while. We couldn't stay in this house forever, that was for certain.

Hailey lay curled up in soft blankets near the corner to fall asleep. Jake and I joined the others on the floor, when I heard Ben begin his story of the passing of his wife. I could tell it was hard for him to build his courage inside so he could stay strong, but there was no hiding the fact that he was hurting.

"Her name was Alice. She was coming home from work. She worked late that night, hoping to pick up overtime. We were planning a family trip for the summertime, and she wanted to make a little extra money to put away for it. She called me in her car, saying the streets were chaotic. People were rioting she said, chasing other people, fighting in large groups." he took a deep breath.

"If she only knew the truth. I grew a little worried, and I think Hailey saw it in my eyes. We waited by the front door so we could greet her when she pulled in the driveway. Hailey just wanted to see her, but I was getting more worried with each passing minute. I couldn't stop looking at my gold watch, one she gave to me on our fifth anniversary." he rubbed his left wrist where a watch used to be.

"I saw her headlights coming down the street, and I saw Hailey light up. There was a group of people I didn't recognize standing in the yard across the street. When Alice pulled into the driveway I noticed the group began walking in her direction. I remembered the baseball bat we kept behind the front door, never thinking we would need it. It hadn't moved in so long it collected a layer of dust. Alice stepped out of the car, but reached back in to grab her purse. Now the group was right behind her. She never saw it coming. A tall man lunged at her. He didn't hit her, he didn't push her, he bit her. He sank his teeth into her neck. Alice screamed in pain. Hailey shrieked out, wanting to not believe what just happened. I grabbed the bat, and ran out the front door. When I rounded the corner of the car, the gang had her on the ground, lashing at her, spilling her blood over the pavement. She was screaming as hard as she could, kicking and punching back at her attackers. I pulled the bat around, using my weight to crush that tall man's skull. There was a sick thud and a splatter sound. I didn't even see his brains spray the hood of the car. I spun to catch the next man in the jaw, sending teeth in the air. Alice continued to scream, but her pleads for help were getting quieter and her yells were finishing with a raspy plea, then the gurgling of blood in her throat came. I kept swinging away at each attacker I could. The last man stood up from Alice, just as her screams had stopped."

Ben took a moment using his fists to muffle himself as he growled a crying damnation for the attacker.

"He looked at me, and I could see his eyes were no longer human. He had blood running from his mouth, that shone bright red in comparison to his pale dead skin. I knew what he was instantly, but I didn't want to believe it. His eyes widened as he lunged towards me. I didn't realize I was already swinging the bat. I caught him in his left temple. I saw his face compress in slow motion, before his skull exploded open. He dropped to the ground. There were headless corpses laying around my wife's motionless body, and blood collecting beneath her. I couldn't believe what just happened. All was silent around me. I stared at her lifeless face. A face I kissed every morning and every night. I heard nothing around me. I didn't hear Hailey screaming at the top of her lungs for mommy to get up. I almost forgot to breathe. When I remembered to inhale, my eyes burst with tears when the air hit my lungs. I dropped to my knees next to Alice. I sobbed as I brought my face inches from hers. I begged the lord to make things right. I wanted her to sit up, so I could heal her. So I could tell her I loved her. Her eyes opened, but not the way I wanted. She possessed the same lifeless eyes her attackers stared at me with. Her mouth opened to expel a horrible groan. At that moment I heard Hailey's cries from the front porch. I knew it was too late for my dear Alice. I leapt to my feet, and ran to Hailey, grabbing her in my arms and running inside, before Alice could see where we went. I locked the door behind us, and turned off the lights. I spent all night trying to explain to Hailey what had happened to mommy. That's just not possible. To this day I don't think she can fully forgive me for leaving mom 'laying in the grass' as she says. I pray to God everyday that someday she might understand."

Ben began sobbing uncontrollably now.

"I wanted to save my wife! I wanted to take her inside and heal her wounds! I wanted us to grow old as a family! Those monsters took her from us and I can't tell my daughter that I couldn't stop her mommy from becoming a walking corpse!"

I felt the sting of tears in my eyes. Jake rubbed his eyes on his shirt sleeves, I could tell he began thinking of his family. Sarah burst into tears with Ben and wrapped her arms around him. They embraced in a tight hug for a long minute. The pain of the end of days was beginning to set in like a sledgehammer to my chest, and we were all in for the hell that awaited.

The sun began to set as the sky grew darker. Most of the walkers had cleared out of the area in search of more food. Food of course, meant fellow survivors. Ben curled up next to Hailey in the corner. Sarah, Jake, and I lay on the floor staring up at the ceiling.

"Do you think our parents are still alive?" Sarah whispered.

Jake tried to offer words to cheer us up.

"Our parents lived miles from here in different cities. Smaller cities. Surely they had a better chance than we do. I bet the military got them out and moved them to a safe location. We just need to find them."

I didn't know how much faith I could put in Jake's statement, but I did feel better hearing it. I found that hope is just as important as food, water, and shelter. Without hope there is no reason to need or even look for other necessities. We have to get to the football stadium. That is where the rebuilding begins.

"Do you remember Ben saying something about the military setting up a safe zone at the football stadium?" I reminded the others.

They knew immediately what I was talking about.

"We have to go there" Sarah urged. "It's our only chance of surviving this nightmare."

Jake agreed.

"The supplies in the houses nearby will run dry real quick. Especially if we have to fight off another horde. We got lucky today, but I don't want to risk that again."

We knew where we needed to go, we just needed to figure out how to get there. There were helicopters flying overhead yesterday, maybe they'll be in the air tomorrow. Maybe they only search parts of the city on different days, I'm sure they don't have enough choppers or fuel to spend all day in the air. We'll need a way to flag them down, get their attention so there is no doubt we are survivors and we're still here. We began discussing a plan, and for the next two hours we created our most brilliant plan. Now we just needed the supplies.

It was nice going to bed with a plan of escape in our minds. We slept a little easier that night knowing there was hope the next day. When the sun shone a thin ray through the window between the blanket and the wall, it was a nice warmth that woke me. Ben and Hailey stirred right after I sat up, and I could tell Ben was awake. I was excited to tell him of our plan to get out of here, but I figured I would let Jake and Sarah tell him with me in case I missed any details. When Ben saw me moving around, he also sat up.

"Got any food around here?"

"Best food in a tin can for miles." I smiled, trying to make the mood lighthearted.

"Just what the doctor ordered" he smiled back, still rubbing the sleep out of his eyes.

The others woke when they heard the cans being opened with a manual opener. The electricity was shut off now; I assumed it was this way all over the neighborhood, possibly the city. We'd have to eat the food cold; starting a fire was out of the question. The walkers couldn't smell human flesh over the stench of their own rotting corpse, but I didn't want to risk the smell of a fire or food cooking to attract them. Over our cold breakfast the five of us discussed the plan to attract the attention of the helicopter, to fine tune the idea as best as possible. This plan was only going to work once, so it had to be perfect. Ben's idea of painting HELP on the roof was a good idea. It was subtle enough to not catch attention from the walkers, but large enough so the helicopter could see it. Just the sign wouldn't be enough though, we would need a way to show the helicopter that we were still alive when they flew overhead.

We would have to paint the roof under cover of darkness so the walkers wouldn't see us. I chose to go next door using the backyard fence jumping method, while Ben and Jake would go to the house on the other side, and in thirty minutes we would meet back in our yard. The house I was going to, I remembered had a very expensive garden in the backyard with a fountain. I knew I could find PVC pipe somewhere over there, I just hoped it was the right size. Sarah stayed back with Hailey, assuring her we would be okay and that her father would be back soon. She also looked at this as an opportunity to try to mend things with her and Ben about her mother.

Through a quick glance out the window the streets appeared to be free of any walkers. The three of us made our way out the back door, and I watched Jake and Ben as they disappeared over the fence. I grabbed the top of the post and pulled my way over the opposite fence.

The neighbor's yard was eerily empty. The fountain wasn't flowing, the flowers not moving with the slight breeze passing through. I saw the shed tucked away in the corner of the yard, and made my way towards it. I don't know what I would have done if the shed was locked, but I was getting into the shed one way or the other. There was no lock, just a fancy decoration hook that held the shed door closed. I slid the door open an inch at a time, trying to prevent any metal on metal squeaking. Not only did I not want to attract attention, but the sound of it made my skin crawl. Surprisingly the inside of the shed didn't smell like a typical backyard shed with gasoline and lawnmowers. They were meticulous about small details to beautify their garden.

I found a milk crate in the corner filled with miscellaneous pipe fittings, some of which I could use. Next to the crate was exactly what I needed, a 2 ½ inch PVC pipe about 4 feet long. *Perfect*. I grabbed the tube, some glue, and a few of the fittings. I got what I needed out of the shed and tossed it over the fence. I still had twenty minutes before anybody would start to worry, so I decided to peruse inside the house a bit. The back door was wooden with a paneled glass window. I grabbed some rags out of the shed and covered one of the small sections of glass with them, until it was completely covered with thick rags. I used a hammer to smash the glass. I was impressed with myself for thinking this well on my feet. Little to no sound came from the glass shattering. I reached in and unlocked the door. The hinges were well oiled, like the attention to detail in the yard.

The house looked normal on the inside. I never met the couple that lived here. They kept to themselves mostly, and I wasn't home very often anyway, maybe a weekend or two each month. I entered into the kitchen and dining room area. They had nice designer appliances, all matching in color. Shiny copper pans hung on the walls over a large, clean but well used stove top. I knew better than to start digging through cabinets before I cleared the house of any threats. I walked through the living room admiring the art work that hung over a wide tan leather couch. *They were living the life here!* I thought. There were no signs of any struggles, which allowed me to relax a little, knowing that maybe nobody was home during the initial attack. The bedroom had a lavish king size bed with Egyptian cotton sheets. The bed was made, with all the pillows arranged neatly at the head.

I looked in the closet for anything we might need. There were some fancy shoes, some nice suits, but that wouldn't do us any good. I made my way to the garage, where a brand new four door Chevy four wheel drive sat under the lights. *What a shame to have such a clean four wheel drive I thought.* It was jet black with a brush guard on the front, all for cosmetic reasons. I couldn't see any sign this truck had ever been off the pavement. Along the wall were the cans of paint I was hoping to find. As much as the couple here had remodeled, there was certain to be some leftover paint. I grabbed the dark colors, hoping to contrast with the roof color so the message would stand out. Two cans should be enough, and I left the garage. I made my way back to the kitchen and began opening the cabinets one by one. I opened a cabinet above the refrigerator and my eyes locked on it immediately. I hadn't planned on it, but that was the prettiest thing I'd seen in a long time.

Jake and Ben made it over the fence at the same time. Jake landed on his feet, Ben went down to one knee in the grass. Jake right away noticed the patio furniture next to the house. The chairs weren't cheap knock offs, the people here spent good money buying chairs that would last.

"Good" Jake said. "Family people."

The barbecue grill next to the patio was exactly what Jake was looking for. He used his multi tool pliers to unscrew the nut off the back of the electric propane igniter on the front of the grill. In less than a minute he was playing with it in his hands.

"What does that do?" Ben sheepishly asked.

Jake gave him a half grin.

"Hold your hand out."

Ben jumped back when Jake shocked him, not thinking it was as funny as Jake did.

"Let's go inside" Ben said, rubbing his hand.

Ben approached the back door and put his still tingling hand on the knob. The door knob wouldn't turn, so they each chose a window to attempt a silent break in. Jake saw the kitchen on the other side of the window as he was feeling around for a place to lift on. Ben saw the living room on the other side of his window. The sight wasn't comforting. Pillows were thrown around the room. There was a broken picture frame laying across the couch, next to a smashed coffee table. There was definitely a fight in here he thought. He was staring so hard in the room looking for clues he didn't noticed Jake right next to him.

"My window wouldn't open" Jake said next to Ben's ear.

"Jesus Jake you scared the hell out of me!" Ben said, trying to yell softly.

"You know I have a loaded gun in my hand right?"

Jake chuckled and threw an arm around Ben in a playful manner.

"I'm just messing with you chief. No harm in a little fun eh?"

Ben wasn't amused enough to answer so he placed his hands against the window and lifted up. The window opened enough he could squeeze his fingers under it to lift it all the way up.

Ben was the first in the living room, Jake quickly followed. He might mess around, but he always got a friend's back in a hairy situation. They paused to listen for any movement in the house. Nothing could be heard. Just like the rest of the neighborhood, dead quiet. Jake's eyes locked immediately on a samurai sword hanging on a wall above the TV. He moved straight toward it, pulling it out of it's case and posing with it for Ben like a child showing off a trophy.

"Let me get this straight" Ben started, "you want a samurai sword to defend yourself against an army of the dead that carry an infectious virus in their bloodstream that's sure to spray on you if you cut them open?"

Jake's smile dropped and so did his samurai pose.

"What a buzz kill Ben."

He tossed the sword onto the couch and continued looking around. There was nothing of real interest in this house, just a bunch of useless crap that looks like it was bought from TV ads. In the kitchen Ben found a bag of birthday balloons tucked away in a drawer of miscellaneous items. He pocketed the bag and closed the drawer.

"Let's get out of here. This place gives me the creeps" Jake said to Ben, with a little shiver.

"I still need to get the tank off the grill."

They crawled out the window, leaving it open behind them.

"We'll save this for the next clan of survivors" Ben joked.

He moved to the grill and unscrewed the large propane tank from the hose. Jake grabbed some lighter fluid and charcoal and they hauled their treasure over to the fence, tossing it over one by one.

"Why don't you hand that to my when I get over" Jake said to Ben, pointing at the propane tank.

"Good idea."

Jake went over first, and grabbed the tank from Ben, struggling to hold it over his head. Once he was relieved of the tank, Ben hopped over the fence and collected the lighter fluid and charcoal off the ground then followed Jake with the tank to the backdoor of the house. They met David at the back door with a big smile on his face.

"Why are you so happy? Did you find an adult magazine?" Jake said crassly.

"Nope. I found something better than that, and I'm sure you'll agree."

I pulled a thirty year old bottle of scotch from behind my back and displayed it for Jake.

"Ha ha! Brother you know how to house shop!" he said as his face lit up.

Ben looked over the bottle's label.

"That's about a $300 bottle of scotch you got there David. It's from Ireland."

Pleased that we found what we needed and with a little bonus, we moved inside to show off our finds.

Jake and I spent the rest of the afternoon crafting this cannon from a spud gun idea we'd seen on the internet. Ben took one of the tennis balls he found in my garage and poked holes in it, enough to squeeze a balloon into, plus a few holes to vent. Sarah crushed up some charcoal into a fine dust while Hailey watched us construct this canon like mad scientists. I put the crushed charcoal in the tennis ball first, then pushed the balloon inside with a pen. Then I filled the balloon with propane and tied the end off. Sarah stapled some shoestrings to the tennis ball to make a tail for stability, then soaked it in a bowl of lighter fluid. Jake and I finished the cannon just in time for the sun to begin setting.

The five of us sat down for an evening dinner before we would go up to the roof. The vegetables were still cold, but they tasted better this time. We were all proud of our accomplishments today, and we were ready for tomorrow. If all goes well, we will see a helicopter flying overhead that can take us to a safe zone. After dinner we shared a toast of the most expensive liquor we'd ever had, going around the circle, each giving cheers.

"I would like to toast two of the best men I've ever known, and to the family I love that's not my own" Sarah began the toasting.

"I would like to raise my glass to our new friends, that can't replace old ones but will always hold a special place in my heart" Ben said, holding his glass high.

Jake spoke up after Ben.

"This is for our friends and family that can't be here, but hopefully are in a better place."

I admired everyone I was with here tonight. We were a very special group, and I was proud to be a part of it.

"Jake, Sarah, Ben, Hailey, you are all family in my heart, and you mean the world to me. Even if we are all that's left in the world."

The scotch was smooth as silk going down, but I sure felt the burn in my chest.

It was late enough now that Jake and I could sneak on to the roof without being seen. The scotch gave us enough liquid courage to have the will to climb up relaxed. The night wasn't too bright, the moon only showed a quarter of itself. The air was cool, and thankfully not windy. We each carried a can of paint and brush with us. We had enough paint for more than a simple HELP sign, so we decided to spread ALIVE INSIDE across the largest portion of the roof we could find.

We were proud of our job, and we stood back to admire it. The distant moans broke our sense of proud accomplishment, reminding us the threat was still there and ready to attack. We climbed down and went in through the back door. We went to our usual sleeping spots to lie down for the night. Tomorrow held all the promise we needed for a good night's rest.

CHAPTER EIGHT

Beams of warm sun pierced the darkness around the blankets covering the windows in the living room, slowly spreading from the dark corner near Ben and Hailey to where we slept in the middle of the room. The morning sun was a reminder we could feel good about the day. We had the food to last us another week without more scavenging, and we had weapons to defend ourselves against a small group of walkers. All night I dreamt of hearing a helicopter overhead, ready to take us to safety. Just one small step remained in this unimaginable situation, then we could say goodbye to the days of living in darkness. I saw Ben sit up and rub the sleep out of his eyes as he looked in my direction.

"Are we saved yet?" he asked rhetorically. I chuckled.

"They said they would be here when their lunch was over."

"They must be Union workers" Ben replied, keeping the friendly chatter volleying.

Sarah and Jake woke to our laughing, Jake immediately wanting breakfast.

"The things I would do for some hot eggs and bacon."

Sarah chimed in, wanting waffles added to that order.

They walked to the kitchen and immediately I heard cans being shuffled around, discussed like they were on a menu. I could faintly smell the lighter fluid the tennis balls were soaking in, even though they were in a sealable plastic case. I was hoping if we had to shoot this fireball in the air the helicopter wouldn't think we were attempting to attack it, but it was a hell of a way to flag somebody down. My train of thought was broken when Hailey woke up violently coughing. Ben hugged her, patting her on the back as she coughed dryly into the bend of her elbow. Ben placed the back of his hand on her forehead,

"Goodness princess you're burning up!"

I heard the forks stop moving inside the tin cans of vegetables in the kitchen as Jake and Sarah froze. I handed a bottle of water to Ben for Hailey to wet her throat with, and unintentionally gasped when she looked up at me. She had deep purple bags under her bloodshot eyes that shone in contrast to her pale white skin. She was weak when she took the water from Ben, her hands were shaking.

"Ben I have to ask you, has she been bitten or scratched?"

"Absolutely not!" He snapped back.

I realized his protection for his daughter, his only immediate family left alive. Jake and Sarah rounded the corner out of the kitchen, both with a look of concern displayed across their faces.

"Ben we have to know." I warned him, for the safety of us all.

"You'll just have to take my word for it sir!" he said defending his daughter.

Sarah came closer, putting a hand on Ben's shoulder.

"Let me take her into the other room and check her for wounds Ben. I'll help her in anyway I can. You can come to if you'd like."

Seeing that we weren't going to give up persistence, he agreed to oblige us.

"Hailey honey, Miss Sarah is going to take you into that room and make sure you are okay. We're going to get you feeling better as soon as we can."

Hailey's eyes started welling up, followed by a heavy tear slowly running down her right cheek before she spoke.

"Daddy am I going to be okay?" She looked at Ben with a heavily worried look on her young face.

"Everything's going to okay honey." Sarah took her by the hand.

"Hailey, sweetie come with me so I can check you for wounds, just like the doctor."

As Hailey's other hand left her father's she asked Sarah if she was a doctor. Sarah's eyes got a little misty when she responded to her that she would do the best she could. They went into the first bedroom and the three of us stood there frozen like statues as the door closed behind them.

"Ben I'm sure she's okay" Jake said trying to comfort him.

"You know we have to be sure Ben. We'll do everything to make sure she's okay."

The next ten minutes felt like an eternity. When the door opened, we were standing there not having moved at all. I think we all exhaled in relief when Sarah nodded that she had not been bitten or scratched, and showing no signs of infection. She was still sick however, and we would need to get medication to her immediately. Jake and I volunteered to search the surrounding houses for medications.

Just before it was noon, I slid my .45 into my belt and put my leather jacket on over a tee shirt and jeans. Jake tried to borrow some of my clothes, but they were too tight so he stayed in his worn jeans and Carhartt jacket. He slung the shotgun over his back and grabbed his trusty wooden bat. I figured this time I would leave the golf clubs and take the aluminum bat Sarah had been carrying.

I looked out the front windows to see if we had a crowd today, but there were only a few walkers scattered up and down the street. I guess they hadn't made it to wherever the horde had gone. We slid out the back door and leapt the fence to the house I had gone into before. Once again the backdoor was open and nothing had changed inside. We made our way down the hall and each chose a bathroom to look through. Jake stopped at the first bathroom as I continued down the hallway. I heard Jake rustling around through the drawers, but I didn't hear any pill bottles rattle. I found the master bath in the back of the house, and it matched the vanity of the other rooms. There were shiny marble countertops and a glassed in shower with gold lining. I saw the medicine cabinet set in the wall behind a lacquered wooden panel. Inside there were bottles of over the counter pain relief, and some other prescriptions I had no idea what they were for. I looked under the sink for travel bag to put the pills in, and of course there wasn't anything like it. *I hope they are on vacation, and nowhere around here, I thought.* I emptied a silk pillow case and put the bottles in it, along with some toilet paper and personal hygiene items that hadn't been taken for their trip. I met Jake in the hallway and he showed me a bottle of ibuprofen he'd found. He put it in the pillow case after looking through the other bottles.

"This one here is an antibiotic, this one is for diabetes. Good score, but nothing we need. We'll have to go next door I suppose."

I'm glad Jake could identify the bottles, but I wasn't going to ask how he knew. We moved towards the back door, and I noticed with every step I took, the pills rattled in their bottles making me sound like a walking maraca.

"David you think you can keep it quiet when you walk so close to me?" Jake said jokingly.

"I'll be a lot quieter if you take this bag from me."

"Ha ha no way dude!"

As we made our way out the back door we could hear gunshots a few miles away. Jake paused for a moment, putting his hand to my chest to stop me. After about fifteen shots were fired there was a moment of silence, and then nothing.

"I hope they are as lucky as we were" Jake said to me, then moving again towards the next house.

We jumped the fence again, slightly remembering this yard when we escaped through here before. There were plastic toys scattered across the yard, and one bench on the patio facing the yard. *The toys are a good find for our situation* I thought, but the house is still new territory in a very dangerous place. The back door was a sliding glass door with the curtains closed behind it. The tall, slender plastic curtains should have been standing still, but they were slightly swaying back and forth. One of them had been torn down, revealing a dark room behind it, with a narrow beam of light across the floor. The back door was locked, and it was way too big to break without making much noise. Jake knew this scenario all to well and was already checking windows.

"It's locked here to" he said disappointed.

I cupped my hands around my eyes and peered in through the door where the shade had been ripped down.

"I think the front door is open."

I was slightly irritated that I hadn't paid attention to it before.

"With the toys here I think it would be worth checking out."

"Alright let's do it." Jake agreed.

We moved to the opposite side of the house from ours and found the gate leading to the front yard. Jake squeezed the handle and quietly opened the gate. The path to the front of the house looked clear of walkers. Jake led us out of the backyard and around to the front door. Sure enough the door was wide open, but the bloody prints in the entryway weren't the slightest bit welcoming. We looked at each other like we were both now on high alert. Jake slid into the house with his bat pulled back ready to strike, and I followed in quickly so as not to be seen by any walkers nearby. Jake stood at the mouth of the living room, ready for any thing to happen as I slowly closed the door behind us and locked the deadbolt. We poured into the open room as quietly as we could, listening for any movement in the house. There was a spilled bowl of cereal on the floor, filling the room with an incredibly horrible stench of spoiled milk. The television sat eerily quiet on it's stand, where life once shone through the picture. There were a child's drawings that looked like they had once been stuck on the refrigerator, but were now scattered across the kitchen floor and replaced by bloody adult sized handprints.

"I don't like this at all" Jake whispered to me.

"Let's just check for medications and get the hell out of here" I agreed with him.

We moved cautiously through the hallway, and I couldn't help but notice the child's room to my right had been torn apart. It looked like a tornado swept through, ripping apart everything in its path. I could tell a young boy lived here. There was a red race car bed in his room, surrounded by walls painted by an outer space them. A small desk with a miniature chair stood in the corner, with little drawings of what looked like his family in stick figure form around a square house. *Everything used to be perfect, once upon a time.* I shivered a little as the scene that might have taken place here ran through my mind. I didn't want to imagine confronting any little walkers. In the hallway bathroom there were little toothbrushes, Spiderman toothpaste tubes, and in a cabinet above the toilet there were cold medications for a young child. Jake began placing cough syrup, child's Tylenol, sinus medication, and some stomach tablet chewable into the pillow case.

"Alright we got what we need, let's get out of here" he said.

With as much medication as the child had, I figured the adults might have a small pharmacy in the master bath, and while we are here…

"Let's check out the parent's bathroom and then we leave."

Jake wasn't terribly excited about the idea, but he pushed himself down the hallway to the end, where the master bedroom door was slightly ajar. With one hand pushing the door open, one hand gripped tightly on the bat, Jake moved into the room first. The stench of death filled our nostrils. The first thing we both saw was the sideways facing bed covered in blood. On top was a woman's body, at least the clothes looked like a woman's, her body eaten down to the bone in most places. We entered at the corner of the room, and across a mirrored dresser was the bathroom door. We must have taken a step forward a minute at a time, because we crept into this crime scene so slowly the only thing moving fast was our heart rates. The French style closet doors across from the foot of the bed were smeared with blood, more so than the blood sprayed white walls. I snapped back into reality and hurried past the dresser into the bathroom. I took a brief pause to glimpse into the mirror and see how stubbly my face had gotten without shaving for a few days. *Back to what we came here for.* I wanted to get the medication, but I also wanted to get out of the bedroom so the images would stop flashing through my mind. I opened the cabinet and used my arm to rake everything into the pillow case. I didn't know what I was grabbing; I just wanted it in the bag so we could leave, not caring how much noise I was making.

"Oh shit David...."

"What?" I said coming out of the bathroom to a frozen in place Jake.

His face was frozen in fear as he stared across the room. I looked where his eyes were glued, and across the bed a corpse was slowly rising. A middle aged man was slowly rising to his feet. His skin was grey; his eyes were no longer human. His mouth was open with dry blood than stained down his shirt covered chest. Bloody hands gripped the sheets as he pulled his way onto the bed coming towards us. We couldn't move at the sight in front of us. *The bedroom door was right there!* The man got one leg onto the bed when we snapped out of our trance. One by one we swapped baseball bats into the top of the man's skull, spilling the grey matter inside into piles on the stained sheets. Jake and I both grunted with each swing we took at the man, hitting him until our arms got tired. There was nothing left above his shoulders when we stopped swinging and dropped the bat to our sides. Standing there in horror, neither of us moved. What came next startled us back into fight mode. The French style doors to the closet rattled open, and my worst fear peered out, about three feet tall.

The little boy stood there, deep sunken eyes staring up at us. He couldn't have been older than eight years. *We could run out of the house without ever having to hurt this child. Would God judge us for not sending this poor child to him instead of leaving him in this hell?* I urged Jake to move, pushing my elbow into his side.

"Are you hearing to hurt me?" the child spoke.

"Oh my God you're alive!" We said in unison, as our chests began thumping with life again.

"What is your name little man?" Jake asked the trembling little boy.

"Adam" he returned, beginning to look around the room. I jumped between him and the scene on the bed.

"My name is David, and this is Jake. Do you know where your parents are?" Hoping not to hear what I knew the answer was.

"My daddy hurt my mommy! And then he tried to hurt me!" The child's eyes burst into tears.

"Close your eyes Adam, and come with us. We'll keep you safe."

I grabbed his hand and we followed Jake out of the bedroom and down the hallway. We were in a race to get out of this morbid house. Jake was the first to the backdoor, yanking up the lock and pulling the stiff door wide open. We stepped into the yard and inhaled a deep breath of fresh air. No more smell of death. No more rotten milk. Slowly the foul stenches were leaving my nostrils as we walked to the fence. Jake was the first over so he could help Adam get across. I followed, wanting to resist the temptation of looking at that house one last time, but I couldn't. I took a quick glimpse, and felt a shutter go down my body. The images started rushing back so I squinted hard to push them away and rolled over the fence.

A familiar sound came roaring up the street, taking a moment for us to realize what it was. It was a truck with loud exhaust screaming up the road. Jake and I hurried to the fence facing the front yard and poked our heads above the fence top with hopes of seeing the survivors. Gunshots rang out from the cab of the truck, shooting at walkers bumbling down the street. A man in the back of the truck saw us, and I could tell by the look on his face he wasn't here to help. He yelled to the driver one hand holding on to the side of the pickup, the other arm fully extended and pointing at us. We jumped down and scrambled the fence into the neighbor's yard. I was carrying Adam under my right arm, and the pillow case of meds slung over my left shoulder running and rattling to the final fence. The truck's tires screeched to a halt in front of the house. They saw us hurdle the last fence, and I thought maybe they wouldn't know what house we were going into. As we rushed in the back door I remembered the front door and my stomach sank. *Alive Inside.* Ben, Sarah, and Hailey's faces changed to panic when they saw us come in with such haste.

"What's going on out there?! Sarah yelled for answers.

"I don't know Sarah, but they don't look friendly" I answered, setting Adam down next to Hailey.

"Who is this?"

"Sarah please just introduce him to Hailey" I said running towards the front window.

It was a red extended cab truck with mud slung on the fenders. They stopped in the middle of the street, the broadside of the truck facing the house. Two men in the bed of the truck had shotguns pointed at the house; the passenger had an AK-47 aimed at the window I was looking out of. The driver opened his door and stood on the door sill to address us with a bullhorn.

"Looters." Jake said.

Where are the walkers at? Oh that's right, they shot them. The one time I wouldn't mind seeing walkers... This was not going to end well. I motioned Ben to take the kids to the kitchen in the back of the house and lay on the floor. The man with the bullhorn spoke.

"Listen up alive inside! We don't want much trouble, we just want your food, water, and any guns you might have. If you comply, you won't get hurt badly." He laughed to his buddies as he finished the last part.

"We're not giving them shit!" Sarah roared to Jake and me.

We stayed quiet, hoping somehow they would just leave. We didn't have the firepower to shoot our way out, even if we did, we'd need the ammo when the horde came. The horde would be coming soon.

"Maybe we can wait them out until the horde comes" I whispered to the others, whispering out of habit.

"This is your last chance!" The bullhorn sounded off again.

We lay there, looking out the window, attempting to call their bluff. The driver lowered his bullhorn and said something to the other three. Flashes came from the truck as bullets and shotgun pellets riddled the front walls of the house, shattering glass and splintering wood into the living room raining down on us.

"Why are they doing this?! What did we do to them?!" Sarah screamed with her eyes shut, holding her hands around her head trying to protect herself from the glass.

The bullets took a pause, and the bullhorn came back to life.

"Y'all don't want us to do that again do you? Give us what you got."

"You're not getting anything from us you assholes!" Sarah screamed back.

I could hear the hatred in her voice.

"Oh you got a pretty little thing in there, do ya? Send her out with the food, and wearing something....simple."

"Oh hell no" Jake said in a flat voice.

"We've got to do something."

The bullet barrage ripped through the walls again as Jake scrambled across the floor towards the kitchen. I knew exactly what he was doing. I crawled behind him into the kitchen. Once I was lying on tile I stretched my arm up to the counter and felt for the plastic container with the tennis balls soaking in it. Jake had the PVC cannon and crawled back into the living room with me right behind him. We waited for the bullets to stop flying, and then peeked through the gaping window from the back of the room. I motioned for Sarah to move behind us and into the kitchen.

"I bet y'all are getting tired of us shooting up your place. You've got one minute to send out the women with the food, or we're coming in to get them, and leaving the rest of you for the flesh eating monsters. I hope you make the right decision!"
The passenger's door was open, with enough room that if we aimed right we could send a fireball into the cab of the truck.

"If we can land one in the cab of that truck, you and I can go out there guns a blazing and kill those assholes." I said to Jake, hoping he had input also.

"Then what? They die, the horde comes, and we die. It's that simple."
He had a point. We were fighting two battles. Survivors can't even band together against the walking dead. I knew if we survived this, we'd just face more looters again some other day. *Looters doesn't begin to describe them. This group is a gang of savages.*

"Thirty seconds!" the bullhorn blasted.
Staring at the truck I remembered it. *There's a large truck next door! We can use it to go to the football stadium!* When my eyes lit up Jake knew I was on to something. I told him the plan, Sarah had her head stretched around the corner listening to the plan. When I finished I could hear her explain the plan to the others.

"Ten seconds!"
I stuffed a tennis ball into the tube and we filled the back end

with propane. Jake brought the cannon over his shoulder, as if to aim it at the opening on the passenger's side.

"Five..."

"Four..."

I pushed the igniter. The belly of the cannon growled, then *BOOM!* The tennis ball shot out as a fireball straight into the cab of the pickup. It struck the passenger seat and erupted into a ball of fire filling the cab with flames. The passenger fell to the ground trying to put the flames on his back out. The two men in the back dove out of the bed hitting the ground hard. The driver's front side absorbed much of the blast, immediately burning his skin down to the muscle. Flames poured around the roof of the cab as oxygen filled back in the truck. The front half of the truck was roasting and we could see the paint begin to boil. We were already on our feet with guns drawn, sprinting across the yard. When I got about ten yards from the passenger still trying to roll the flames out, I shot him twice in the chest, fresh blood staining his shirt. His body went limp, dropping the AK on the concrete. Jake gave each man behind the truck a load of buckshot to the torso, keeping them down, but not killing them. I had plans for the driver after I picked up the assault rifle from the passenger. I came around the front of the truck seeing the bullhorn smashed and the man trying to crawl away.

"Please kill me! It hurts so bad! Shoot me!"

I decided to fulfill one of his requests, so I shot him in the knee.

"I'll let the horde finish you off."

I could see the numbers growing at the end of the street, moving our way slowly. I took the pistol out of his belt and dropped the magazine into my pocket. I tossed the empty gun back to him, giving him the feeling of helplessness I'm sure he pushed on so many people. Jake collected the ammo and guns from the others before we sprinted back to the house. The horde surely saw us, but the fresh bodies outside should slow them down.

CHAPTER NINE

Once in the house Sarah already had the back door open and waved us to hurry up. We met Ben and the kids in the back yard with a bag of canned food and the medical pillow case, and helped each other over the fence. Running to the house next door was easy, and getting in was easy, now we just needed to find the keys to the truck. I heard screams come from the street as the savages were being eaten by the horde. In a way I felt a little better inside about the justice that was being served. *Those men were killers* I kept telling myself. Ben held the kids' hands as we looked for the keys. Sarah was going through drawers in the kitchen; Jake was digging through couch cushions in the living room. The people that lived here were very organized. *I bet the keys were....exactly.* The keys were hanging on a key rack fixed to a wall beside the garage door.

"I've got them!" I exclaimed.

Everyone moved at once towards the door, almost smashing me against the door as I tried to open it up.

"Back up! Back up!"

As soon as there was room I swung the door open and I couldn't have been more excited when I saw that black truck sitting there, shining under the fluorescent bulbs. It chirped when I pressed the unlock button on the keyless and we piled in wherever there was a seat. Ben and the kids sat in the backseat, and like a good father he instructed them to put on their seatbelts. Jake followed Sarah into the passenger's side, Sarah taking the middle seat. The truck roared to life as I turned the key, spewing black smoke out of the loud exhaust and rock music blaring out of the subwoofers under the seat. As I predicted, the garage door opener was attached to the visor above me, I dropped the shifter in reverse and pushed the garage open button. Nothing happened. Jake and I looked at each other, thinking the same thing. *There's no electricity.* He jumped out of the passenger door and grabbed the release string hanging from the cable. He grunted as he lifted the door, its wheels screeching in the tracks as it opened up. This got some attention of a few walkers I could see in the side view mirror, but most of them were concerned with the meal at hand. Once Jake closed the truck door behind him I punched the gas and we were flying backwards out of the garage and into the street. The sound that came from hitting some walkers was a sick thudding, but they were no match for the V8 that powered this beast. I threw the shifter in drive and again mashed the pedal, lifting the front of the truck. The exhaust screamed louder as the rpm's climbed. *Just ten miles to go.* In the rear view mirror I could see the horde devouring our attackers, gnawing them to the bone. A walker was coming towards us in the middle of the road so I decided to test the brush guard. We hit the teenage zombie with such force his head snapped off at the neck and bounced over the truck as his body splattered on the ground.

"Woooooo!" Jake yelled holding onto the truck's interior handles for dear life.

We were screaming through the streets of this neighborhood, turning the head of every walker we passed. I didn't care who saw us. We would be in a safe zone soon. Many of the houses we passed looked the same. The front door was wide open, or the windows were busted out. There was even a sedan parked in the living room of a house on the corner. Ben was in the backseat assuring the children we were on our way to a safe area, and those things couldn't hurt us there. Sarah was trying to balance between consoling the children with Ben and calling out walkers to hit in the road for points. I'll admit we took a little pleasure in our sick game. We were finally on the offensive, and we still had food, medicine, and plenty of guns.

I saw the sign I had been looking for. The green sign that told us the stadium was our next left. I barely slowed down for the turn, chirping the tires as I gripped the wheel through the intersection. A mile ahead we could see them. Two huge armored tanks guarded the entrance to the stadium, with a couple of humvees beside them, machine guns positioned down the streets.

Our excitement wouldn't last long however. The scene looked all wrong now. There were sandbags built up to funnel people in, but there was nobody there. Nobody stood ready behind the machine guns. Nobody stood there to guide us in to the safe zone. There were bodies in the streets leading up to the entrance, and a few bodies slung over the sandbags of the machine gun pits. No sign of life around. *This is where the horde was going. There was a large supply of food on the other side of those gates. The Army couldn't push back the numbers of the dead walking towards them.*

"No, no, NO! Where is everybody?" Sarah asked, not wanting to believe what she was seeing.

"I think we're late" Jake replied.

"That might be a blessing."

"What is it? What's happening? Where is everybody?" the kids kept asking anybody that was listening.

Ben told them the drive was going to be longer than we thought which eased them a little. He was staring at me through the rear view mirror, and I could read his thoughts. *What's your plan now hero?* I was at a loss. What could we do? Everything we planned led us to this moment, and now there was nothing. This explains why the choppers weren't flying overhead anymore. This explains the endless number of walkers we kept seeing in the streets. I slowed down as we got closer to the checkpoint, hoping at some point somebody would wave us in and everything would be okay. Nobody appeared. No welcome mat. I looked beyond the chain link fence into the stadium. There they were. The dead were walking about, looking for their next meal. Some groups were on their knees around a corpse. I'm sure they were cleaning some poor soul's bones off. I made the right turn before the large tan tank and continued driving up the street. I looked down at the dashboard gauges. We had a half tank of gas to take us away from this spot.

"What do we do now" Sarah asked.

Jake began filling each shotgun with the remaining shells.

"Shooting your way out of this truck isn't an answer

Jake!"

Sarah grew more and more frantic with each empty intersection we passed through. Ben did his best to keep the children calm, but like me he was running out of ideas and the children were growing impatient. I wasn't thinking clearly, and it hadn't occurred to me we were driving deeper into downtown.

The intersections were getting closer and closer to each other the further we went down the road. That had to mean one thing. We were in the red light district, and we're running out of daylight. I asked Jake to load as many rounds as he could in the magazines of my 45, wishing I had enough ammo left to do so. *Maybe if I think about it hard enough he'll hand me a full shotgun.* We came onto a long, open road, with what looked like apartment complexes on each side. The street was covered in scattered bodies of the dead. The dead weren't walking, but they were actually head split open dead. I slowed the truck down, not liking the situation we were coming into. The windows and doors downstairs were boarded up, but the windows upstairs were open. The mood in the truck was shared, as silence fell upon us. These buildings were fortified, and ideally we were saved. The paint on the doors said otherwise. DO NOT ENTER was painted in bright orange on the closest wall to our right. Across the street someone had painted NO TRESPASSING on a garage door and 'Pit Bulls' on the apartment next to it.

"I don't think we're welcome here..."

Before Sarah could finish, two trucks sped out of the driveways at the corner apartments, coming together touching grills to block the road ahead. The driver of the black truck and passenger of the blue truck stepped out and pointed shotguns at us. The tires screeched as I slammed on the brakes. I wasn't completely stopped when I threw the transmission in reverse, getting a grinding noise as the truck clunked into gear. The rear tires made donuts of smoke as the kids were screaming behind me, Sarah and Jake racking the shotguns. The truck was accelerating faster and the steering wheel was getting harder to control. I took my eyes off the rear view mirror to see flashes from the muzzles of the men in front of us. In the split second I wasn't looking behind us, I didn't see they had done the same maneuver with trucks behind us. I slammed the rear into the bed of a single cab pickup, trapping the gunman inside. Fenders groaned as I drove the truck away from the roadblock. I could see men of all ages pointing rifles out of the second story windows, not firing yet. The end of the street was blocked with the two trucks, and privacy fences along the driveways they came out of. *More fences to cross* I thought. I floored the gas pedal and the truck roared with life, picking up speed towards the roadblock. The windows opened with flashes as bullets riddled our truck from both sides. I couldn't hear my own screaming over the screams that were filling the truck. I had frozen with my foot all the way on the pedal and one thing in mind, crashing us out of here. The men at the roadblock ran away from the trucks as we got closer. Just as we were about two car lengths away from the other trucks I jerked the wheel to the right, missing the black truck by inches. Our front grill struck the fence, squeezing between two posts, sending chunks of wood flying in every direction. The bullets stopped hitting the truck; I'm not sure if they were missing or stopped shooting altogether. Our screams turned to joyful cheers as we sped down the empty street. Well, all but one of us. Ben was still screaming in the back seat.

"I'm hit! Oh God I'm hit!"

"Oh my God Ben, are you okay?!" Sarah yelled out of habit, knowing he wasn't.

Ben had been shot in the leg from one of the rifles used. It had to be a rifle, I don't think the shotguns could have done that much damage at the distance they were. Thankfully the kids were not hurt, but they were screaming when they saw the blood on Ben's hand. Hailey screamed at the top of her lungs for God to let her daddy live. I could barely think to myself with her high pitch screams in my ears, but I didn't blame her. Ben was all she had left of her family.

The truck was sputtering some, and it really rattled over fifty mph, but I wasn't going to slow down. I wasn't sure what I was looking for anymore, I just had to find Ben help. Sarah wrapped her belt around his leg, with one of Ben's ripped off sleeves stuffed in the wound to keep pressure on it. The bleeding had slowed, and the fact that he was still alive meant they hadn't hit his femoral artery. I tried to take every road I could find that would get us further from downtown. Those apartments were well fortified, and they had planned how to trap someone inside, or prevent someone from coming in. *The tribes were already building.* I took a deep sigh of relief as we came upon a street not filled with walkers or armed survivors. The truck had really taken a beating getting us out of that ambush. Steam was spewing from under the hood, and I knew we didn't have much longer before the engine would lock up.

Everyone was exhausted from everything that's happened in the past few days, along with getting very little sleep. Our faces showed it. Ben was still in severe pain, and his skin was getting pale. His shirt was soaked from Hailey's tears. We were now several miles from the apartment complex we labeled Pit Bull Alley. We had passed a few walkers, occasionally bumping one with the side view mirrors, or vindictively with the front brush guard. The truck sputtered along, barely able to accelerate at all. The area we came into now looked a little safer, but again I knew nothing was what it seemed anymore. We came into a homely looking suburban area that still had cars parked in front of the stores. There were some shops along the left in a row, and a large hardware store across the street. It was an old fashioned hardware store, and just like the other shops across the street every store looked like it was Mom and Pop operated. It could have meant a pleasant drive aside from the few walkers stumbling about. A loud hiss followed by a pop came from the engine and the truck grounded to a halt like a sled on concrete. The engine gave a few last clunks before finally settling, leaving us in the middle of the road. *What in the hell do we do now?*

Every walker in sight noticed we weren't moving anymore and they moved towards us, like lions stalking their prey. I knew the truck wouldn't hold them back very long. *When are we going to catch a fucking break?!* The sun was on the edge of the horizon, only an orange dot.

"David if you have an idea I'd love to hear it!" Jake said while racking the shotgun.

"We've got to get into one of these buildings!"

But then what would we do? Most of the stores had reinforced glass doors, and if we broke the glass it wouldn't do us any good to be inside if we couldn't keep the dead out.

"We can't stay here!" Sarah yelled, pointing at a walker, just steps in front of the truck.

I opened the door with my pistol ready to shoot, forgetting about the dome light. We were now lit up as if under a search light for all to see. The nearest walkers groaned and began walking faster towards us, each with a stiff limp. *They know where we are for sure now* I thought. I had a moment before each shot to aim so as not to miss. A headshot meant instant stopping power. After two carefully placed shots, I heard the deep bark from Jake's shotgun followed by thuds on the concrete. Once the immediate walkers were down, I helped get everyone out of the truck. Ben was able to walk with assistance, which meant one less gun to our advantage. Sarah helped him along, holding Adam's hand with her other. Hailey stayed glued to her Dad's side, encouraging him through tears. We moved underneath the walkway of the hardware store and followed the wall down, hoping for an unlocked door. There was a set of double glass doors between showcase windows, but they only rattled when we tugged on them. I could hear the bell on the other side of the door hitting the frame with each tug. We continued down the walls, shooting a walker when they got within twenty feet. We were running low on ammo, and options. Nearing the corner of the store I could see an alley that separated this hardware store from the two story building next to it. I prayed there were no surprises around that corner, because we couldn't handle much more. Ben and Sarah were doing their best to keep up with us, but we couldn't face a horde if there was one around the corner. I heard a boom ahead of us, but not that of a gun. There was loud pop overhead, showering the sky with bright colors. *Fireworks?* We hesitated reaching the corner, but in that moment Jake and I lowered our weapons. The walkers stopped in their tracks and looked up at the sky, as if curiosity took over the need to feed.

"PSST!" a voice said across the alley.

A man had his head and arm poking out of a door in the two story building, frantically waving us to come in. I took a deep breath; I hadn't noticed that I stopped breathing for a moment. We hurried as fast as we could before the showering embers burnt out. I ran to the door, Jake and I helping the others before going in ourselves. As the heavy door slammed behind us, I heard the moaning again. Jake and I peered out of a nearby window, amazed at what we saw. To the walkers we had vanished into thin air. They had no idea we were inside, so they continued down the road for the next hunt. *But it wouldn't be us.*

CHAPTER TEN

I was shaking the hand of a middle aged man, his name is Hassam. I couldn't thank him enough for his hospitality. He was a frail man. He looked of Middle Eastern descent. He had a very friendly face, and a very trustworthy feel to him. Despite the conditions outside he maintained a starched button up shirt and creased slacks. He had immediately taken Ben over to a table in the back of what looked like a grocery store. After we introduced ourselves he welcomed us into the store, offering us anything off the shelves and some fresh chai. Hassam knew quite a bit about first aid, and was able to get Ben stitched up.

"He's lost a lot of blood, but your friend is going to be okay" he assured us.

"We can't thank you enough. You've given us food, you've saved Ben. We'll find a way to repay you sir I promise." I said, putting a hand on his shoulder.

Hassam smiled. I knew he was thinking of something already.

"I would like you to meet some of my family" he said kindly, moving towards the staircase. He whispered upstairs, and I could hear the stairs creak as soft footsteps came down. A tall woman, around the same age as Hassam, was the first down, followed by a young teenage girl.

"This is my wife, Eesha, and this is my daughter, Aamani."

He paused long enough for us greet each other, but we didn't shake hands. Eesha was a tall woman, with long strait brown hair. She was dressed equally nice as Hassam, with a mid-calf skirt topped with a soft canary yellow shirt. Aamani was a typical teenager, in jeans and a shirt of some band I never heard of. They were a quiet pair, and after our introduction they tended to Ben, bringing him water and bread.

"We have some blankets I'll bring down for you. I apologize, but we do not have room upstairs. I will make up for our inconvenience with extra blankets and pillows." He smiled before he turned to the staircase and disappeared to the second floor.

The front windows to the store had been painted over, backed up by empty shelves for support. The store was about the size of my house, appropriately so seeing as there was a home above us. The shelves were stocked, and still in order. Hassam's place had not been ransacked by looters. There were candles of all sizes burning, providing a mellow glow that lit the back of the store. Hassam was right about the blankets. He provided large, soft blankets that made incredible pallets on the floor. Soft goose down pillows encased in smooth fleece covers lay in two's at the head of each bed. Ben and Hailey took the corner as usual, this time with Adam beside them. He had really taken a liking to them, but he still hardly spoke. I don't blame him. Eesha and Aamani helped Sarah and Jake to their cozy beds on the floor. I could tell Sarah wanted to stay up and talk but she was so tired. I jokingly told her if anything exciting happens I would wake her. Eesha and Aamani went upstairs as soon as everyone was comfortable in their pallet. I decided to stay up and enjoy another cup of Hassam's chai. It was hot and sweet, but it packed a caffeinated punch. We took a seat on a couple of stools by the register, somewhat simulating the counter as a bar top. He told me how he kept his family indoors when the whole thing started. Just like each one of us, this situation approached us on a small scale. They already lived above a grocery store, so they had to need to explore outside the safety of their home. I told him about the oil rig incident, wanting to doubt that was the origin, but I knew what I saw there.

"What do you think of all this mess Hassam? Do you think this is God's wrath bringing judgment upon us?"
I hadn't considered thinking we might have different gods.
He took a long sip of his chai, and paused to let the hot drink soak his pallet.

"A forest can flourish from the tips of mountains, to the plains below. Every inch of the forest floor is occupied with life.

112

On a day that would seem as normal as any other, a lightning bolt crashes into a tree, igniting the tree and those around it. Soon a fire spreads uncontrollably. The fire will rage for weeks, sometimes months, destroying everything in its path. Or so it would seem. When the smoke clears, all is black and dead. Shortly after a green sapling emerges from the ashy soil, more sprout around it. Life is returning to the forest floor. It may take years and possibly decades, but the forest will flourish again."

"You think this is all just a cleansing?!" I got a little upset at the idea.

"You're telling me God is a janitor just doing his rounds?"

"I don't mean it that way David" he kept his calm, "but would I be correct to say you believe this is an apocalyptic event?"

"An event? There's only one apocalypse Hassam, and this is it."

"On the contrary David. Sodom and Gomorrah experienced an apocalypse. The Mayans experienced an apocalypse. Many fallen empires have experienced an apocalypse. Do you feel there is hope for survival?"

"I think we can survive this mess, and I'll do my damn best to ensure that." I said confidently.

"Then it couldn't possibly be the end, David. Do you think if God wanted to punish us by ending existence he would hold back any punches? Mountains would crumble, oceans would flood the land, and fires would rise from the broken crust of Earth. There would be no question the end of days had begun. All hope would be gone. That would be the point."

He had a valid point. Maybe it was the lack of sleep and sugar high from the tea I had. Hassam and I both took a gulp of tea and savored it.

"You did say this started on an oil rig off the coast of Iceland? Sounds like mankind started this mess. Again."
Now he had my attention.

"Again?"

"Yes." He brought his smile back this time.

"Since the beginning of time man has had a fascination with genetics and the altering of those genetics. Hieroglyphics in ancient Egypt depict a man with an eagle's head, also a wolf's head replacing his own. Greek mythology believed in a monster that was half man and half bull. Simply put, man has always chased the dream of evolving into something better. History is written with stories of global life forms getting annihilated by a natural disaster. Those events completely wiped them out. They weren't given a fighting chance."

"I see, because we have a fighting chance against the undead."

"A common bond amongst yesterday's enemies brings closer tomorrow's allies. It is inevitable that some day we would run out of fossil fuels, the economy would collapse. Because our strong desire for convenience, the food we have gotten so used to having at our disposal would have stopped arriving at the local superstore. Mankind would have eventually ripped itself apart, killing all those within itself that opposed the purpose of it. In the end there would be no discerning factor of those that came out as survivors. The fact that the battle for man's survival would have been fought against man itself, there would have been no common bond for mankind ever again. Every man and woman would be perceived as an enemy. What we are experiencing today gives mankind something that binds us together to fight against."

What the hell is in this god damn tea?

He left me speechless. It's not that I couldn't find anything to say, it's that there was too much going through my mind. I've heard nut job theories about the end of days, but that's not what he was saying. I could tell Hassam wasn't going to make accusations about world leaders plotting the destruction of mankind. He wasn't accusing at all. He spoke soon enough to relieve my brain from trying to think of a response.

"You have had a long day my friend. Why don't you get

some sleep David, we can talk in the morning."
I looked at the thick blankets that lay next to the potato chip aisle. The soft pillows beckoned me, and my aching mind agreed.

"I can't thank you enough for everything you have given us. I will find a way to repay you Hassam."

"I'm glad I could help you friend, you have already become a part of my family."

That was nice to hear him say family. I had thought before if that word would ever mean anything again after what has happened. We had met some of his family, and he let us in. That thought reminded me of what he had said earlier. *Some of his family?* I got his attention again before he went upstairs.

"Hassam, earlier you said you would introduce us to some of your family. What did you mean by some?"
He paused and he looked down at his feet, still in casual dress shoes. When he lifted his head and brought his eyes to mine. A smile came across his face, but not with his usual friendly cantor. I could see in his eyes the gears in his mind were turning.

"You have had a long day David. We can discuss your payment in the morning."

CHAPTER ELEVEN

The weather was getting warmer as summer was quickly approaching. Texas' summers are known to really bring the heat, and I wondered how that would affect the walkers. Would they slow down or speed up? Could they reach exhaustion or dehydrate and dry up? One issue was for certain, they would begin to smell worse than before, and I just hoped it would be somewhat bearable. Besides the moaning and constant shuffling, the smell was by far the worst aspect of the walking dead.

I had slept better than I had in a long while, despite waking up wrapped up in blankets on a tile floor. Eesha and Aamani were already awake, sweeping and dusting the aisles, like daily chores. I thought it was strange after all that had happened they would continue something as simple and routine as cleaning, but I suppose it beat the alternative of being bored. I remember long afternoons sitting in the living room of my old house, watching the occasional walker stagger by, and nothing for me to do. Boredom can drive a person insane, and fighting it becomes a war all in it's self. I heard footsteps coming down the stairs followed by Hassam appearing in the yellow walled doorway. A large thermos in his left hand and a few coffee mugs in his right, he looked determined. He had changed clothes, but still kept his neat appearance. Walking directly to a storage room near the back of the store, a single light bulb flickered to life when he hit the switch on the outside of the room. My curiosity got the best of me, and I was already awake and wanting to get off the floor before the broom came through to avoid the awkward shuffling around, so I folded my blankets as neat as I could and placed them in an empty space on the shelf next to me. Hoping one of the coffee mugs was for me, I gently knocked on the open door marked STORAGE to get Hassam's attention. It took a moment for him to acknowledge my presence. I could tell he was thinking hard about something as he blankly stared at the wall in front of him, stiffly holding his steaming coffee. He was sitting in a metal folding chair next to a fold out table with something large on top, covered by a canvas of sorts. It didn't look much like a storage room, but I could tell where there used to be a metal shelf system that left scrapes on the tiles from where they once stood.

The present came to him suddenly as he snapped out of his daze, shaking his head and blinking quickly.

"Good morning David" he started with false motivation and a forced smile.

"Did you sleep well?"

"I slept better than I have in a long time my friend. I couldn't have wrapped myself any tighter in the blue and gray blanket."

"I'm glad to hear it. Have you talked to your family since everything happened?"

He couldn't have asked his last question quick enough. I could tell it was painful enough just to go through the formalities of saying hello.

"I don't have a lot of family Hassam. My dad and I kept our relationship more on a professional level and I'm not sure where my mom is living now, and for her I have a few phone numbers that won't do any good nowadays anyway."

"That's a shame David. Family is always important to have. Who else can you rely on when everything goes wrong, much like our present situation?"

I thought about what he'd said and many of the situations I had been in with Jake and Sarah came to mind. We had relied on each other so much there was definitely a bond between us that couldn't be shaken. I realized how important they were to me, and it shocked me that I had never thought of them this way until now.

"Blood isn't the only thing that makes a family. I think of my friends as I would my close family. I would like to think of your family as my family too Hassam."

"My friend you hardly know us, how could you possibly

view us as family?"

"I know good people Hassam, and the world needs your family values to rebuild from this mess. I would do anything to help you in that sense."

"I'm glad to hear you say that David. As a matter of fact I do need your help. When this mess began, my son was at school. I haven't seen him since that day, but I know he's still alive. You are a very healthy man David and I think you can help me find him."

Hook. Line. Sinker. Hassam had orchestrated this conversation perfectly. Now that I knew his intentions, I began to wonder if all his hospitality had been for deception. I couldn't say no to his request, not after I just told him his family was mine.

"What exactly do you mean, find him? Do you know where he his?"

"He was enrolled at a nice college about twenty miles from here; Spring Gate College off of Red Oaks drive. The school is in a nice community and has a gated entrance. His name is Samir. He is a great man, very smart and I am so proud of him."

Hassam was adamant about referring to his son as a man.

"I want you to find a way to bring him back home to his family."

I wasn't mad about Hassam tactfully handling our situation the way he did. His request wasn't unreasonable either, I could understand his position. He could tell I was already thinking of the supplies we would need to do this, so he unveiled what was beneath the canvas on the table. There was a large radio, with an old fashioned push button microphone. A large auto battery, probably for a work truck, sat next to the radio with a 120v converter plugged in between the battery and radio. Hassam never stopped surprising me of his intelligence.

"I've been in contact with a few 'outposts' if you will, about the status of the world outside. I've talked to posts as far as

Amarillo, but the signal was weak and clarity depends on the weather. Just like a chain, one link is connected to another and eventually one end is connected to the other. Through communications down the line we have received reports from as far west as Nevada, and as far east as Kentucky. The virus took a snowball effect, starting off slowly and soon spreading like wild fire across the plains. Our nation is at a total loss, but I'm unsure of the conditions overseas. It's likely the virus spread to Mexico, and then to South America if they didn't already have it. Little factions have established safe havens around the country in hopes of rebuilding, but state lines as we knew them no longer exist."

Hassam's manner had changed from gentle shop keeper to something of an amateur militant officer as he gave me his finding from radio transmissions. I wondered if he had ever talked to 'Pit Bulls' that tried to kill us for whatever reasons. It made sense that tribal groups would be the first step towards rebuilding, and it was clear territories would be fought for all over again. There would be bloodshed aside from the horror created by the creatures outside. The virus has been devastating, and it wasn't showing signs of slowing down as long as there were fresh bodies to infect. I wondered if Hassam would have shared this information with me had I not agreed to help find his son, it was like a reward for playing along.

"It's a pretty simple drive from here to his school, provided the roads are open. A majority of structures between them and us are residential, with a few stores, but nothing guaranteeing safety. A few blocks from here there's an on ramp to the highway, and the school is right off the highway. You have guns; I will provide you with food for yourselves and some for anybody that might be at the school. I regret however, to tell you that I do not have a means of travel for you. I know I am asking you to risk your life for a stranger, but my son means the world to me, and I will forever be in your debt for your services."

This whole scenario seemed like a madman's plan to me, but we were in his debt. If I was to say no, there's no way I could face him again, and we would inevitably have to leave the store.

"I will have to talk with Jake and Sarah about a plan to do this. I want Ben and the kids to stay here with you. I'll let you know when we can leave."

"Thank you my friend" Hassam said, extending his hand out to shake mine.

Whether this handshake was a friendly gesture or a silent binding agreement, we would have to do this for him.

Leaving the storage room I was glad to see everyone was awake and moving around. Ben was helping Hailey tear the wrapper of a little snack cake, but Adam had already ripped into one and started on another. Jake and Sarah sat together sharing a bag of beef jerky, washing it down with a soda. Eesha and Aamani went into the storage room, I'm sure to ask Hassam how the conversation went. The expression on my face told Jake and Sarah everything but the details of what we were about to do. I explained to them about Hassam's son, and the gated school, and that we would need to find him and bring him back. They didn't have to ask about why we would have to do this, I think they understood.

"We are running low on ammo, but we should have enough to get us there, provided we don't have to shoot our way out of any ambushes" Jake informed.

"That also depends on our way of travel. Certainly you don't expect us to walk, right David?

"No we're definitely not going to walk. Hassam has no vehicle here, and I don't know of any around. The truck was able to stand up to some abuse, but I don't want to get stuck in a sea of walkers again either. What we need is armored transport."

Sarah was staring blankly between Jake and I, I couldn't tell if she was listening or spacing out.

"There's a construction site not too far from here!" She blurted out, coming out of her trance.

Jake and I looked at her, puzzled.

"I saw it on the way in. There was a big dump truck there,

and that would be perfect."

I was impressed. She was right, a dump truck would be perfect if it had enough fuel, and most contractors don't like to let their trucks get low on diesel so it could be a safe gamble. We had a plan put together relatively quickly, and it sounded safe with just a few 'let's hope' factors involved. At sundown we would leave the shop, and have to move on foot to the construction site a few blocks over, roughly a mile away. Depending on how many walkers we would have to avoid, it would take us about twenty minutes with the gear and guns. Providing we were in luck we would drive the dump truck to the school, pick up Samir, get back to the shop just in time for dinner and good night's rest. *The theory is sound.*

We were able to hold a few conversations with the others, and find way to spend our time avoiding boredom until the sun went down. The daytime hours passed slowly. We were both excited and worried about tonight. As the sun got closer to the horizon, we began packing what we would need. Hassam gave us Aamani's school bag full of canned food, a can opener, some candles, and waterproof matches. The bag was styled by a popular children's movie, and pink with purple borders. We laughed now that our mentality had changed from silent night mercenaries, to a trio of pink backpack musketeers. The shotguns and handguns were loaded, and with tradition we slung the weapons and carried melee bats and pipes, flashlights in our non swinging hands. Upstairs Eesha was watching through the window for any dangers down the street, both dead and alive. There were a few walkers down the block in front of the hardware store, but nothing we couldn't handle with a few hard swings. The sun slowly slipped out of sight, and the streets grew dark. The moon shone half full, providing the perfect amount of light, not too dark, not too bright. I opened the back door slowly to prevent any metal on metal groaning, and then the three of us slipped into the alley undetected. Hassam closed the door behind us and now there was no mistake we were back in the urban jungle. We jogged through the alleyways as quietly as we could, as the openness of the main roads provided a bigger chance of being seen. After passing two blocks it was time to cross the main road to get to the construction site. There were two walkers in our way crossing the street, but they were easily brought down by Jake's bat and my crowbar. Back in the alleys again we continued what I guessed was north, quickly passing by mounds of built up trash piles and the occasional sign of where an attack had taken place. The night was eerily still. There was no breeze to cover any sound we made, making our journey that much more cautious. The alley opened up to a field of orange plastic fencing and barrels, the true sign of a construction site. A dog was searching for something to eat around the site, its collar tags shining off the moon's light. A collar meant the dog was probably domesticated and no real threat. It lifted its nose out of a trash pile and began barking at us immediately.

"Shhh shut up dog!" I whispered as loud as I could.

I assumed once the dog realized we weren't going to try to eat it, it began wagging its tail excitedly and trotted towards us. I could tell the dog was a male, he had not been neutered and by the size of his pride he was a mature dog. He stood about two feet tall, with shaggy hair and droopy ears. We kept moving through the site, the dog following us closely. Moving over the concrete foundation and through upright two by fours, we came out of what would have been the front doors, to more bare dirt ground and sawhorses. Gleaming in the moonlight was the truck. The paint was a faded orange, and the bucket a little rusty, but it looked more beautiful than the custom truck we had taken. I moved to the driver's side while Jake and Sarah stood watch for any threats. The door stood wide open, with bloody handprints on the outside. It looked like the driver had been dragged out and most likely eaten, only to join the undead shortly after. There were no bodies around; I just prayed the keys were still in the truck. There was no dome light on, hopefully the battery still enough juice to turn the motor. I climbed onto the bench seat and felt around for the ignition. No keys. I kept my flashlight close to the seat as I looked around for any keys.

"What's taking so long?" Jake whispered from the front of the truck.

"No keys!" I shot back, frustrated at the situation.

"Truckers always have a backup! Check the....never mind." Jake said moving to the driver's side fender well, feeling around blindly underneath. His face lit up as he found it.

"Here!"

He handed me little black box that slid open from the top, opposite the magnet. *God bless Plan B.* Sarah opened the passenger door and jumped into the cab.

"You'd better hurry. We've gotten their attention."

She was referring to the dozen or more walkers across the site making their way towards us. The key went in smoothly and the engine gave a low groan trying to start. Jake jumped in the cab and closed the door behind him. The diesel engine roared to life, sputtering black smoke out of the stacks and clamoring like a loud diesel would. The dog barked outside the door, looking up at Jake.

"Hold on David" as Jake opened his door and helped the mutt jump into his lap.

"We can't just leave him here."

"He's your problem now."

I shifted into gear and rolled the truck across the bumpy terrain and onto the street. The headlights caught a walker's face just before smashing him to the side. The truck wasn't slowed at all by the impact. Once we were moving and navigating our way to the main street, I looked at the gauges to see we had almost a full tank. This mission was going so well it scared me a little. Jake couldn't hold the dog back from licking his face. Who knew what that dog had been eating?

Besides the occasional stalled car, the highway was empty. We passed by a few neighborhoods on the way, all dead still. Most of the fires had burned out, and those that survived had probably left the area. The houses were just lifeless shells now, full of someone else's memories and sometimes a family's demise. Those were the houses easy to identify. There were usually broken windows, open doors, and the usual blood trails. It was scary to think how comfortable I had gotten imagining blood puddles and body parts as a way of telling a story.

The green signs along the highway were telling us we were going in the right direction. Like Hassam had said, we were about twenty miles out when a sign read: NEXT EXIT RED OAKS DRIVE. I steered around a wrecked Mercedes along the off ramp. *We must be in the right area.* The off ramp to the access road led further away from the highway, but still within sight across an open field. The right side of the road was lined with tall, majestic oak trees. The area was very well groomed and landscaped with precision. As we approached a stop sign I had no intention of stopping at, the intersection opened up revealing a large field with a single winding road leading to a black steel gate with a brick wall at both ends. The school stood ominous behind the wall, black windows and no sign of life. There were three floors, built with natural red brick and a large entrance held up with pillars. I killed the headlights as we came to a stop at the gate.

"What do we do now?" Sarah asked, unable to take her eyes off the amazing structure on the other side of the gate.

"I don't know, but plowing through the gate doesn't sound like a good idea. We might have to walk this one."

I nudged the bumper into the gate so we could use the truck to climb over the fence, as the vertical steel supports wouldn't provide a foothold. Switching off the ignition, the truck sat in silence as darkness draped over us and the fields surrounding the school.

"No sign of walkers around, we should be safe to make our way on foot."

Jake opened his door and let the dog loose. The dog squeezed through the fence and ran as fast as he could to the school. I rolled my window, hoping to hear a sign of life as the dog got closer. *Please bark dog. Bark!* The speaker on the wall scared the hell out of us as it crackled to life, getting a jump out of all three of us.

"Could you please get your truck off our gate? We can open it for you." A female voice instructed.
Sarah breathed a deep sigh of relief, grabbing my hand and putting it on the shifter knob nudging me to hurry.

The gate was well lubed and hardly made a sound as it pulled apart. Once the truck was through, the gate closed behind us. I didn't need the headlights to find my way to the front entrance. I was still cautious about approaching the school. The speaker showed there was electricity here, but the surrounding area was blacked out. *They must have their own generators* I thought to myself, getting hopeful. The loud diesel broke the silence surrounding the school, and now being next to the entrance the sound echoed off the large building's brick walls. There were four young males and a female ready to greet us, standing on the steps leading to the double wooden doors. They didn't have weapons. I assumed they meant us no harm, but how would they defend themselves from walkers? Silence came again as I turned off the truck. One of the men was petting the dog and feeding him potato chips. The eldest of the group, who couldn't have been more than 25 years old and with an athletic build, was the first to approach us, offering his hand to Jake.

"Welcome to Spring Gate College. You are more than welcome to stay as long as you are peaceful and are willing to work for our community."
I was the last to shake his hand, but he still had plenty of squeeze left in him.

"Bring your bags, please come inside."

CHAPTER TWELVE

The entry opened into a huge foyer that went up all three floors, topped by a glass ceiling. There was a round desk in the center of the lobby, a security station that most likely controlled the gate. Along the right wall was a glass cabinet housing trophies of all sizes, but most of them big. The left wall had plaque photos of the staff, some of them had been taken down. From our immediate left and right were stairs that curved up and around the room connecting to the second floor in the rear of the room, and curving around again to the third floor directly above us. There were a few strategically placed lamps lighting the room, giving it a mellow, but still professional feel.

We had exchanged introductions as we came in, by the leader I assumed, who introduced himself as Philip Terry Marshall, a professor I guessed by his clothing. Two students, Jim and Chad I think, helped Jake out with the supplies, asking about his shotgun. I didn't catch the names of the other man and woman; they left down a hallway as soon as we came in. Philip walked us into the large room to the security desk.

"A majority of us were in class when the school got attacked. Some student's parents lived in the neighborhoods nearby. It was horrible to hear them tell us about seeing their parents' lifeless faces try to tear down walls to attack them. Most of the student body collected in the courtyard, and together we fought back the army of undead, mostly with textbooks and office supplies. When the fight was over and the dead no longer moved, we were left with educated students, and the necessary means to survive."

He walked us to a map of the campus posted next to the staff wall.

"We are currently in the West Wing. This was the math and sciences wing, which we have modified into residential rooms. The North Wing, which you are facing now, provides classrooms for botany from the science wing, and the rest is housing for the students that provide care for the farm in the courtyard. The East Wing is strictly medical, and we have students there constantly working to find a cure. The South Wing has been converted to storage and housing for newcomers like yourselves. Do you have education in a particular field you might be able to help us with?"

"We know how to kick ass." Jake said jokingly, but kept a serious face.

"Actually," I interjected, "we're looking for someone that might be here. His name is Samir. His father Hassam sent us to bring him back home."

Philip stood there a moment; I could tell he was running faces through his mind.

"Yes I believe he's here, if I'm thinking of the right guy. We call him Sam; he's in the medical wing. I'll take you to him."

We entered the courtyard, which was just as impressive as the main entrance. There were street lamps lining the walk from each wing, which led to a large water fountain in the middle of the courtyard. Only four lamps were lit however, I assumed to save power. The power came from generators in the basement under the main building Philip informed us. I could see the garden to our left that had been created before day zero. There were ripe tomatoes, squash, pumpkins, and some others I couldn't identify. The water fountain had hoses leading out of it into large plastic bins for clean drinking water. Groups of students had gathered around the gazebos placed throughout the yard. The entrance to the medical wing was a set of double glass doors the students kept clean. Inside East Wing was everything a college would look like. There were flyers posted on the walls, with new flyers advertising jokes about the undead, and survival tips, and recent information the group heard about different groups trying to start over like the students were. A young, energetic female approached us first, greeting us with a handshake.

"You must be the dump truck crew! Hi my name is Robin." She said with a Texas twang.   She was tall, with long blonde hair and a slender frame accentuated by her grey spandex pants and lime green shirt. I knew the look on Jake's face when he shook her hand. I had seen it only a few times when he'd meet somebody new in one of our late night outings.

"So y'all are into medicine huh?" she said, looking at Jake.

Before Philip could answer her Jake spoke up.

"We're not really doctors; we're looking for a fella named Samir."

Her expression slightly saddened at his response.

"You're not going to stay? Why would you want to go back out in that mess? You're not taking Samir with you are you?"

She tried to not sound desperate to keep us here, and she didn't want us taking Samir. If he was as smart as Hassam had said, he might be important at the college. I knew it would hurt Jake to give her a solid answer. Before he could reply to her I informed her we just wanted to talk to him. While she led us down the hall Jake kept small talk with her, laughing at her jokes, and telling stories about our backyard adventures, slightly stacking up the truth. She took us to a door marked Bio Labs and knocked three times. A small wiry kid with glasses answered the door. His thick glasses magnified his eyes, giving him a fishbowl appearance.

"Hi Mathew we're looking for Samir." Robin said with a mercy flirt.

The boy answered in a small mousy voice.

"He's in his lab shooting up rats, Robin."

He smiled as he said her name. *He's shooting up rats? I thought labs were supposed to be clean?*

"This Samir is harder to reach than the president!" Sarah getting a little frustrated said. Mathew led us through a couple lab doors to a man sitting at his desk, pulling a needle out of a rat and placing the rodent back in the cage. *Oh, shooting up rats.*

"Samir, these people are here to talk to you, something about your father?" Robin introduced us.

128

"You know my father? Is he okay? Where is he?"
I stopped him before he ran out of breath.

"Your father is fine Samir. He saved us from a horde and was very nice to give us a place to stay and food during our stay there. As a favor to him, we are here to escort you back to your family."
His response was the opposite of what I was expecting to hear.

"I can't go back."

"What do you mean you can't go back Samir? We're here to take you."

"I'm sorry. It's not that I don't want to go back; I pray that I can see them again. I am so important here in developing medicine that I can't just leave. Besides, we are self sustaining here. His little shop will run out of food soon."
What are we going to do now? He doesn't want to leave, but I owe Hassam my word that I will bring his son back home.

"Listen I promised your father...."

"Bring them here!" His eyes lit up with excitement as he said it.

"What?"

"You came in the dump truck, yes? You could bring them back to the college; they can stay in my living quarters! I know my father would understand if he knew how important I am here."

He made a valid argument. I owed his father this favor, but he was right about the food supply at the shop. The shelves were running low and most of what was left was junk food anyway. There was really no argument in Hassam's case, his son was much better off here, and so would the rest of his family. The three of us talked it over, and decided Sam was right. All we had to do now was go back and get them.

Samir and Robin walked with us to the front of the campus, back to our dump truck. Robin and Jake really took a liking to each other, so I knew when we got back we would be here a while. In the front lobby we were greeted by a group of students I could tell were waiting to talk to us.

"Sir could we ask you for a large favor when you go out?"

The students explained to us that while they had food and water here, they were lacking in tools and a means for security. I knew it was only a matter of time before looters heard of this place and would break in, possibly hurting somebody. I had faith in this group of students. They wanted to rebuild, replacing violence with hospitality. The tools we could get from the hardware store next to Hassam's shop. The guns were going to be a little more difficult. I explained to them we had the weapons we did because we came across them, more so out of luck. I didn't know where the nearest gun shop was, and besides that, there were probably bars over the windows and doors.

"Here it is!" A young student yelled, bringing a phone book from the security desk to us.

"The yellow pages will tell you where the nearest gun store is!"

Oh thank you, you little brat. The store wasn't too far off the highway, but it was on the other side of the college from the direction we needed to go. The fact remained that we were going to do this for them in return for shelter, and we ourselves were running low on ammo. The plan was made to pick up Hassam and his family, Ben and the kids, and grab everything we could from the hardware store. An older student in dirty jeans gave us a list of tools he would need, and we would need as many hands as possible to gather that much in a short time. I guessed we would need chains to rip the bars off the doors at the gun shop, and we could also get those at the hardware store.

Leaving the college without Samir made this night feel like it was going to last a lot longer than we had anticipated. Our original goals had instantly grown much more difficult, with a lot more risk but with better payoff. The wind had picked up from the Southwest, as if the night needed to be creepier. The dump truck roared down the interstate, this time with no dog licking Jake's face. About a mile ahead of us I could see red tail lights glowing. We weren't far from Hassam's shop, and I wondered if we would come across more survivors, or more pirates. I kept the speed at eighty miles per hour, and we were coming on the tail lights very quickly now. *They slowed down.* We were a block away from the tail lights of a medium sized SUV. The tail lights took an immediate right turn, hitting the guard rail, sending a shower of sparks into the night air. The front bumper clipped the end of the rail, lifting the rear end in the air and toppling on its side. I hit the brakes so hard the truck groaned to lose speed. After two flips the SUV settled in the ditch on its roof. I switched my glance back to the road, and had the street lights been on I would have seen the horde ahead. There were about forty of them, spaced out far enough to cover all lanes, but close enough we wouldn't be able to squeeze through. I knew we would need speed to punch our way through, but part of me wanted to help those trapped in the SUV. Without thinking I brought the truck to a stop on the road beside the upside down wreck.

"What the hell are you doing!?" Sarah yelled, before we saw someone crawl out of the driver's side window.

"We have to help them. This won't take long, just grab the survivors and get in!"

Jake and Sarah grunted sighs of disgust as they leapt out and sprinted to the wreck. The nearest walkers were a hundred yards in front of us now, staggering towards us as fast as they could. The driver was a young girl, probably high school aged. I could hear her screaming at Jake and Sarah that her friend was still in the car. Sarah helped her up the embankment into the bed of the truck. She had blood coming from her forehead, and a few visible cuts on her arms. Jake yanked so hard on the passenger's door the whole SUV was rocking. The walkers were fifty yards away now. Sarah screamed at Jake to hurry, when he finally ripped the door open. The passenger was laying there unconscious, blood all over her face and clothes. Jake slung her over his shoulder and slowly made his way to the truck. The walkers were close enough now they could push their bodies to lunging speed. I could hear Jake's boots hit the rungs of the ladder on the dump bucket, but I wasn't leaving until everyone was in. Jake pounded his fist on the roof of the cab, screaming.

"Go! Go! Go!"

I jerked my foot off the clutch and mashed the accelerator. The turbo whined as the grill began smashing bodies in our way. It was a very powerful truck, but the engine lagged trying to pick up rpm's. There were so many undead they were stalling the truck! We couldn't stop now so I kept the pedal down, thinking I was about to shove my foot through the floor. It took every bit of first gear to get us through this medium sized horde. After the last skull was smashed on the bumper the truck's engine finally wound up rpm's and was ready for second gear. In the rearview I could see the walkers turned around and following us at the speed of undead.

We were in front of Hassam's shop within five minutes of leaving the horde, which meant they weren't far away. There was no light coming from the shop, but I knew they still had to be there. I parked the truck in the alley next to the door we used before, hoping Hassam would hear the rumble of the diesel and have the door ready for us to pour in. When I cut the engine the wind carried the moans of the approaching horde to us. Thankfully Hassam was at the door, his face lit up hoping to see his son. His hopeful smile turned straight when I leapt out of the cab and hurried to the bucket. Jake was already down and helping the first girl out of the truck. Sarah had taken the girls top shirt and wrapped it around her head to keep pressure on the wound. She staggered to the door and Hassam helped her in, sitting her down inside next to the storage room. Sarah helped Jake get the other girl on his shoulders then hopped down from the bucket. Jake carried her in followed by Sarah. I took a last look of the street hoping no walkers saw us enter before I closed the door behind us. I didn't see any of them so hopefully we would be safe. For now.

It looked like a primitive ER in the back of Hassam's

shop. Eesha had a pot of water and rags cleaning the conscious girl's wounds. The other girl suffered from severe head trauma and wouldn't be alive much longer if she didn't get serious medical treatment.

"What happened David? Where is my son?"
Hassam bombarded me with questions while I was trying to figure out our next move.

"These girls flipped their SUV avoiding a horde on the highway. We were on our way back from the college. Hassam, your son is fine, but plans have changed."
I told him the new plans to get his family to the college along with tools and weapons, but we needed to get these girls there fast if we were going to help them.

"Hassam, grab everything you need but be reasonable, only things you can carry. If possible, grab the radio. Get into the truck and Sarah is going to drive the rest of you to the college. Jake and I are going to stay here."

"What the hell are you talking about David?" Jake was not thrilled with the idea of leaving the two of us behind. Sarah wasn't thrilled about it either, but I knew she could handle it.

"Sarah it's midnight now. Drive to the college and drop everybody off. It should take about an hour and a half before you can get back here, give or take some time considering walkers. When you get back, we'll be on the roof of the hardware store. Try to get a mattress for the bucket of the truck."

She knew where I was going with this, so she nodded in agreement and ran to help the injured girl up to her feet. She took charge of the situation, giving everyone a responsibility for getting into the truck quicker. The horde was still approaching, and we needed to get in hardware store before they saw us, and Sarah needed to be on the road. Sarah slung a shotgun and helped everyone stage by the back door. I gave a quick glance outside as I cracked the door open, and the path to the truck looked clear. I stepped into the alley with the shotgun's stock tucked deep into my shoulder. As soon as we could get loaded into the truck, Sarah was going to back it up close to the hardware store so Jake and I could jump onto the roof. With the crowbar in stuffed between my belt and pants, all we needed now was luck. Jake and I were the last to board the bucket of the truck, and Sarah did as she was told. The roof was still pretty high, but with a boost from Jake I pulled myself up. Once up I reached back, extending a hand for Jake. He was heavier than I remembered, but with a few grunts I pulled him high enough that he could get himself up. Hassam banged the roof of the cab to tell Sarah she was clear to leave. Her hand stuck out of the window and gave us a wave goodbye as black smoke billowed from the smokestacks. The truck picked up speed leaving the store, and then the smashing of corpses against the front grill began.

CHAPTER THIRTEEN

The roof was quiet once the audible diesel could no longer be heard. I could hear the scuffing of feet on concrete as walkers milled around the store beneath us.

"David I hope this plan of yours works. I would really like to see Robin again." His tone never changed. I could hear the slight disappointment in his voice.

"You really like her don't you?"

"Maybe" he chuckled.

"Did you keep me hear to ask about her?"

"Well you know me Jake, always dating vicariously through you."

"What about you and Sarah? I've seen some sparks fly here and there."

I didn't answer him. He laughed out loud as we walked across the roof. I knew exactly what I was looking for; I just hoped it was here.

"On these older buildings, architects would build a ladder to the roof from the inside, and they didn't start putting locks on them until someone installed the pull down ladder on the wall facing the alley. This store has an external pull down ladder with a lock on it, so there should be a way in from the roof."

"If you're wrong I'll kick your ass" was all he could say back, jokingly.

After a few minutes of searching, there it was in the opposite corner of the store. I noticed a large rusty lock holding the door shut. Using the crowbar, I pulled as hard as I could to pry the lock open, but it wouldn't budge. Jake had to help but with both of us the lock popped open. Before I lifted the potentially loud door, I reminded Jake that the windows had not been painted, and we would most likely not be able to use flashlights, but be ready for anything. *What could possibly go wrong?* The door opened with the loudest metal on metal screeching my skin began to crawl. I bet every walker for miles around heard the door squeal. My thought was answered by a crowd of moans from the street below.

The ladder led down into total darkness, and immediately I didn't like the plan I made, but we had to do it. I decided to go first since it was my idea, Jake aiming the shotgun below me. The ladder seemed to go forever, and it seemed darker with my eyelids open. Finally my foot rested on the tile floor. I paused briefly to listen for any sounds. Nothing. The only noise was my heartbeat, thumping loud enough that's all I could hear. Jake's foot stepped on the first rung, followed by his second. I turned so I could have security for him while he came down. It was wishful thinking, I couldn't see anything. I hadn't stepped far from the ladder, and Jake's foot stepped on my heel as he stepped on the tile. He also stood still for a moment, listening for any movement. We couldn't just stand here, so I threw caution aside and filled myself with false motivation to take a big step forward. I placed my right foot ahead of me and pushed my body forward. I almost blacked out as something smashed into my forehead and I fell to the floor.

Even in absolute darkness I was stunned and had blurry vision. Risking another attack and further injury, I flicked on my flashlight, revealing my attacker. My attacker stood in front of me; a gray metal door. We were inside the janitor's closet. I threw an elbow into Jake's leg to stop him from laughing, but I couldn't blame him. I would have laughed to if my head didn't hurt so badly.

"Ha ha brother I'm sorry but that was funny!"

If there was anybody in the store, dead or alive they knew we were there. I wrapped my hand around the cold knob and prepared myself for anything on the other side.

"Alright Jake, just grab everything on the list and whatever else we can grab, throw it into a tool bag, and let's start a pile on the roof."

"Yeah you told me already, let's get this over with. No need to lose your *head* about it."

I didn't think his comment was funny, at least not right now anyway. The door swung inwards, and my flashlight met the face of an enraged old man swinging an axe handle at my head, cracking it against the steel frame. I ducked in time to miss it, and Jake was quick with the shotgun pointed at the old man's head.

"Put it down old man. I don't want to shoot you."

"Get the hell outta my store! You'll have to kill me if you want anything here you fucking pirates!"

I wasn't questioning the fact that Jake was quick on the trigger, but I was sure he wouldn't kill an innocent man. Just in case I was quick to interject.

"Calm down everyone! Sir we aren't here to rob you." Well, kind of. "We can help you sir, please just put the stick down."

He backed away, but wouldn't put down his axe handle. He was a husky man, in his seventies. He wore a light red flannel shirt tucked neatly into his jeans that barely reached the ankles of his boots.

"How the hell are you going to help me? I don't need your help."

"Sir there is a college up the highway that has food and water and they are looking to establish a safe outpost. We can take you there. I can see you have a wedding band on, we can take your wife also."

"My wife is dead son."

I couldn't imagine what might have happened to an elderly woman with the threats we are now facing. This old man probably has a horrible story to tell.

"I'm sorry sir. Did the walkers get her?"

"No, she died of a heart attack three years ago."

In a way, that was a relief.

"Do you have any family or friends with you we can help?"

I was trying to be polite, but I would have helped him if it meant we could take his tools with his consent. I really didn't want to have to fight him.

"I don't have anybody nearby. My son is in the Army. I'm sure he's helping us win this war against these punks."

The old man had spunk, I'll give him that.

"My name is David, this is Jake."

We exchanged firm handshakes.

"My name's William Bradley Johnson, but you can call me Bill."

His name was so appropriate for his style.

"Bill we want to take you to Spring Gate, but some workers there really needs your tools. Because I want to be respectful, I'm asking your permission to bring tools with us to the college."

"What kind of tools do you need?"

I showed him the list. As he looked over it with the flashlight he gave an occasional *oh* and *uh huh.*

"I have everything here. How did you say we were going to get there?"

"A friend of ours is driving a dump truck back to pick us up. It's important that we're on the roof when she gets here."

"Oh you're the ones that have been making all that racket! God damn son you've woken the dead!"

I couldn't tell if he was joking or not, but we were running out of time. He agreed to help us, so we began filling tool bags with saws, screwdrivers, pliers, anything that would fit. The bags got heavier with each addition. Some bags would take two of us to get up the ladder. Jake would pull from the top as pushed from below. Bill sat back with a cup of fresh coffee, watching us sweat. I looked down at my watch and flicked the Indiglo button. 1:19 a.m. We were running out of time. A total of five heavy bags made it to the roof. For each power tool we grabbed extra blades and batteries. Each screwdriver had a twin. Without a doubt we had the best tool collection around. Jake helped Bill up the ladder, and he grunted as the cool wind hit his face. Once the three of us made it to the top, Bill yelled at Jake for not closing the roof cap. He didn't want rain falling into his store. I laughed at the man's pride that would never falter. We lined the bags up beside each other next to the lip of the roof, and waited for our ride. I could see there were walkers up and down the street. There weren't as many as the earlier horde, but enough that Sarah wouldn't be able to stop for long. I explained our plan to Bill; he jokingly responded that we should just leave him in the store. The pickup time came and there was no Sarah. I knew better than to worry this close to our estimated time, but I couldn't help it. We had made three runs down the highway so far, and her trip back would make four. A loud truck like that is sure to attract walkers from miles around. That could explain the horde there earlier.

"Sarah's smart, David. She'll find a way back here."
Jake could see the worry on my face.

Another thirty minutes went by, and no sign of Sarah. We were sitting down now, leaning against the bags. Lying on a bag full of tools is exactly as comfortable as it sounds. The night air was a little chilly, mainly because there was no escape from the wind on the roof. I tried not to think of the possibilities. Jake was right, Sarah was a smart girl and she would find a way to get here. She had to. Each bag weighed close to a hundred pounds, and we couldn't carry that weight quickly enough if we had to leave. Maybe we wouldn't need the tools anymore. Hassam would see his son soon, and that would be true to my word like I promised. *What if they never made it to the college?* I couldn't stop thinking negative thoughts about what might have happened. I closed my eyes and tried to shut out the thoughts.

I jolted upright, suddenly realizing I had fallen asleep. Jake was asleep to, lying on the bag next to me. Bill was nowhere to be seen. *What the hell happened?* I looked at my watch. 3:42 a.m. *Where the hell is Bill? Where the hell is Sarah? What is going on?* I shook Jake until he woke up.

"What happened Jake?! Where is Bill and where is Sarah?!"

He realized now something was wrong. He looked around for Bill, and we both shot to our feet. The street was crowded with walkers. *Boom!* The sound broke the silence. *Boom!* Again. Bill was on the store's awning with Jake's shotgun, shooting at walkers in the street. There were about fifty, squeezing together to get closer to Bill, all with their arms raised trying to grab him.

"Bill what are you doing?!" I yelled, running over to him.

"Your lady friend never showed! We're gonna have to shoot our way out!"

I grabbed the shotgun from Bill, as he squeezed off the last round in the gun.

"Get back to the bags Bill! Sarah will be here!"

Something had to have happened to her. *She would have honked the horn to get our attention right?* What were we going to do now? We don't have a vehicle; we can't run back to the college. My plan was quickly crumbling.

"Bill do you have a truck?" Jake asked, putting his last five shells in the scattergun.

"You mean my old Ford? How else would I get to work?" He replied, sounding like he innocently forgot.

"Bill you're telling me you've had a truck here the whole time?"

"Yes, but you said we were taking the dump truck. My truck is parked there in the front, but it's surrounded by those assholes."

I took a deep breath to calm down. Could it really be this hard to get anything done?

"Bill do you have the keys to your truck?"

"Yes."

"Okay great, let me have them. We're going back into the store."

He handed the keys to me with no resistance, but confused about why we would go back into the store. Jake knew I had a plan, and he was content just going along with it instead of clouding the issue with questions. We brought the bags down in the store, and placed them as close as we could to the entrance without being seen.

"Bill does this set of keys have the store's keys on it also?"

"Yes the big gold one, it goes to the front and back door."

Perfect. I went down the aisles collecting what I needed. Hassam's radio setup gave me the idea. One lawnmower battery, one power converter, and one circular saw with the safety cover taped back. I knew there couldn't be any walkers in the alley; they were all circled around Bill's truck trying to bite the idiot making noise. I unlocked the back door to the alley and placed the saw on the concrete blade down. I pulled the cord under the door and locked the deadbolt. The converter was hooked up to the battery; all I had to do was plug in the saw…. Rin-din-din-din-din-din! As the saw came to life it made more than enough noise to attract attention to the alley. I crept through the store where Jake and Bill were, watching through the front glass like kids spying on a girl they liked across the playground. Few from the group left the horde to the alley, but like the snowball effect they all followed. Soon there were no walkers left in front of the store, but the saw wouldn't keep their attention long since it wasn't food. We dragged the bags to the door; I fumbled getting the key into the lock. Finally the lock gave and we were out the door. In just those few steps my arms were throbbing from carrying two bags and it was hell getting them into the bed of the truck. Around the corner a walker appeared, and began moaning loudly at us, moving in our direction. I yanked open the driver's door once the lock popped up and dove through the cab to unlock the passenger's side for Jake. Jake helped Bill get in quicker than he was used to, and Bill kept his grumpy attitude about it. I turned the ignition, but the motor was lazy to start. *Is there anything about Bill that's not old fashioned?* The motor finally belched life out of the exhaust, as the moaning walker was arms length away from my window. I was too frustrated with what had happened tonight to not do it, so I rolled the window down and placed my .45 six inches from the bridge of that walker's nose. His skull expanded sideways as the top of his head flew off his body and splat on the concrete beside him, his lifeless corpse following. Now I felt a little better. I straightened the truck out on the street and mashed the pedal, but the truck had the acceleration of a golf cart. I followed the signs to the highway and took the nearest on ramp. We were running dangerously low on ammo now. It struck me that if we didn't go to the gun shop now we might not ever get the chance. I mentioned the idea to Jake, and he agreed. We have the chains, let's do it.

I kept the gas pedal pushed to the floor the whole way down the highway, but we were still doing just over seventy mph. My eyes followed the Red Oaks exit sign as it passed over us. Our exit would be coming up close to five miles from the Red Oaks exit. There weren't any new cars stranded or crashed along the highway, especially any dump trucks. There was some relief in that fact, maybe they made it to the college and they were safe. The exit was approaching; now let's hope nobody looted the store before we get there. The neighborhood was so much different than the houses in Red Oaks. I had heard some students in one of the gazebos saying that was the reason for the walls. Apparently when the college was founded many decades ago, the wall wasn't in the design. It was added later because the crime from the nearby community was flowing over into Red Oaks. It was a neat history lesson, but I hoped the crime wasn't the same now as it was then. Jake was getting the chain ready when we turned onto the street. I could see the shop, now just a few blocks away, with a big yellow sign advertising military surplus.

There were just a few walkers on the street, but we wouldn't have much time before more arrived after we rip the security bars off the wall. I swung the truck around the front of the store, and then backed the rear bumper as close to the doors as I could get without hitting the curb. Jake and I jumped out, Jake pulling the chain and looping it over the trailer hitch. I wrapped the chain around the bars once, and set the hook tightly on the chain. Jake stood clear, with his shotgun raised for any intruders. The truck grunted at first, but pulled the bars off with relative ease. The glass doors were locked, but that was nothing a hard swing with the chain wouldn't take care of. Once inside the store Jake and I both grabbed two duffel bags, and began shoving every gun we could grab in one duffel bag and filling the other with arm loads of ammo at a time. I gathered everything from hunting rifles to tactical shotguns, and a few assault rifles with plenty of magazines. I hadn't realized how heavy the bags got until both Jake and I paused our looting and glanced at each other. We agreed silently and moved back to the truck. Bill was admiring a lever action rifle, and grabbed as much ammo as his other hand could hold. Getting back to the truck there were a few walkers nearby, I quickly handled them with my pistol. We jumped in the truck, this time Bill helped himself in so as not to be manhandled by Jake. As soon as Jake's door was shut, I mashed the pedal and we were flying down the road leaving dust between us and the walkers. In just a few minutes we would be at the college, and we would have our answers.

CHAPTER FOURTEEN

Across the highway I saw the college sitting there in the darkness, as still as it could be. There were never any initial signs of life in buildings after Day Zero, but I guess that was the point. I steered the truck down the exit and made a left under the overpass. The college was so close but relief was not what we felt when we got close to the gate. The burnt shell of a dump truck sat outside the gate. The fire must have been intense. The tires were melted to the pavement, and the metal itself looked like it would crumble if something hit it too hard. The dump truck blocked the entrance, but I could squeeze the truck through when they opened the gate. I drove right up to the gate, with speaker near my window, and flashed my headlights. Nothing. I waited a moment, and then honked the horn twice. Nothing. *This isn't good.* I rolled my window down to yell at the speaker.

"Hello? This is David Sangora, I was here earlier, I have everything you requested, let us in!"

There was no response. The sun would be up soon, and I'd prefer to be indoors when it did. Not to mention the three of us were very tired. Maybe that's what the problem is, everyone is asleep. They are college kids. I laid on the horn, risking the walkers hearing it and coming to the campus. Jake couldn't make anything of the situation either.

"We have everything they could possibly need in the bed of our truck, and they won't let us in."

"*Our* truck?" Bill responded to Jake, letting his property be known.

"You don't drive it anymore" Jake said back, pointing at me.

"I'll kick your ass son, that's for sure."

Bill always stood his ground, but now they were sounding like a couple of school girls. Had I not been so exhausted and the situation was completely different I might have laughed. I scanned the grounds for any clues as to what happened here. I was quick enough to notice the gun barrel pointing at me from

144

around the corner, but not quick enough to draw mine in defense.

"Don't move or I'll shoot you!" came a voice from behind the rifle.

"Don't shoot. I'm David and this is Jake. We were here earlier. Did a woman named Sarah get back here safely with Samir's father Hassam? She was driving this dump truck."

I figured if I dropped enough names the kid might pick up on it. Someone had been listening over the speaker, and the gate slowly opened. I offered the kid a ride to the front door, so he hopped in the bed of the truck. I felt the weight of the world lift off my shoulders when I saw the smile across Sarah's face, waiting for us at the front door. I hit the brakes at the last minute; the truck skidding to a halt. I leapt out of the door to hug her. The kid in the back slammed into the cab, and for that I felt bad, and I could hear Bill bitching about my driving but it just didn't matter any more. I hadn't realized how much I missed Sarah.

"What the hell happened here Sarah?"

"I'll tell you all about it inside. We're not done here."
I saw Philip approaching, Hassam and Samir behind him.

"We got everything you asked for Philip. You might want to get some help unloading those bags though."

He smiled at my statement, and waved some athletic students over to help with the bags. As we walked through the doors I could hear the students' comments of joy over the bags we brought them. Philip made his way in front of us, to lead us somewhere.

"David if you'll follow me I'll take you to a conference room where we have water and food for you. Jake and uh, grandpa we'd like you to come to."

"Who the hell you calling grandpa boy?"

The conference room had a large wooden table in the center of the room, surrounded by several comfortable looking chairs. Jake and I sat on the same side of the table, Sarah sat across from us. Bill wasted no time getting water and a snack cake from a table in the corner. Hassam and Samir sat beside Sarah. Philip sat at the end of the table, ready to address us.

"David your plan was a very good one. Sarah told us how you decided to stay back and collect supplies while she brought the two injured girls and Samir's family. I'm sorry to tell you the girl, Erica, with the serious head wound did not make it. Her friend Amy has suffered a concussion, but she's going to be okay. Ben and his two children are safe, they are sleeping right now. When they arrived at the gate, they were ambushed when two trucks blocked them in and threw a Molotov cocktail at the cab of the dump truck. As you know, everyone made it away from the truck and escaped the attackers by slipping through the gate. There were six of them. They were armed with rifles and large capacity magazines. They gave us an ultimatum. We have one week to hand the campus over to them or they will come back with numbers and take it by force. A few of us have discussed different options, but we would like to ask your opinion before we come to any final decisions."

Not only are the living trying to survive an undead army, but the living are trying to kill the living. Hassam was right when he said we are at a total loss. It felt like we were back in ancient times, but with newer weapons.

"We've all had a very long day and an even longer night Philip. Give us a day to think about it, and we can come back to this conference room with an answer."

"That sounds good David. Would you agree Jake?"

"Sure."

"Okay, let me take you to your rooms. We have beds made for you in the south wing; I encourage you to catch up on sleep."

Everyone in the room stood up at the same time with a sense of urgency, but we stumbled like zombies leaving the room. Nobody was interested in conversation this early in the morning. I just hoped my room was dark enough the sun wouldn't bother me when it rose, which would be soon. Hassam and Samir said goodnight and exited towards the courtyard, I assumed to the medical wing. Philip was escorting us to the south wing when a student approached him with a sheet of notebook paper.

"Professor here are the numbers you requested."

"Thank you James" he said, taking the paper and folding it in his pocket.

We finally arrived at our rooms, on the second floor. There weren't many goodbyes, each of us eager to crawl into a warm bed. I stepped into my room, greeted by the smell of fresh cut wood and clean linen. It made for an interesting combination, but considering my state it was the greatest smell in the world. The room was larger than I anticipated. I'd guess around 250 square feet. The twin size bed was against the left wall, with a homemade nightstand beside it. It was wobbly and poorly constructed; now I understood why they needed tools so bad. The bed was made, with the crisp sheets pulled tight and the pillow fluffed. I was quickly undressed, pulling the covers back, feeling the softness of the sheets. I eased beneath the covers as my body thanked me for this gift I was receiving. I laid my head on the soft pillow, sinking in. Sleep would come soon and I promised myself I wouldn't wake up for another day.

My comfort was broken when a speeding car screeched to a halt outside the front gate and laid heavily on the horn. The passenger stepped out screaming, pleading for the gates to open.

CHAPTER FIFTEEN

I woke up feeling well rested. I hadn't moved since I laid down early this morning. The sheets felt soft as I stretched under the covers, reaching for my watch on the shop class quality nightstand. Most people would normally be getting off work at this time. Apparently the car that came screaming up the drive last night wasn't such a big deal, at least it didn't involve me and I was fine with that. I remembered leaving my clothes on the floor last night, but now they were folded in a neat stack on the cushion of the lounge chair. I didn't even hear the door open. I slowly crawled out of bed, giving my body one last stretch before starting the day. It felt nice to put on clean clothes. My pants had been starched, which was definitely a change from what I was used to. A growl came from my stomach as I slid my shirt on. I slid into my boots and I was out the door.

There was animosity in the air. People were quiet as they walked through the hallways. Everyone was thinking about the pirates and the choice we would have to make soon. I remembered Jake and I would be needed in the conference room sometime today, and maybe we could find out what happened after we'd gone to bed. I smelled something cooking down the hall and I followed the scent. It led me downstairs to a modified cafeteria that was changed from what could have been a science classroom. I noticed Philip sitting at a table enjoying a cup of coffee. The cooks had prepared steaks and potatoes, and I grabbed the largest steak I could find, accompanied by a pile of skillet cooked potatoes. Grabbing a seat across from Philip, I knew he was here for conversation.

"I knew the food would bring you down" he smiled, and then took a sip from his coffee.

"What happened last night with that car?" I said bluntly, in no mood to sweeten the conversation.

"Let's meet in the conference room in one hour, okay? That car came from the pirate's outpost. They aren't called the pirates however, they call themselves the Pit Bulls. They have taken control of a survivor's outpost in a superstore about thirty miles from here. They used violence to assume control, and now they use the people there to produce food, much like slaves. They were a couple in their thirties, and they'll be at the meeting to fill us in on the details."

"Do you think they can be trusted?"

"I believe their intentions are true."

"Okay. I'll see you in an hour."

Philip finished his coffee and left the room. It was nice to enjoy my steak in peace and quiet.

After a walk through the courtyard enjoying the sun for a few minutes I made my way to the front hall for our meeting. I had forgotten how great the sun feels on skin. We had been locked indoors for a majority of the past few weeks trying to hide from the walkers. I met Jake in the hallway, asked if he slept as well as I did. His calm demeanor answered my curiosity. We were the last two to come in for the meeting. I noticed Bill wasn't there. I shut the door behind me, and Philip started talking the moment we sat down.

"A majority of the people here are scared about our current situation. Some are talking about giving in to their request in the hope of peace. I am not comfortable with the idea of rebuilding our world in slavery. I would like to introduce Andy and Kelly. They came here from the Pit Bull outpost, otherwise known as the superstore thirty miles west of here. I will let them tell you their story."

Andy was an average man by every standard. His height, build, demeanor, everything was middle of the road.

"My wife and I sought refuge at the superstore when the outbreak occurred. We'd heard there were survivors there and they had the means to sustain shelter there for quite some time. For a few weeks everything was great. Everyday more survivors showed up. Together we had established a new post, capable of producing food, shelter, and simple first aid. We would broadcast over several radio frequencies of our capabilities, welcoming anybody that could make it there. It wasn't long before we let in the wrong survivors. They seemed like a decent couple. They worked hard the first day, and then they just got lazy. We kept the doors locked constantly, and when someone would leave for supplies there were dry erase boards posted of the times the doors would be opened. One day a convoy of vehicles showed up, and that couple opened the garage bay doors for them to move their trucks into. They came in with assault rifles and told us we could either work for them or join the undead. They are monsters. Women were getting raped, husbands getting beaten almost to death. They killed a man because he wouldn't let one of them sleep with his wife. They told him he could be replaced in an instant. They didn't shoot him to death however. Seven of them beat him unconscious and dragged his body to the roof, laughing and joking the whole time. They dumped his body over the edge and watched the undead devour him. The next day the wife was forced to tend to the garden on the roof, and she saw her husband milling around with the undead in the crowd below."

Kelly was in tears, Philip handed her a tissue. Andy was getting pretty choked up telling the story. I wondered if they had experienced the same torture, but I was quick to shake those curious, horrible thoughts out of my head. Andy reached down to comfort his wife.

"Thank you for sharing with us your tragedies, Andy. I hope that is a fate none of us will ever see."

"Kill every one of those mother fuckers!" Andy yelled out, surprising me with his ferocity.

Bill came in and escorted the couple out. I noticed he wore a holstered pistol around his belt now. I could tell he wanted no part of our battle plans, and I respected him for that. Bill was able to console the couple in his strangely abrasive ways. Once the couple left the room, Bill closed the door behind them.

"Now you've heard what these monsters' intentions are.

150

I'll be damned if I let them onto this campus and ruin what we have worked so hard to achieve. Here is a manifest of the weapons and ammo you brought in last night. I believe we have the firepower to defend ourselves."

When Philip handed me the list, I felt a sense of pride surged through me at what me and Jake had accomplished. The list read:

7 shotguns-230 shells
8 assault rifles-900 rounds
10 deer rifles -410 rounds
14 handguns-1,200 rounds

"What are you talking about Philip?" I wanted him to come out and say what he was planning.

"I'm saying we have manpower and firepower to defend the campus in case of attack. Guns and ammo are being stored in an office near the front entrance. We can draw up battle plans for defending the campus," he paused, "defending this post from any direction. What do you think?"

We looked around the room at each other; nobody was sure where to start. I decided to speak up first.

"Philip I understand the importance of establishing a good defensive drill for any attack, but I don't think that should be our offense also. If we stay here, waiting for an attack, we'll get just that. We will lose lives and risk being overrun. The idea is to keep the peaceful people safe. What if we were to take the fight to them? We have people here that have worked inside the Pit Bulls' post, and we can gather good information from them about weaknesses in the security."

"Well David what about the people inside their post?"

"I'm not saying there won't be casualties. Looking at the odds however, they stand in our favor to attack them. The Pit Bulls are centrally located there, the people they've enslaved are ready to revolt, and there is an army of undead surrounding the building!"

Silence fell in the room as everyone considered the options to themselves. I was a little surprised at myself for coming up with such an idea. The last thing I want is for this place to get attacked. I love the people here. I love the atmosphere. I love what this outpost stands for. Philip finished his thoughts with a quick multiple pen tap on the table.

"What would you need to attack the Pit Bulls?"

I didn't realize I was staring at him blankly, processing numbers in my mind.

"I'll have to get back with you. In the mean time I want twelve athletic men on the roof with me, with rifles and ammo. We'll begin tomorrow at 8:00 a.m."

"Are you setting up defensive positions?"

"No sir. I think I can teach these boys how to shoot."

CHAPTER SIXTEEN

A thunderstorm blew in after midnight, pouring down rain until sunrise. A light fog rests on the lush green grass surrounding the college. Large clouds float in the sky, giving the city a bluish gray hue. David wakes up at sunrise, and begins his day with a cup of coffee and the latest reports from Hassam's radios, now installed in a classroom turned intelligence gathering operations. He had never been in the military, unlike his father, and now David is feeling the pressure of his decisions. He vowed to train up young men to fight other men and risk their lives, all for the hope of survival. David did however, feel confident with the decisions he'd made up to this point, and knew it was only a matter of time before his minimal, but tactical know how would be needed.

I knocked softly on the slightly open door to the radio room telling myself it was so I wouldn't alarm anybody, but secretly I didn't want to catch them sleeping. A voice from within gave a quick 'yeah,' which was all the permission I needed. The room was still, except for the hum from the equipment. The room had a smell of old coffee and electronic dust. At the table with a headset on was a young man I'd come to know as Kevin, but he liked to be called Sippo, some kind of computer nerd jargon. He was husky, but looked like he could have been athletic at one time. He was listening intently to the voice in the headset, so I took a seat beside him without disturbing him. After a moment and a few sentences jotted down on a notebook pad, he removed his headset and looked at me with droopy bloodshot eyes.

"You know some people sleep at night Sippo."

"Believe me I had every intention to do so but the radio hasn't stopped chattering since dinner last night. Using Hassam's radio and some networking equipment we have here we were able to get a much stronger signal and we are now communicating to separate locations from coast to coast through a string of piggy backed connections."

I was really impressed with Sippo. Communicating with other outposts was crucial for rebuilding.

"What's the network saying this early in the morning?"

"Well they've been talking about the same thing all night. A post in northern New York has confirmed that New York City is at a total loss. There are million of the undead there, and getting any supplies is almost a lost cause because no one returns from there. They even named an event as the Manhattan Massacre after a group of twenty men and women went deep into the city for food and only one man returned, infected, but alive long enough to tell the story. Rumor has it the remaining portion of the military is going to drop a nuke in Times Square to prevent further spreading."

"Let's hope they don't get any ideas around here" I interrupted.

"Uh, well that's another issue. A majority of the factions that are surviving are trying to rebuild their communities with their own laws and techniques. The existing federal government is still trying to operate as one nation, and they are considering doing what is best for the nation. Let's face it, the big cities are where the undead are collecting, and we can't use biological or chemical weapons against them, so the only option left is nuclear."

"Do you have any good news Sippo?"

"As a matter of fact I do. I have been talking with Jessica, a girl at the Pit Bull superstore post. She's been communicating with me when those pirates aren't around. She sounds hot." He finished smiling.

"What has she told you? Can she tell us how they operate?"

"She's a very smart girl. They are horrible to the innocent people there. They watch over them with rifles, and treat them like slaves."

"What's keeping them from revolting?"

"Well it's not that easy David!" he said as if defending Jessica.

154

"They are friendly people, and those pirates have guns and there are just too many of them!"

"Okay, tell her not to worry, we will have a plan to eliminate the Pit Bulls."

Sippo thanked me, I don't think for having a plan, but for being confident that we could do something for Jessica. I had about an hour before the recruits would be on the roof, and I wanted a hot breakfast before we began so I gave praise to Sippo for the work he had done and told him to go to bed.

As usual, Philip was in the cafeteria enjoying a cup of coffee. He was concerned about the news of the events in New York, but delighted to know we had a contact in the Pit Bull post. I could tell his attitude towards our attackers had changed overnight, he wanted to kill every one of them for treating innocent people the way they do. I assured him we would find a way to eradicate them and soon that post would be on our side. Philip asked about the training I was going to do with the young men, but to be honest I was going to play it by ear. I knew a few marksmanship tips I'd learned from my father, along with some battle techniques I'd read about in his magazines. The same factor that kept bothering me was keeping Philip awake at night also. How were we going to eliminate the threat with so many good people around and not get them hurt or killed? We would have to create the ultimate plan. I finished my bacon and eggs, trying to enjoy them but I couldn't stop thinking of different scenarios. I said good morning to Philip and left the cafeteria to the stairwell.

When I made it to the roof, there were fifteen able bodied men waiting around anxiously, each with a rifle they chose from the arms room. The weather was cool for spring. The clouds produced a mellow overcast, which would provide tougher target practice with the limited visibility. There weren't many options for targets, so we had to improvise. The night before I asked Jake to bring some targets up, but he was with Robin. He must have passed the info along, because there on the edge of the roof stood a row of dirt filled milk jugs and soda cans. The edge of the roof made a wall, and stood about four feet high giving us almost optimal height for practice. Using a telescope I borrowed from the science lab, I scanned the area for the nearest group of walkers. About a mile out was a group ten I counted, possibly more behind buildings. I suppose we were doing things right here and not attracting attention, but that would soon change. After a brief class on weapon safety they were ready to shoot. Some of these students had never held a gun before, let alone shoot one. *This should be interesting.* They drew their weapons up, tucking the stocks in the pocket of their shoulder like I said, and ready to fire.

"Fire!"

At the first shot I started the timer on my watch. Most of the students hit their targets; after all they were only fifty yards away. A few students would need some extra practice.

"I want to emphasize precision shooting gentlemen. There are fifteen of you, and at ten rounds apiece we have used one hundred fifty rounds. We are not a well supplied army so each shot must count."

I called a cease fire so I could look over the roof. There was the group of walkers, along with a few stragglers from nearby. Fifteen minutes was the time it took them to reach our walls from a mile out after the first shot.

"Now it's time to put your shooting to the test! Everyone will load one round at a time and you *will* hit your target, because that one round might be your last. Shooting at multiple targets will require communication so everybody's not aiming at the same target. Everyone get ready! You have thirty seconds to hit fifteen dead heads with one shot each. Your time starts…..Now!"

Each man began calling out the color of the shirt their target was wearing, until somebody would declare that one theirs. Some would argue over targets, some would stand by quietly

156

anxiously awaiting the shot.

"Five seconds!"

Many of them drew their rifles up and jerked the trigger in a panic. At the end of the thirty seconds I counted the bodies that fell.

"Eight bodies dropped. Of those, three stood back up. Three of you need shotguns. Seven of you need baseball bats."

We stayed there on the roof for another hour, until everyone felt comfortable with their rifle, and as of now, it was *their* rifle. Walkers were coming from every direction now. They functioned much like we did with the radios. They would use the actions of others to find out what was going on around them. I could only assume they would see another zombie walking towards something and they would join them, as they tended to move in groups. We went downstairs for lunch, and in the stairwells I could hear them bragging about who shot what.

The cafeteria was bustling with activity. Rumors were circulating that I had a plan to get us out of this mess with the Pit Bulls. If I didn't have enough stress before, it was coming down on me like a ton of bricks now. I was getting looks from other students I'd never met. The cooks made a delicious garden salad with homemade vinaigrette. *What I would give for a steak right now.* My craving gave me an idea for a training operation for the transformation from student to soldier. We would have to find and slaughter a cow.

After lunch I decided to check in with the radio guys for any information along the east coast. I figured Sippo would be in bed, but it's hard to sleep when information keeps coming in. Sure enough, there he was with a fresh cup of coffee. I could smell the bitterness of the coffee when I walked in the room. Sippo poured a cup as strong as they come.

"A nap just wasn't exciting enough was it?"

"I got a few hours of sleep, but I woke up and came right

back here. Things are moving fast in New York."

"What do you mean? How fast?"

"The outpost upstate has had many survivors coming in from across the Appalachian Mountains in fear of fallout. If the rumors are true, detonation will occur soon. The people near ground zero say there was a lot of military activity the past few days broadcasting the impending 'sterilization'."

"Do you think they'll do it?"

"It's too early to tell, but the posts there are preparing for it as fast as they can."

We both looked at a map Sippo had enlarged from a history book and stapled to the wall. Geographically everything was pointing to mass evacuation from the New York City area. The survivors that were gathering across the mountains should be safe from the fallout we agreed.

"Have you heard anything from Jessica?" I asked, trying to brighten the conversation.

"Yes but for just a moment. Those tyrants are watching her carefully."

"Hmm. Well let's give them something to talk about."

"What do you mean?" He asked with a confused look.

"Tell her to report to them that there are rumors the college campus is planning an attack on them."

"Are you out of your damn mind? That would put crosshairs on us, even more so than now."

"Exactly. They'll plan for an attack and set up defenses, putting the attack on us off for a while."

He thought about it for a moment, and with a nod he radioed to Jessica as if he was leaking information out. Once he was done, we knew it went perfectly. They would believe it, and that would buy us some time. I gave Sippo a pat on the shoulder and nodded approval for a job well done.

That evening the eight recruits with solid aim, Jake, and me met in the parking lot beside two pickups. They were standing around the bed of a white extended cab swapping tales about what tonight's mission might entail. I let their stories continue as Jake and I stood by the other truck catching up on today's events. He was truly happy being around Robin. I hadn't seen him smile like this in a long time.

"Are you sure you want to come along?"

"David I really like it here," he was speaking of Robin, "I'm going to stick around and start something here."
I could appreciate that Jake had found something or someone worth staying for.

"Alright gentlemen gather around. Tonight is your first mission. There is a small ranch about thirty miles from here. We're going to kidnap a cow tonight. We're going to bring it back here for steaks tomorrow night!"

The crew roared with cheers at my last comment. They were definitely motivated for the mission. Jake and I separated and sat in the passenger's seat of each truck. Rifles and shotguns loaded, we left the front gate and set the cruise to ninety when we got on the highway. A few miles down the highway I really noticed how dark the world had become. Buildings had become black shapes. Roads had become black snakes. I was slowly getting used to the absolute silence that engrossed us. The recruits were breaking the tension by whooping and hollering. I knew the loud yells wouldn't help our cause by attracting attention, but I was somewhat curious to see how these young men would react to a horde. To be honest I didn't know of any farms nearby, I just assumed we would drive until the street lights ended. It's hard to do though when the lights aren't on and we can only see by moon light.

After an hour of driving we came across a long white metal wildlife fence. We had passed a few walkers leaving the city, but as we got into the rural areas everything around us just got quieter. The trucks rolled to a stop beside the fence, the loud exhaust carrying across the fields. There weren't any cattle nearby; I hoped they hadn't run off. We decided to leave two men back to watch the trucks; the rest of us jumped the fence and began our search across an empty field. Occasionally someone would step in a cow pie, reassuring us we were on the right track. After a few minutes of walking a barn appeared in front of us that we hadn't seen until we were right up on it. The red barn was large, with wide double doors closed shut in the front. I didn't hear any movement inside, so the cattle must still be in the field, which could be hundreds of acres. There was a white two story farmhouse a little over a football field away; four of the recruits went to search for anything we could salvage inside. The rest of us saw what we came for when we came around the barn. There stood a dozen cattle, inside a small gated area with no more grain in the troughs. They were weak from hunger, and now we had to figure out how we were going to get this large animal into the back of the truck.

"I used to work on a farm! We need the harness, I bet it's in the barn!" said one of the recruits, excited to help.

I nodded him the okay to search the barn, with another recruit to watch his back. They disappeared around the front of the barn while Jake and I picked out the largest cow to take. The slamming of a screen door from the house followed by yelling spooked Jake and me into jerking our heads around in surprise. The four recruits were yelling something, and running towards us in fear. As they got closer, my chest began thumping louder when I understood what they were saying.

"There's a whole army of them! Get the hell outta here! Run!"

"Where?!" I yelled back.

The first recruit stopped near us briefly, panting while trying to spit out a sentence.

"The field....other side of house....hundreds of them! We have to leave!"

We turned as we all heard the moans round the corner of the house. It was a sea of zombies pouring around the house like a tidal wave. I ran to the front of the barn for the other two, everyone right behind me. As I gripped the handle to the quick access door I fell to the ground as a bullet splintered the wood inches from my face. A scream followed the shot and as I ripped the door open I saw the four walkers eating the two recruits alive. The visions of horror came flooding back as I froze in place. It took Jake to pull me to my feet and get me running. Running to the trucks all I could see was a walker ripping into the recruit's throat, biting and thrashing, ripping flesh apart while he screamed. The dead army was right behind us, coming in waves, tripping over each other. I swear everyone in this one horse town was infected, and they were after us for their next meal. The trucks were running when we hurdled the fence and jumped into the beds.

"Where is Steven and Jacob?!" One driver yelled, but we didn't have time to tell him. The tires squealed as the trucks whipped around to take us home.

The drive home was silent. A few of the recruits had watery eyes; the rest of us had faces of stone. No emotion. The realization that everything outside the walls was against us began to set in on the young gunslingers. I wondered now if we would be able to uphold all the promises I had made to Spring Gate.

The heavy gate creaked as it slowly opened for us. As usual Philip was waiting for us near the front doors, but before he could ask about the absence of a cow he saw the expressions on our faces.

"What happened out there David?"

"We weren't ready Philip. We weren't ready."

He knew something awful happened. I could see him silently counting each of us as we stepped out of the trucks and came inside. I stayed on the porch with Philip until everyone was inside.

"Tell me David, why are we missing two young men?"

"There was a horde. It seems like everywhere we go we run into an army of undead. They never lose numbers, and whenever the living loses a life the dead gain another. We need more training before we will be ready for such ambitious goals."

Philip took a deep breath, like he was absorbing what I told him, but I could tell he knew something I didn't.

"You're not going to have time to train these boys David. We heard from the superstore tonight about an uprising they had. The rumors you spread there that we were going to attack worked and our friends believed it."

A sudden glimpse of hope stopped me in my tracks, but his solemn expression told me otherwise.

"The good news is our friends there have taken control of the store once again."

"And the bad news?"

"The bad news is those pirates need a new place to build their strength, and rumor has it they are coming here. I wanted to tell you before I made an announcement to the campus, but we are running out of time."

Philip led me through the lobby to the courtyard doors. The dim lamps inside the lobby didn't allow me to see the courtyard until the doors swung open. There stood everyone from the campus, probably two hundred people, each with a dire look of concern. They were expecting bad news, and Philip was ready to reveal our latest troubles.

Philip started of with a traditional ladies and gentlemen opening. I could tell he was no stranger to speeches, and I'm sure he's done hundreds of them, but never with this message. The hush over the crowd turned to cries and moans with every detail he gave, and I could tell everyone was losing hope fast. Questions were shot out of the crowd like gunshots, each from a troubled mind but too garbled to understand. When the crowd grew too restless, I did the only thing I could think of to get their attention back.

BOOM! And the crowd immediately fell silent. Everyone turned their attention to me as I stood there with my big bore pistol held above my head and pointed to the sky.

"I know this is all very frightening to hear. However, this doesn't change our situation. We don't know for sure that they are coming here, and on top of that we don't know that they are looking for a fight. Regardless of their intentions, we can assume that they have taken loses and are not at full strength. I suggest we prepare for whatever may come. Tonight we will set up defensive positions and wait for sunrise."

I felt a twinge of hope circulate through my spine, and half expected a round of applause after my speech but the crowd remained silent. Most of the students shuffled back to the buildings, their heads hung low and already a feeling of defeat. Those with rifles stood in place, ready for their instructions. Tonight every rifle we had would be used to defend Spring Gate.

CHAPTER SEVENTEEN

The night air was warmer than usual. Summer time must be getting close. The warmer air both spread and preserved the smell of rotting flesh. It was a horrible smell. With every whiff my senses wanted to cringe, like a child pulling his bed sheets over his head when he heard a frightening noise outside. The light breeze that lofted across the rooftop was cool on my skin, but was strong with the smell of the dead. I could see for miles. That's what it felt like. Everything was darker than night. I would see a light come on for a moment in the distance, which was sure to attract the undead. Once a light would come on, it would go out shortly after. I just hoped the lights would go out before the walkers would see them. Of the recruits that were most accurate with a rifle, I brought them with me to roam the rooftops, looking for any signs of attackers. I assigned a group of men to the second floor that weren't as close a shot but were excited to help out.

The night was still, silent. The kind of silent that could drive an awaiting force mad. The relaxing hum of nature couldn't be heard. There were no birds chirping, and no movement through the trees. The light breeze was the only sign that time was actually moving. My radio hadn't made a noise for a long hour now. I glanced at my watch, the Indiglo light growing dimmer with each day. *Three thirty in the morning. A few more hours and the sun would be up, lessening the chance of an attack.*

"Over there!" One of the recruits at the other end of the roof yelled out.

I ran to him, huffing from sprinting so hard.

"What is it?"

"A truck sir. He's driving so slow, just idling down the street."

As strange as it sounded, he was right. A truck was coming towards us about a half mile away with its lights on, moving no faster than walking speed. *Walking speed. Oh Shit!*

"Everyone get ready for an attack!" I yelled into the radio.

"Lock the doors, brace them with furniture!" I hoped nobody was trying to talk over the radio while I was; they had to know what was coming.

The truck made the final turn and was on the drive towards the front gate. There was just enough moon I could see that far with my binoculars. I recognized the truck as a member of the Pit Bull's gang. A few car lengths behind the truck, was the beginning of an unending horde of undead. They moved as a solid force, led by a crawling truck, fueled by vengeance.

The truck's headlight beams leapt to the second floor when the driver mashed the gas. With no hesitation the truck plowed into the main gate, blowing the gate off its rail and smashing the brick wall as it warped around like a smashed aluminum can. One headlight remained as the single cab truck screamed up the drive. The building shook when the two ton truck smashed through the front doors and stopped just short of pushing through the lobby and into the courtyard. The giant mass of undead flowed through the gate like a torrent of water that just broke free from a dam. Shots from the rooftop and second floor crackled like popcorn.

"Save your ammo!"
I ordered those that could hear me. It was like they were shooting pellet guns into a swarm of bees.

The roof door slammed against the wall as we ran down the stairs and into the hallway.
Doors were opening in the hallway as students were poking their heads out, asking each other if they felt the building rumble.

"Get back inside! Lock your doors!"
I yelled at them, trying to help as much as I could before I made it to the second floor. A few of them took my advice and locked themselves in; others followed us, curiosity getting the best of them. We made the stairs to the second floor in four bounds, flooded with adrenaline. The second floor hallways were

swarming with students, all in a panic to rush past us and to the third floor. With another jump I was just outside the door to the first floor, where I could hear the screams. As soon as the door opened the volume of screams hit me like speakers at a rock concert. Chaos filled the hallways, students waking up to an invasion and trying to escape, and the only way out was up. We pushed through the current of students, some trampling others to get to the stairwells. I saw the source of the panic, at the end of the hall in the lobby. We made our way past the last bunch of students trying to escape and were now faced with the horde just twenty feet away. Without hesitation our rifles belched flame and bullets at the nearest skulls we could hit, sending black fluids and gray matter into the air. Like spit wads hitting tanks, our bullets did nothing to slow the horde. The lobby was full of the hungry dead, and they were quickly filling into the hallways.

"Run!" was all I could yell, but they didn't need instruction.

We clearly couldn't handle the threat and the dead were moving in fast. The horde must have grown hungry, I had never seen the dead so vicious. They moved with little bursts of sprints, capable of catching an out of breath human. We ran as fast as we could down the hallways, barely making it in the stairwell before rotting bodies smashed the door we slammed behind us. Inches from my face and through the glass pane of the door dead faces were pressed against the glass so hard pieces of flesh were rubbing off their decaying bones. The door had no lock on it, at best we could make it to the second floor before one of them accidentally hit the door handle and they pushed through.

"Help the others on the next floor! Get them inside their rooms and lock the doors!"

The men disappeared into the second floor hallway as I held the door as hard as I could. My fingers were turning purple I was squeezing the handle so tight, but there was no way I could hold it. The door burst open as I leapt away from it, my left foot landing on the first step of the stairs and I was at the second floor door in four jumps. I slammed the door behind me, knowing I didn't have much time. The door had the push lever facing the stairwell, nothing that would stall the walkers. I saw doors down the hallway slam shut, must have been the last of my recruits getting behind a locked door. The hallway was silent, but not for long. I ran down, yelling for someone with an open door. I heard the stairwell door behind me burst open, moans and growls filling the quiet air throughout the hallway. A door halfway down the hall opened, a young man waving me in excitedly. My lungs were burning by the time I made it to the door, I collapsed on the floor as soon as I was in and he slammed the door shut behind me.

Footsteps thundered through the hallway as we lay there in silence. Bloody fists were pounding on the door, sounding like ripe tomatoes smashing against the metal frame. I stumbled out of the way as the young man pushed a dresser against the door. In the living quarters of the room there was a window to the courtyard, where I could see people running across the lawn and through the gardens with the undead snapping their jaws behind them. The window slid open with ease. Shoving the barrel of my military styled rifle out, my sights rested on the head of a walker near the fountain. I squeezed the trigger and felt the recoil against my shoulder. The walker stopped where he stood, and slowly collapsed to the ground.

"Move over!" the young man yelled at me, getting his rifle positioned on the window frame for a steady shot. We did what we could for those fleeing into the rear building, but there were just too many walkers. Each time someone was bitten, they would stand and join the army of undead.

The living no longer occupied the courtyard. The last living beings I saw closed themselves off in the door marked 'Basement' at the far end of the courtyard. There must be two dozen hungry, soulless walkers pushing in on the door. I know the door won't hold for long. The pounding against our door stopped, I guess they moved on to easier prey. There were three of us in the room. I hadn't noticed the young girl curled up in the corner. She looked to be in her early twenties, staring blankly at the opposite wall, rocking back and forth clutching her legs.

"Her name is Becky. I'm Brad" the young man said, white knuckles wrapped around his rifle.

"She's in shock."

"My name's David. We need to put a blanket on her."

I ripped the comforter off the bed, handing it to Brad to wrap around her. She flinched when he touched her, like he woke her from a bad dream.

"Are we going to die?" she asked.

"No Becky, we're not." I comforted her, trying to convince myself also.

Our heads jerked towards the window as we heard the loud crash from the courtyard. Jumping to the window, I saw the ravenous group of walkers push into the basement door. *May God help you now.* Across the yard on the second floor I saw a woman pounding her fists on the window as the room behind her filled with hungry flesh eaters. Her mouth opened wide as she screamed behind the glass, blood pouring from the mouths that latched onto her arms and neck. I saw the life leave her as she slid down the window pane, mouth still open; her face frozen in horror. The walkers rushed out of the room, leaving a trail of blood behind them along the walls and floors. Brad stood beside me, as still as a statue watching in horror. A moment later the woman stood up; she slowly stumbled to the door, all life in her gone. The lights in our room went black, snapping us out of our daze. The entire campus lost power.

"They must have wrecked the generators!" Brad said, looking at me concerned.

Becky started crying, pulling the blanket tighter around her body. The footsteps in the hallway slowed to a walk. I could hear screams down the hall, which always followed the crash of a door being smashed in by sheer weight. Brad helped me prop a couch against the dresser, and anything heavy we could find to hold the door shut. Once the door appeared secure, Brad sat beside Becky trying to calm her down. I stood next to the window, watching the courtyard. The yard was still, other than the grazing walkers, but I knew the hallways and dorms were the exception. Hundreds of them had raced through the halls, filling every building with flesh eaters.

I began to think about Jake and Sarah. Hassam and his family. Philip and the students. The faces of every person I'd met here flashed through my mind. Faces of those I'd never talked to, only seen around campus flashed through my mind. The sun broke the horizon and cast a warm, soft light on the courtyard. The grim scene below me could now be seen clearly. Half eaten bodies lay scattered around the yard. A girl across the yard pulled herself across a walkway, leaving a bloody trail from her legless torso. Body parts resting in puddles of dried blood lay around the fountain. There were groups of the dead around the yard, gathered around a lifeless body, eating someone like a pride of lions on a kill. The dead were a plague. They moved through an area, leaving nothing but death in their wake.

A window on the second floor of the science building burst out, a fireball spewing out behind it, grazing the canopy of the trees below. The flames licked the outer walls of the building, climbing to the third floor. Another window four rooms down did the same, sending flames to the roof. Emerging from the flames was a screaming man, leaping to the yard below. I could hear his legs break as he crashed into the soft grass. Moaning corpses hung out of the window, flames covering them. Flesh was melting off their faces, dripping on the window sill, showing white bone where their pale cheeks used to be. The fire was slowly taking the animation from the undead, their bodies slumping out of the window. Windows of the third floor went foggy, and then melted like cheese on a hot plate. Flames leapt of out every window on the third floor now, roaring loudly, like a train passing by. Only the screams inside could be heard over the burning of structure and flesh. Students were leaping out of the burning rooms to their death below, avoiding the flames and walking death behind them. A woman burst out of the first floor doors into the courtyard, narrowly dodging a corpse falling from the third floor. She screamed when the sunlight hit her melted face, falling to her knees in the garden. Three walkers chased her out, taking advantage of her pain, sinking their teeth into her like wild dogs. Several yards away I could feel the heat from the science wing as the entire building went up in flames. Black smoke filled the sky, the breeze carrying it over the medical wing. The smoke was thick enough I could see the sun through it without squinting. The bright orange ball was black as charcoal.

Beauty and hope burned in that building, leaving nothing but the black smoke that covered the glow of the sun. *My friends are gone. Our hope of rebuilding is lost.* I hoped that by some miracle that if Sarah had died, it was peaceful. If Jake had died I hoped he was with Robin.

"Robin was in the medical wing!"

"David shut up!" Brad yelled through tight lips, trying to stay quiet.

"We have to get out of here Brad, you and Becky need to come with me."

"I'm not going anywhere!" She yelled with a dry mouth and red puffy eyes.

"Listen to me! There are survivors in the medical wing, and there are cars in the parking lot."

"Where are we going to go David?" Brad asked pessimistically, but curious.

"Let's go to superstore."

CHAPTER EIGHTEEN

We made a plan to go through the medical wing, picking up survivors along the way. I wasn't leaving here without Jake and Sarah. The only problem was the few hundred zombies that were in our way. The hardest part would be waiting them out. Exhaustion was setting in, and we felt like we were dragging anchors around our necks. I sat on the floor beside the bed, doing my best to keep my eyes open. Brad fell asleep holding Becky in one arm, rifle in the other. I could still hear the shuffling of dead feet outside in the hallway, all signs were pointing towards sleep. My eyes closed for just a moment.

I woke up startled, immediately searching the room for any threats. My shirt was sweaty, and the room smelled like smoke. There was no smoke in the room; I just prayed the fire didn't spread to our building. I woke up Brad, he jumped like I did. He rubbed the sleep out of his eyes, looking out the window.
"What time is it?"
I had to check my watch, unaware myself.
"Almost five. I don't see any walkers in the courtyard. Maybe they moved on."
"When should we leave here?"
I thought for a moment, tossing around what-ifs through my mind.
"Now."

Brad woke up Becky; he already had a change of clothes ready for her. We were gentlemen and gazed out of the window while she changed. At first I felt uncomfortable seeing her reflection in the glass, but something about her changing clothes relaxed me. Her changing clothes reminded me of times before day zero.
"Okay I'm ready" she announced.
We did a last check, making sure our weapons held as many bullets as possible, though we didn't have many left. I

approached the door first, Brad behind me. Becky didn't have a gun, and I didn't believe she would use it if she had one.

I turned the knob slowly, and then opened the door enough to peek through. The hallway was dark. Three doors down across the hall a door was open, sunlight shining in lighting a portion of the hallway. I knew already, but I hoped it wasn't a door we heard smashed open with a meal inside. I could see movement at the end of the hall near the stairwell. We would have to go that way, since the building was only connected by breezeways at each corner on ground level. Unfortunately Becky didn't keep baseball bats lying around her room, so any bark from our guns would surely attract attention. I checked the hallway in the other direction, there was no movement. We crept into the hall, slowly making our way down the dark corridor. The figure at the end of the hall was standing still, and dark. As we got closer I could see she was a tall woman, with long, straight hair. She stood there in a white long sleeve, with a blood stained grey skirt. Her arms were by her sides, not moving. Her feet were moving like she was walking in place.

"Hello?" Becky called out.

The girl turned around slowly, very stiffly. Her long dark hair covered most of her face, but I could see into the deep bloody sockets where her eyes used to be. Dry blood streamed from her eye sockets down her face, filling in the scratches where they were clawed out. Her expression turned from lifeless to savagely hungry in an instant. She lunged towards us, but was unable to bite any of us without her vision. I motioned for the others to slip into the stairwell as quietly as possible. There's no reason to use a bullet on something that couldn't see us, risking the others hearing us. I looked back as we slid into the stairwell. She was thrashing her arms wildly, looking for a nearby victim. *If she's here, I hope her soul is somewhere else.*

Despite the carnage that surrounded us, the fresh air in the breezeway was a nice change. A walker across the yard spotted us, but was too far away to be any real threat. We slipped into the stairwell of the medical building, quietly shutting the door behind us. *Where do we begin our search?* I feared that Jake or Sarah had been in a room that was broken into or worse yet stranded in a hallway.

"Where do you think they are?" Brad whispered to me.

"I'm not sure. I hope they're in a sealed vault with armored walls."

"Oh you mean like the medical lab?" he replied so innocently.

My eyes lit up with excitement when I'd realized what he said.

"Brad you're a genius!"

"Yes actually. That's been confirmed. Two years ago…"

"Quiet. Let's check the hallway" I cut him off.

Peeking through the little window in the stairwell door, I could only see partially down the hallway. I could make out what I thought were the lab doors about a hundred feet away. The door was silent as we crept through and into the hallway. When the door shut behind us there was very little light to see with. The sun was going to be down soon, and we had no flashlights. In other words, if we didn't find our friends or shelter soon, our troubles would multiply by the minute. Every footstep we took down the hall sounded like an elephant's hoof smashing the ground in our opinion, but in actuality we were being very quiet. It's amazing how loud something soft can be in absolute silence. Moving past an open door on our left, I could see a figure slowly pacing the room in front of a window, looked to be male, but definitely not living. I pressed my finger to my lips to remind the others to stay quiet, but I doubt they saw me. We were getting very close to the labs now; I could tell when the carpet turned to tile. A deep gurgle came from our direct front, and very close. I pressed my hand against Brad's chest, stopping him from walking further. In the silence I heard the shuffling feet in front of us. I guessed maybe a dozen of them were filling this part of the hallway. The smell of rotting flesh was so strong I almost gagged. Brad had not stopped Becky and she had no idea we were feet away from the undead. She bumped into him, catching her off guard as she let out a loud gasp trying to hold her scream in. That's all it took. The silent hall filled with grunts and moans and the feet went from shuffling to hard, directed steps.

"Shoot 'em all!" I yelled to Brad.

The burst of fire from my rifle briefly illuminated our targets, showing their lifeless faces warp into demonic flesh eaters. Each flash from the rifle showed our enemy's faces, getting closer with every shot. My ears were ringing from the blasts in such a confined space. I pulled the trigger as fast as I could, but they were only getting closer. My heart stopped when the bullets stopped. My gun was empty. Brad fired as fast as he could from his bolt action, but he would run out soon also. My .45 made a lonely bark with each shot, not as accurate as I wanted but the hall was so dark. I felt Brad step back when he ran out of ammo. This is it. 4 rounds. 3 rounds. 2 rounds. *BOOM! BOOM!* I felt cold, sticky goo hit my face. This time the gun blasts were coming from a door down the hall.

"Get the hell in here!"

That's Jake's voice!

I grabbed Brad's sleeve and pushed him towards the door, reaching around in the dark to find Becky. I felt her hand reaching out. I squeezed the warm hand and pulled. She must have been apprehensive, because it took some effort to get her moving, but she would have to trust me. I followed Brad into the lab door, pulling Becky behind me. Once inside, I heard the door hiss behind us as it closed. A small lantern gave us some light, and it was nice to see Jake's face. Becky's hand went limp, so I let her go. I'm sure she was still a little frightened. When I let go however, I heard a thump hit the floor at my feet. It was Becky's forearm, chewed off just before the elbow.

The doors were thick; I could barely hear the pounding coming from the other side. Inside there were people gathered around the lantern. I recognized Robin, but I didn't see Sarah or Hassam's family. There was a large muscular black man, named

Darius, who I recognized from football pictures in the hallway from our first visit. Beside him sat a smaller man named Kameel. There were two girls I'd never seen before, and furthest from me was Sippo.

"Jake, where is Sarah?"

I instantly started denying any answer he might give when he put his hand on my shoulder.

"We haven't seen Sarah since the attack began. From what I'm told she was in the science wing."

"Well what you were told is wrong Jake!"

He didn't begin to argue with me. I had never thought of Sarah in a way as a significant other, but I had grown attached to her. She never let me down with her abilities, and I loved her spark. *There's no way she's gone.* He also told me Hassam and his family had not been seen. Last he heard they were in their rooms upstairs, but the second floor took a hard toll of casualties.

There wasn't much difference between the way we looked and felt compared to the undead. Nobody had eaten in the last day, besides some muffins that were left in the lab. Sleep came in small doses also.

"We can't stay here. We are hungry, tired, and running out of ammo." Jake reported.

"Our plan was to come here to find you and Sarah and take a few trucks to the superstore." I told Jake.

"That sounds great David, but we don't have the keys to any trucks in the parking lot."

He was right. There's no telling how many of those keys were in the pockets of a corpse walking up and down the hallways.

"Take the spirit bus. It doesn't use keys, just a turn knob." Darius spoke up.

"The spirit bus?"

"Yeah. The bus we take to out of town football games. It's always gassed up, and it doesn't need keys. We keep it next to the locker room."

"Darius I could kiss you right now" Jake said jokingly, giving him a playful hug, pretending to move in for a kiss.

"Get off me honky!" He laughed back.

"How do we get to the locker rooms?" I enjoyed the horseplay, but I couldn't get past the fact Sarah could be gone.

"They didn't play a significant role in our survival here, so we hardly used them. The showers aren't exactly private, so the building ended up never getting used. We'll have to go around the building through the courtyard to avoid the horde in the hallway, and from there the athletic complex is about two hundred yards across the lawn."

"Well what are we waiting for? Let's go!" Sippo spoke up, excited about getting to the superstore to meet his radio girl.

The nine of us grabbed anything we might need, from miscellaneous batteries to a few small containers. A laboratory doesn't have much useful gear to someone who doesn't know how to use it. Leaving a sealed lab out any other door than the main door would be tricky, but we lucked out with a changing room that was attached to it. It was the size of a janitor's closet, lined with small lockers, but it had a frosted glass window that faced the courtyard. I pushed the top of the window with a good amount of strength but with my other hand slowed the bottom from coming in too fast. The center pivot window was now open, and we began crawling out one by one.

Once the nine of us were in the yard, we moved to the breezeway Brad and I had come through earlier. It reminded me of losing Becky in the hallway. She never made a sound. After the breezeway I could see the athletics building a couple hundred yards away, like Darius said. In the parking lot there were several walkers surrounding a small import car. I thought we could sneak by, but the open field left us nowhere to hide. One of them grunted as he caught us in the corner of his eye. Their focus quickly turned to us; I guess whatever meal inside the car wasn't worth their effort. We sprinted to the football locker rooms, out running our chasers. The metal double doors were unlocked, but took a hard pull to open. Darius shut the door behind us, wrapping a chain around the push bars, locking us inside.

"The bus is in the back, next to the groundskeeper's shed."

CHAPTER NINETEEN

Sarah woke up with a pounding headache, buried under wooden rubble that smelled of ash. She pushed a large wooden plank off her abdomen, suddenly feeling the pain from her right leg. Her instincts told her to stay quiet, but it was all she could do to keep from screaming. Looking down she noticed a section of rebar jutting out of her thigh, with blood around the wound. The bar was too long to leave in, but if she pulled it out she could bleed out. Beside her laid a man with his face frozen in terror, eyelids wide open. *He must have been killed in the fire, or the collapse of the roof* she thought. He didn't show signs of infection. She reached down with both hands and grabbed her thigh, slowly pulling it off the rebar. The pain was excruciating. She grit her teeth, tightened her jaw, doing anything to take her mind off the pain. Little relief came when the bar was finally out of her leg, but now she was left with large hole in the largest muscle of her leg. The wound was hours old she determined, most of the blood inside was dry. Her belt and torn off sleeve made an excellent pressure bandage. There was debris everywhere, some piles still burning. The ashes between her and the lifeless man a few feet away were still hot. Her arms burned as she crawled toward the corpse. The pain from Sarah's leg radiated through her body each time she moved. Hoping to get lucky, she reached into the man's pockets. A smile spread across her face as she felt what she was looking for in his right pocket. The keys clacked against the keyless entry when she pulled them out of his pocket.

It took all her might to climb to her feet. Using a piece of fallen wall, she propped herself up, finally able to see the destruction. She was still on the third floor, but the roof had collapsed, leaving her exposed to the grim images that lay around the campus. The science wing was the only building that burned, but there was so much blood everywhere, nobody could have survived the attack. She hoped her friends made it out alive, somehow. Every step she took towards the stairwell shot pain up her spine. The stairwell was now a concrete skeleton, char marks covering the walls. She winced at each step on the way down, just two more flights to go. The sun was almost below the horizon when she made it to the bottom of the stairs. She stood at the stairwell door, readying herself for the quick run to the parking lot. Once she would be in the breezeway she would be exposed, and there would be walkers around as long as there was food. The metal door warped during the fire, it took all her might to push it open. Stepping into the breezeway, her shoulder hurt now from slamming into the door, but it took no attention from her leg. As she followed the wall and came to the corner of the medical building, she heard the slurping and chewing just feet away. The dead were in her way to the parking lot, but she had no other way to go, so she would have to out run them. She took several deep breaths before making the dash, convincing herself she could make it, and getting the keyless entry ready to beep. *One..Two..Three!* She darted past the corner, but moving only as fast as she could limp her bloody leg. The walkers noticed her immediately and abandoned the corpse they were feeding on. The pain was so intense; she prayed she wouldn't pass out while running to the car. Once Sarah was near the parking lot, she repeatedly pushed the keyless entry remote. In the far corner of the lot, a small little black car chirped. *Of course it's that far away.* She could barely keep distance between her and the walkers. At times the pain would be so intense she didn't notice the walkers were gaining on her. It seemed like an eternity before she reached the little black car. The car was a two door hatchback that looked more like a roller skate than an automobile. She would be able to leave the campus in a hurry, but the car provided no real security. Worried that she might open the wound in her leg, she tried to pull the homemade bandage tighter while she limped closer. She swung open the little door, gritting her teeth again as she bent her leg to get in. When she pulled the door shut the dead surrounded the car. They beat their fists bloody against the car, the windows chattering as she started the motor.

Suddenly the pounding stopped. The walkers took an interest in something completely new. Sarah wasn't sure what it was, but they left her car and moved quickly to another target. *Whatever it is, thank you.* The tires squealed as she left the parking lot and down the drive way to the broken gate.

Sarah wasn't sure where she was going, but she had to get somewhere safe. She would need medical attention soon. The makeshift bandage had done well, but the run through the parking lot had opened the wound up, soaking the cloth and running down her leg. Weaving in and out of the parked cars along the highway, she drove as fast as she could respond to the steering. As she sped down the blacktop, the cars were turning into blurs of color. Her reaction time was slowing fast. As if someone poured water over the windshield, her vision became blurry and she couldn't distinguish car from truck, pavement from grass. Darkness began at the corner of her eyes, steadily growing inwards. Her hands left the steering wheel as her head slumped downward, eyes shut and losing consciousness. The car drifted to the side of the highway, grinding against the guard rail, sending a shower of sparks in the air. She'd reached the end of the rail, and without its support the car veered into the ditch. The front bumper struck the opposite side of the ditch, bouncing upward unevenly, flinging the car on its side. Her body tumbled like a rag doll inside, the airbags filling out around her. The little black car rolled over several times before landing on its roof at the bottom of the ditch. Her world had gone black.

"I think she's still alive!"

"No way man; she's been bitten!"

"I don't think so. The wound's not infected, and she still has a pulse. She must have been out for hours."

"Whatever just help her out and we'll take her to Doc."

CHAPTER TWENTY

The bus didn't have much acceleration, but once it was moving it could plow through a light horde. Sippo chose to drive the bus, his excitement to see Jessica was getting the best of him. The highway was dark as usual. I'm glad Sippo knew his way around town; even with the bright headlights it was difficult to see road signs until we were right up on them. It occurred to me as we were leaving one suburb and entering another that this was the farthest I had been from my house since day zero. There were burned out buildings along the highway we'd already been down, but this road was different. Businesses were missing walls. Entire structures were demolished. A semi truck had plowed through a grocery store, leaving evidence of the building's demise. The infection must have spread rapidly in this town, because the chaos that ensued certainly overwhelmed it quickly. The drive was like a tour of downtown London after WWII. The piles of rubble which used to be buildings were the lightest of the morbid scenes, if there was such a case. Upon exiting the main road we drove past a bus stop that sent shivers through each of us. The Plexiglas windows used to create a bus passenger's shelter from the elements was stained blood red. Body parts were strewn out over puddles of dried blood inside. I felt remorse for those poor souls inside when a horde came through, cleaning out the bus stop like locusts over a field of crops. A mile down from the bus stop was a sea of wrecked cars that stretched over a football field. The carnage was evident there, as we had to drive slowly on the sidewalk beside the cars, Sippo doing his best to avoid the occasional grinding from nearby buildings. There wasn't a car there that hadn't collided with another, and the driver pulled out through a pulled open door or a broken window. I couldn't stop staring at an eighties model gray hatchback with two blood streaks across the hood. There's no telling what was on the other side.

"We're almost there!" Sippo yelled out as he wheeled the bus around a wide right turn.

The mood was suddenly lighter in the cab of the bus, each of us hoping to be safe soon. The headlights cast long white beams down the wide, dark road. At the tip of the beams I could see small objects moving around the road.

"Are those animals?" Sippo asked me, steering straight but looking up at me as I now loomed over his right shoulder.

"No. Those are shoes." I hesitated, thinking. "Don't let off the throttle."

His foot pushed a little heavier on the pedal when the lights revealed the bloodied torsos atop the staggering legs. I couldn't tell how deep the horde was, but it was too late to slow down now. The bus immediately lost speed as we crashed into the first wave of walking dead. The sound of flesh tearing and bones breaking could be heard over the struggling diesel engine as we pushed through. The headlights disappeared into the nearest walkers, shutting out all light. From the light of the moon I could see the hungry faces down the road as far as I could see staring directly at us.

Before we turned into the parking lot I could see flashes from the rooftop, probably riflemen clearing the way for us. Sippo drove the bus to the bay doors of the tire shop, and before he could honk the horn light spread across the ground as the door lifted before us. Two men with shotguns stepped out and sprayed a nearby walker in the face, leaving a headless corpse to fall to the ground. The two gunmen followed the bus inside and closed the door behind us, closing off any light from the garage leaving the building looking lifeless once again. The windows were painted black, to hide the well lit interior of the garage. Large floodlights hung from the ceiling. There were a few trucks with us in the garage; they'd been fitted with makeshift armor from metal shelving racks inside the store. We were greeted the moment we stepped off the bus. The introductions were friendly, but I could tell they were determining our intentions of being here. I don't blame them, after what they had been through.

"Hello, my name is Peter. Welcome to Rooftop Gardens.

What are your intentions here?"

His glasses gave him a nerdy appearance, and his parted blonde hair didn't help, but under his polo shirt he was well built, stocky even. I was a little taken with the blunt approach he used, and I noticed the men with shotguns standing by a little on edge. We did just step out of a bus with rifles, so I wanted to make it clear we had no foul intentions.

"My name is David," and I introduced the others as we shook hands.

"We came from Spring Gate. Unfortunately we were overrun last night by a major horde, and we are all that remains of the post."

"I'm sorry to hear that David, but by now I'm sure you've heard about the uprising here? I believe Jessica talked to your man on the radio?"

Sippo stopped him to ask where he could find her, but Peter calmly replied he would get his chance.

"I understand you are very tired, just let our medic check you over and you will be given a place to eat and rest. It's our way of making sure the infected don't make it inside. Lately it's hard to trust the living, let alone the living dead."

We agreed to his request, I think we were all too tired to put up an argument anyway. One by one the medic checked us for bites or scratches in the waiting room of the garage. After the 'Infection Inspection' as we called it, we were treated to steaks and reheated frozen vegetables. The steaks had a spice to them I couldn't identify, perhaps to cover up the aging gaminess of the meat. Sippo finally got to meet Jessica, and I couldn't have imagined an odder couple. He was the nerdy type, but she had an hourglass figure, with creamy olive skin. Her dark hair complemented her mysterious eyes, and I could tell Sippo was lost in them. We sat around a large patio table in front of an oversized flat screen television, watching a DVD we voted on. After dinner Peter led us to the sleeping quarters, a partitioned off area in the back of the store, with camping lanterns to lead the way. It was nice to lie in a soft bed again, but I couldn't shake the faces of those I was so close to, but would probably never see again.

I didn't know how long I'd slept when I woke up in the dark room. The small night lanterns were still glowing, but with no windows I couldn't tell if it was day or night. Part of me wanted to stay in bed, and sleep this whole nightmare away, but I couldn't do that. I was in someone else's home. There was a blue digital clock on the floor a few cots away, it read 9:27. *The sky's going to be really bright or really dark when I walk out of here. Another day in these boots,* I thought as I slid them on my sore, aching feet. I followed the dimly lit wall to the door separating us from the main room. Opening the door, the light hit me like walking out of a cave into a sunlit field. I hadn't realized the vastness of the store until now, when the light shone throughout it. The building was designed with shaded Plexiglas windows built into the ceiling, to save money on power usage during the day. This building was actually perfect for survival.

I was now in what used to be the electronics section, but now was sectioned off with partitions with what looked like makeshift communications equipment in each one. There was someone sitting at each post listening in headphones, three posts total. Most of the shelves had been emptied of anything that was useful, even the video game cabinets. They were smart to keep the model TV's along the wall turned off; there was no need to attract attention, or burn electricity for that matter. I'm not sure how they were getting electricity here either. Batteries would last for only so long, even the amounts supplied by a super store. Two of the radio operators were quietly listening, slightly daydreaming. Only one of the operators was intently talking into the microphone.

The aisles were surprisingly clean for an apocalyptic fortress. My stomach growled a little when I smelled something tasty coming from the produce section. I crossed through the pet department on the way towards the delicious smell, noticing nothing had been removed from the shelves except the kitty litter. The produce department was nothing like it was when the doors were open for business. Aisles were turned sideways, blocking the food off from anybody coming by and grabbing food. There was an opening in the wall of shelves, with two folding tables breaking the barrier. A man in an apron sat on a stool behind the tables, a clipboard full of papers in front of him.

"What's a guy got to do for some of those eggs cooking back there?" I asked the man.

He stood up from the stool, but there wasn't much difference in height. He wore a stained white V-neck shirt over brown slacks. His short gray hair circled the top of his shiny bald head, behind thick glasses.

"What's your section buddy?" He asked.

"My section?"

"Yeah, where you workin?"

My confused look gave me away instantly.

"Oh you must be one of the new guys. Alright, this one's on the house." He turned and yelled to someone behind the barriers.

"One breakfast special Alonzo!"

"You say it's on the house, how do you do currency here? Obviously money isn't worth anything."

"We call it a Work for Food system. It was Ray's idea. You put in time on your assigned station, and you earn a meal for working that part of the day. Breakfast is a large meal for what it's worth, so the hours someone works until lunch earns them a sandwich. Afternoon shifts earn you a sizeable dinner. It works the same way for the night shift, that's why the morning and evening meals are proportioned the way they are."

A young Hispanic man brought a Styrofoam plate full of scrambled eggs from the kitchen and set it down in front of the man as he finished. He marked something on the clipboard then handed me a plastic spoon.

185

"Don't throw away your trash, we use everything we have at least twice." he smiled as he handed me the plate. There were picnic tables set up not far away, underneath a skylight, providing me a great place to enjoy this hot meal.

There were a few people sitting at the tables when I walked up, one table full of younger kids in their teens. I chose the table with three others that were closer to my age. They were quick to start a conversation as soon as I set my plate down.

"You're from the college aren't you?" a heavyset woman asked me first. Her red hair was plain, complementing her plain round glasses that sat on her cheeks.

"Rumors spread quickly here."

"Hun, we live in a building. Nothing goes on here that everybody doesn't know about the moment it happens."
I smiled a little, agreeing with her trying to be friendly, as I shoveled a full spoon of eggs in my mouth.

"It's amazing how well you function here. Despite what's happening outside you've established a barter system and have somehow built a thriving community."

"Everyone has played a role building what we have here" the slim man across from the woman spoke. His red flannel shirt and light framed silver glasses gave him an educated look.

"Everything from the Work for Food program, to the electricity provided here."

"I was curious about that," shoveling another bite of eggs in my mouth, chasing the mouthful of bacon down.

"How do you have electricity here?"
The slim man put his fork down and crossed his arms, as if ready to explain everything.

"The biggest impact on electricity we have here is minimizing use. We have troughs of water on the roof that are heated by the sun, and then routed down to the kitchen and showers by garden hoses. The troughs are slender and long, so as not to put stress on the structure, and to reach different parts of the post. The electricity that powers the televisions, radios, and freezers come from the in house gym. Magnets and copper wire around the wheels of exercise bikes are wired into a battery box, much like the alternator in a car. The bikes provide power and fitness."

"That's genius." I couldn't help but be amazed.

"Thank you" he responded, looking quite pleased with himself.

"Oh you'll have to excuse Ronnie" the woman said laughing.

"Those were his ideas."

"Very impressive." I gave him a nod of appreciation.

"What about the Work for Food system?"

They paused for a moment, looking at each other. The third man who hadn't spoke yet, picked his plate up and moved towards the man at the kitchen tables with the clipboard, where a young boy took it out of sight. The woman spoke first.

"The Work for Food system was created by Ray John, but we call him Ray. He's been a valuable member of the community, but he keeps to himself."

"Incredible soldier though" the slim man interrupted, "he volunteers for every scavenger mission we send out."

They continued swapping encounters they'd each had with this man, but he still remained a mystery to them. All I could gather was that he was a Jamaican man in his thirties, quiet, but very tactful on his feet. The more stories I heard, the more I wanted to meet him, regardless if it was curiosity or advantageous.

"Where can I find Ray?" I broke into their conversing.

"He's always on the roof, where we have the vegetables growing."

"You have vegetables growing on the roof?" I didn't want to get sidetracked, but I had to make sure I understood what she said.

"Oh well sure hun. There were plenty of pots and potting

soil in the gardening department. We carried it all to the roof and established a farm right above us. Protection from animals, protection from thieves, and protection from, well you know..."

"You say I can find Ray there?" I asked her quickly, I could tell the thought of the walkers made her uncomfortable real quick. Like a bolt of lightning she snapped back.

"Yes he'll be up there."

Just like the silent man at our table, I took my empty plate back to the man at the kitchen table. He put a check next to my name when I handed my plate over to him. The woman at the table told me there was a rope ladder that led to the roof in the old sporting goods section. It was easy to find, there were tents set up around the area with little shops inside. There were gym weights tied to the bottom of the ladder to keep it stable. *They got everything figured out here don't they?* Blue skies shone down through the open hatch to the roof. The warm sun's rays felt great on my skin. Summer was here, and it felt great. Despite the hot air, the breeze washed over my skin bringing goose bumps to the surface. I actually felt alive. There were workers in large straw hats tending to the young saplings in the carefully arranged pots. Garden hoses laid across the pots, with cuts in them to water each pot. I held my hand over my eyes to block the bright sun, and scanned the rooftop for Ray. After a moment I spotted a man standing with his back to the roof, looking over the parking lot across the roof from me. He was a tall, muscular black man wearing a loose yellow shirt and brown cargo pants. He looked more Jamaican than anybody else, so I made my way through the rows of pots to him. As I got closer I noticed a pair of durable hiking boots on his feet. I had imagined he'd be wearing flip flops, but then again we weren't at the beach.

"Ray?"

He turned to look back at me, but kept his arms crossed and said nothing. His expression never confirmed he was Ray, but his patchy beard gave him an island look. I walked up beside him, crossing my arms trying to mimic his stance. The smell hit me hard. Death flowed through my nostrils like waters flooding a valley. I took a step back, not prepared for the smell, or the sight. Below us were hundreds of living dead. Possibly more than a thousand. Despite their attempts to camouflage the activity inside the building, it was no secret life was flourishing inside. I composed myself, and managed to inhale enough air to speak without bringing my breakfast back up.

"Are you the infamous Ray John?"

He said nothing at first, and then spoke while he stared into the vast expanse before us.

"Does the smell make you uncomfortable?" he spoke in a strong island accent.

"Wha…What? Of course it does. You're not comfortable with the smell of death are you?"

"The day the dead began to walk was not my first encounter with the smell of death. Before, the smell of death brought pain, fear. Now the smell of death hovers around the enemy. Now death is a smell of alarm."

"So can I call you Ray?"

He smiled, this time looking at me.

"You may call me Ray."

"Why do you watch them?"

"I do not watch them. I let them watch me."

"Isn't that why they don't leave?"

"They know we are here, they're not leaving. A horde moves like hundreds of small magnets. I stand here for an hour, they get as close to me as they can, pushing against one another. When I step back from the edge out of sight, they decompress and spread out. One man can control the actions of hundreds, even beyond death."

"That's some heavy shit Ray. You study them?"

"Are they not the enemy? We must know them to defeat them."

"Do you think we'll ever defeat them? What we lose, they gain."

"Three weeks ago where we stand was an empty shell. Today it is a self sufficient civilization."

"Ah yes and speaking of which, I heard Work for Food was your idea?"

"It was. The signs were there all along."

Before I made a fool of myself by asking, I thought for a minute about what he'd said. I could tell enough about him by now that he was an intelligent man, but he liked for others to find the answers themselves. Work for Food. Signs. *Will work for food. Was Ray a homeless man?*

"I don't want to offend you Ray, but were you homeless?"

"If I was homeless and holding the sign, the letters would be facing away from me and I'd never see them. No I wasn't homeless, but I saw many who were, and they provided the answer for me."

"It's genius Ray."

"Don't thank me; thank those that never got the loose change in our pockets."

Our pockets. We aren't so different after all.

"I didn't mean to hit a nerve, if I've offended you." I was still trying to get a definitive response about his life before.

"I never got your name, but you know mine."

"I'm sorry Ray. My name is David."

"Named from a hero of a great story in an even greater book. There is your Goliath, David." He motioned with his palm up towards the giant horde beneath us.

"I don't think you've got the right David."

"He was nothing more than a man with a slingshot. We've spent enough time standing here David. Would you like to see something interesting?"

"Lead the way..." I caught myself from rhyming his name in my willingness to follow. I liked Ray's demeanor and intelligence, but I didn't want to sound too eager.

I followed Ray down the rope ladder and through the aisles to the kitchen, catching double takes from the others as we passed. Ray approached the same man on the stool behind the table I met at breakfast. It seemed a little early for lunch, and I didn't feel like I'd pulled my weight so far.

"I don't think I've earned a sandwich yet Ray."
He paid no attention to my comment, and addressed the bald man with direct intentions.

"Jerry I'd like to show our friend here The Project."
"The...Oh the Project. Sure thing Ray."

He pulled away a red bed sheet, revealing an entrance into the walled kitchen. Ray led me into the area, past more folding tables with several camping stoves on them. He pushed through two folding doors into the storage area of the kitchen. The open room had just enough light coming in to see where we were going. The walls were gray, the concrete floor was gray. This was the butcher's section of the market, and still very clean. Shiny diamond steel plating lay as an entrance to two walk in freezers, where Ray stopped.

"There was concern we would need the second freezer, but through some negotiation I was able to keep one for my experiment. I hope it has paid off."
"Experiment?"
"See for yourself." He pointed to the little window in the door.

As I got close to the window he flicked the light on inside, revealing a walker staring straight back at me, eyes intense. I jumped back instinctively, getting a laugh from Ray.

"What the hell is that?! Why do you have one of them in there?"
"Take another look David." His smile couldn't have stretched wider.

I was a little apprehensive to take another look, but Ray was persistent with his hand motions. There it was standing, but leaning against a stainless steel rack inside. It was an early

191

twenties aged male, athletic build in a t-shirt and khaki pants.

"Why isn't it attacking the door?"

"Flesh will always be flesh, dead or alive David."

"You're telling me he's frozen to death?"

"I prefer dead and frozen. I trapped him using blankets and bungee cords to wrap him up. I separated him from the others by the magnet method. I set the temperature inside to thirty degrees Fahrenheit. In one night he was frozen solid. The following day I turned off the freezing unit, and within hours he thawed, and was just as lethal as before."

"How long has he bee frozen now?"

"He hasn't been thawed in a week."

I could see the advantage of freezing the lifeless corpses. It would be several months before the weather would get cold enough here to drop below freezing temperatures, but many possibilities would open up then.

"Is it easier to kill it once it's frozen?"

"I haven't tried yet, but I imagine it would. We won't use bullets though, too valuable. I want you to try this."

He handed me a wooden baseball bat he kept near the freezer. I could tell he had been waiting for the day he would have an audience. I gripped the bat firmly and readied it as he opened the freezer door. The cold air whirled out as a mist, and the walker's eyes locked immediately on me, but he didn't move. I paused for a moment, allowing the corpse to move if he could, to determine the capabilities of a frozen zombie. Only his eyes rolled. I pulled the bat behind my head, taking a batter's stance to swing for the fences. A harsh breath rolled out of the walker's mouth as I released my stance and contacted with the side of his head. Like concrete shattering and falling to the ground, his head split apart in pieces after a dull smash and crumbling sound.

"Yeah mon!" Ray shouted behind me, jumping and clapping his hands.

"I thought that's what would happen! Death to them all!"

"Ray have you been saving this for a special occasion?"

"I've been waiting for a partner David. I'm tired of

running from them."

I thought for a moment about what he'd said. He was tired of running from them, and to be honest I was to. This was no way to live.

"Ray I know you'll want to hear this!" came a voice from the double doors.

Ray and I looked at each other, we would have to dispose of the headless ice block later, and there was urgency in the man's voice. We quickly shut the freezer door and jogged through the double doors and into the kitchen area. The bald man was waiting for us.

"There's something big happening around the radios, everybody's running over there." The man said calmly, still holding his clipboard.

Ray and I jogged alongside others on the way to the radios, more and more people collecting beside us. Once there I noticed a large gathering, as quiet as a church. A woman's voice could be heard from the center radio booth.

"Are you sure? Can you confirm that?" Her transmission was followed by a pause.

"Dover are you there?"
Radio silence followed for another long pause.

"D..llas..this..s..Dove.." Came a scratchy, cut out response.
I could hear the radio operator in the booth talking to someone.

"We found a signal that stretched to urban parts of New York. It was a little distorted but we could communicate. Now we can't get anything back from them."

"Try the reliable connections. We have to know if what they're saying is true." came a male voice also in the booth.

I heard the female operator try a few locations in her headset, but getting no responses. The crowd was growing impatient.

"What's happening Peter?!" yelled a man in the crowd.

His question sparked the impatience of the others and soon most of the crowd was yelling questions or opinions out loud.

"Quiet! Everyone quiet please!" Peter said as he stood in a chair to address the crowd.

"We don't know exactly what happened yet. We are getting reports from all over the nation and the radio signals are flooded with people talking. Remain calm, and I will let everyone know as soon as I find out anything, you have my word."

"Are we in danger?" said a woman a few feet behind me.

"We have no evidence to say that we are in any danger," Peter responded. "If everyone can remain calm I will get everyone together and tell you everything I know."

"Why do you get to know everything?! You could keep something from us!" came an angry voice in the back.

His outburst sparked another flurry of angry questions guided towards Peter, and the crowd was growing more impatient with every passing minute. I looked at Ray beside me, still keeping his calm with his arms crossed.

"This is absolute madness." I said.

"You said it mon. Everybody wants to hear the news, not knowing what they would do with the information anyway."

I couldn't help but laugh a little with my response to him.

"Almost safer dodging dead heads huh? Ha!"

Ray kept a straight face when he responded with a 'yes'.

"Quiet! Quiet!" yelled Peter, finally calming the crowd.

His burst was followed by silence, until we heard the female radio operator speak again.

"Atlanta are you sure?…That's three total correct?…Okay thank you Atlanta, that confirms our reports from the North. Dallas out."

"Standby everyone!" Peter shouted before the crowd could yell aimlessly again.

Between people and crossed arms I could make out the radio operator's face, whispering in Peter's ear. He did a good job of not letting his expression reveal anything, after all there were almost sixty sets of eyes staring at him. He nodded his head to the woman, confirming he understood what she said, then stood up in his chair to broadcast to the community.

"Ladies and Gentlemen I want you hold your questions until I'm finished, because frankly I don't know how to tell you this so I'll just say it. The former United States government has frantically come up with ideas to salvage the major cities, all from inside Air Force One, which has been flown to Nevada with most of the President's advisors for safety. Most of you were aware a few weeks ago the President declared this state of emergency as a total loss. What's left of the CDC has no way of combating this virus, so the mission status from the President has gone from salvaging to annihilation. At six o'clock this morning, Project Wildfire went into effect. New York City, Philadelphia, and Baltimore we destroyed by nuclear warheads because they were deemed 'beyond repair'. The President is beginning a nationwide cleansing from the east coast, and spreading west to eradicate the major cities, or cities his advisors say are past the point of saving. We are unsure how much time we have here, but there is a plan in action to move all of us away from Dallas and to somewhere safe. In the meantime, please remain calm."

Like an explosion from a dormant volcano, the silent crowd erupted in tears and frantic questions. Their voices echoed off the ceiling, almost shaking the roof above us. The faces slowly turned in our direction as I saw Peter pushing through the crowd.

"Excuse me. Excuse me. Oh David there you are! Please come with me, you to Ray."

Ray and I exchanged glances at each other, shrugging our shoulders in agreement. Not giving in to the chaos by asking questions we followed Peter to the rope ladder and up to the roof, the mob right on our heels.

"Just a damn minute everybody! We're going to discuss our options, and we'll let you know what we come up with. Just go back to what you were doing and stay calm, it's not like we can walk out of here anyway." I said to stop the mob from following us up the ladder.

Once on the roof we walked through the seedlings over to the corner of the building. I noticed despite my pleas to the crowd, Jake and Robin followed us onto the roof.

"How are you always getting suckered into this Dave?" Jake asked with a smirk grin.

"The curse of accomplishment I guess."
Peter brought us into a circle and without hesitation began talking.

"I've told everyone we'd have a plan. Who am I kidding I don't have a plan! They assumed my role as leader because I spoke well and showed intelligence. I'm an English teacher for God's sake! I don't know anything about escaping nuclear attack and saving dozens of people!"

In an instant he grew as panicked as the crowd below. I knew panicking wasn't the answer and it wouldn't help anything so I stayed quiet. From Ray's also quiet demeanor, I assumed he was thinking the same.

"How are you going to get us out of this one David?" Jake said, throwing me into the puddle of fire that was now the leadership position.

"Where can we go?" Peter asked as soon as Jake finished.

"I don't know" was all I could think of. "This whole continent is about to be fire and hungry dead."

It must have hurt the others to hear that, their faces fell when I didn't have the answer they were looking for, until Ray spoke up.

"Well you're not going to my damn island!"

"Why the hell not Ray?! What's so special about your island?" Peter targeted him with his questions.

The bickering between Ray and Peter now sounded like two kids fighting, and it wasn't helping the situation. I crossed my arms and looked down at my feet, trying to separate myself into my own thoughts. *God my feet are killing me. I've had these oil stained boots now for too long.* Then it came to me.

"Both of you shut up! Bickering isn't getting us any closer to a solution!"

"I suppose you have an idea now David?!" Peter barked.

"As a matter of fact, yes….maybe. We're not going to Jamaica, the infection could be there. Everywhere else in the states has the infection. Jake, do you remember the one place we went that had nobody there?"

Jake thought about it for a moment.

"Are you talking about the ghost rig?"

"Yes, but just in principle."

Peter's face filled up with questions.

"What? A ghost rig? What are you talking about?"

"Never mind that. We have enough supplies here to sustain for a while yes?" I continued after Peter's nod, "Let's take them with us, and the only safe place that doesn't have numbers of people, and minimal infection if any at all, would be an oil rig off in the Gulf of Mexico. It would be like the superstore, but surrounded with water. It's perfect!"

I could tell they were considering it silently, and one by one they nodded in approval. Peter was the first to speak.

"How do we get to the coast, and how do we get to the rig? We will need bigger and better vehicles than we have now, and where do we find a boat large enough?"

Ray responded to Peter's question quickly, wanting to and knowing how to help.

"There is a trucking company not far from here with big rigs. With some armor they could take us and supplies to the coast, provided we avoid hordes as best as possible."

"David you know where Aquafex's boat docks are located, and I'm sure they have a few ferries they wouldn't mind us borrowing." Jake said, getting in on the plan.

"We can take Highway 45 all the way down to Galveston, load the ferries, and sail out to a rig. We can send a group in first to clear the rig, and once it's safe bring everyone on."

We looked at each other with smiles as wide as we could stretch them. There were a lot of details to the plan, but if done correctly we could save so many people. Peter knew what he had to do.

"I'll go downstairs and get everyone together. I'll tell them how the plan will function at each step, and I'll get names of who can drive big rigs. We'll have people begin stocking supplies near the maintenance department, ready to load on the trucks once the armor is on. Let's go to the beach, ha ha!"

CHAPTER TWENTY ONE

A kerosene lantern was all that lit the room when Sarah woke up. She woke up in a soft bed, and by the white sheets and light blanket, she recognized the room immediately as a doctor's office. As she sat up, pain shot through her body, reminding her of her injuries. She yelped out, grabbing her leg where the pain was the most. Her hands were squeezed into fresh bandages, recently applied and done professionally. Her cry of pain was heard, and was followed by a soft knock at the door.

"Hello? Are you awake dear?" came a soft voice from the slowly opening door.

"Who are you? Where am I?"

An older woman with glasses walked into the room. Her gray hair was short, her clothes were clean.

"Calm down dear. My name is Doris. You've had severe trauma to your leg, but Dr. Benson says you'll be dancing in no time. I brought you some water. What's your name dear?"

"Sarah. How did I get here?"

"Our ambulance crew was lucky enough to find you Sarah. They saw your car flipping into the ditch, and were quick to get you out before the monsters came. You are at a clinic now dear, and there's nothing to be worried about."

You mean despite every hungry creature that walks the streets right? but Sarah didn't have it in her to be tacky. After all, they did save her life.

"Where is David?"

"David? You were alone in the car when they found you dear."

Doris helped her sit up, and then she slowly walked to the bathroom with a limp. Her leg still hurt, but it wasn't keeping her bed ridden. A dusty mirror was the first to greet her in the bathroom.

"Doris what happened to my hair?!"

"Oh dear I should have told you before you saw it. Your

hair was burned and had melted glass in it, so I gave you a trim."
Sarah could tell she was smiling from behind the door.

Sarah liked her new short hair. She'd always worn her hair to her shoulders, but now she had a nice cropped look she never had the bravery to get before. She came out of the bathroom a few minutes later, Doris sitting in a chair waiting for her.

"I did the best I could with your hair dear, I tried to copy a movie actress I saw in a magazine we had in the lobby. Everyone will be pleased to see you walking, especially Dr. Benson."

"I love it Doris, you did what I never could, ha ha. Do you have anything to eat? I'm starving."

"I thought you'd never ask dear. We've been feeding you intravenously for almost a day now. We were running out of liquid food!" Doris smiled at Sarah.

"I wish we could offer you better, but we've been eating the remaining MRE's since we got trapped in this clinic."

Sarah had many more questions that would need to be answered soon, but she needed food so badly her stomach hurt. Doris led her down a hallway and into the break room, where there were bagged rations stacked in the corner.

"How does beef stew sound dear?"

"You don't have any prime rib do you?"

"Ha ha, no dear, we don't have any real food but this stuff isn't bad heated up. All you have to do is put water in the bag."

Sarah did as she showed her, and in minutes she had a hot bowl of beef stew. She hoped the taste was better than the appearance. As she blew on the spoon to cool off her first bite, a young kid in dirty army fatigues walked into the room.

"Ahhh beef stew that's the best!"

Feeling a little more confident now; Sarah ate the spoonful of stew. If beef stew was the best, her confidence in the rest of the meals was now gone.

"Glad to see you're awake, Ilene! The name's Pearson."

He reached his hand out to shake hers.

"Could you keep the motivation down soldier; my head is killing me. The name's Sarah actually, why do you call me Ilene?"

"Oh sorry. A few of us figured with such a leg injury you might not walk straight again, hence the 'I lean'."

Sarah wasn't as amused as Pearson wanted, and he knew it.

"So tell me Pearson, how did you end up here?"

His energy slowed to a halt. She had hit a nerve, but he took a deep breath like he was willing to talk about it.

"My platoon was assigned guard duty here for the clinic. People were coming in by the dozens, so we had to set up medical tents outside. The rest of my company was assigned to set up aide stations at the football stadium, and we were going to rotate platoons out with this facility. One morning the radios sounded off with gargled transmissions from the stadium, just as our rotation was beginning. We were the initial platoon here so we brought a truck of medical supplies and MRE's, but were supposed to get more supplies when the next platoon came. I was on break from the machine gun position when I heard my buddy Palmer yell out 'Here they come Sarge!' He was told to fire on the horde that approached us, so he opened up with the 50 cal'. Brass was flying everywhere as he sent a wall of bullets down the street. The four gun trucks joined in, chopping up waves of zombies, sending body parts flying. They just kept coming. Some were walking, some were crawling, but they just kept coming. One by one the guns went black on ammo. As the gunners tried to reload, the walkers plowed through our defenses. I saw my platoon leader get pulled apart by his arms, the poor looey. The truck gunners climbed inside and locked themselves in. The horde surrounded the trucks and stayed for days. I never saw them again. Myself and a few others made it inside the clinic. After a while we convinced the zombies there was no life inside by staying quiet, so they moved on. We've been here ever since, living off of MRE's."

A tear rolled down his cheek, his face didn't move from

staring at the table. Sarah could tell he was playing back the whole scene in his mind. He was too young to know how to turn it off. She had to stop him before he went mad.

"Pearson I'm sorry, I didn't mean to bring up bad memories."

His eyes blinked again, and she knew she had his attention.

"Have you communicated with any other posts? We can't stay here forever, what resources do we have?"

"You want to go somewhere else? Out there? Then leave! More food for us anyway!"

He stormed out of the room like a little kid.

Well I got your beef stew kid Sarah thought to herself, halfway convincing herself he was just a kid and was afraid, she herself denying the real threats that existed also. Finishing the last bite of her stew, Sarah decided to meet the rest of the survivors here. Outside the break room and down the hallway was the waiting room, but there was no sign of life. The windows had wool army green blankets hung on them, blocking out any light. Peeking through a window, Sarah could see the tan trucks outside, blood puddles and body parts rotting around them. She noticed a corpse by the machine gun nest, everything eaten but the torso under the body armor. There were assault rifles lying around where she guessed they'd been dropped. After seeing enough of the morbid sights outside, Sarah limped to the back of the clinic hoping to find someone. She heard voices and laughter at the end of a hallway, and the flickering of a flame coming from a patient room. She was excited to see new faces, but was always skeptical about the people she'd meet nowadays. When she was just steps away from the doorway, she heard an outburst from Doris.

"Oh now you're just cheating! Bless your heart, pocket kings."

"I told you that money was mine!" she heard Pearson jokingly return to Doris.

Sarah poked her head around the corner, seeing Doris and

Pearson sitting with a younger man and a very handsome man around a table of cards. Doris took a double take at Sarah, then quickly stood up and invited her into the candle lit room. It was daylight outside but dark as a cave in here. Doris started with the introductions as soon as she pulled Sarah in the room.

"You all know Sarah, and Sarah this is Pearson, Cretes, and Sergeant Mason. They are part of our ambulance team. This is Virginia, she's a nurse here, and in the corner, that is Dr. Benson."

Sarah shook hands with each of them. Cretes and Pearson looked about the same, as most young soldiers do, but each had a full beard, probably wanting to rebel from the shaved face appearance. Virginia was a petite blond girl but full of attitude. Dr. Benson was a large man, very tall and athletically built. He was in his late sixties. His silky gray hair was combed perfectly, and his glasses appropriately sized to his face. He paid attention to his appearance, and was very meticulous about it. Sergeant Mason was a wall of a man, and he captured Sarah's interest immediately. He stood to shake her hand, tipping his chin slightly in a flirtatious way. Sarah couldn't help but gaze at his solid physique and silky complexion. His arms rippled like his shirt sleeves had rocks in them, his chest puffed out in two solidly defined masses. The only soft exterior he had were his baby blue eyes and Sarah was instantly trapped in his gaze. She had to shake her head, as if trying to break free from his intimate eyes, and rethink what she wanted to say.

"It's very to nice to meet all you, and I can't thank you enough for saving my life. Pearson told me you are running out of food. Do you have radio communications? Have you talked to the other post yet about getting supplies or going out searching for any?"

Dr. Benson interjected before anyone else could; he was trying to be a sensible voice in the group.

"Sarah we like your ambition, but we aren't trying to get anybody killed. It's dangerous enough out there searching for survivors, and we are safe in here. Our radio can only receive transmissions, we can't broadcast. We have no idea where the other post is."

"Doc I appreciate your concern for safety for everyone, but you can't stay here forever. A shelter can be safer, but not safe. Those things will find a way in here. You are running out of food, and it's only a matter of time before you will be forced to leave, but without supplies!"

"Sarah I don't like your attitude right now. We are safe here, and we are staying. These boys have seen what's out there, and they don't want to leave here either."

"Fine. Stay here. Give me a gun, a pack of food, and the keys to one of those trucks out there, and I'll leave you here. Please."

"I'm afraid we can't do that Sarah. You will be safe here, and you will grow comfortable with it the longer you stay."

Sarah couldn't take any more without yelling at the old man. He might have known the medical world, but she was used to surviving. She stormed out of the room, ignoring the pain in her leg. She made it to the waiting room before the pain was too much. Falling into a soft maroon chair, she dropped her face into her hands and began to cry. *They don't understand what those things are capable of. We aren't safe here. I need to be back with David and Jake.*

"Been out there too long huh?" came a velvety smooth voice with a deep, tender rumble.
She looked up through teary eyes to see Sergeant Mason standing beside her, offering her a cold beer.

"I've been to so many different places already. They all fall through eventually, no matter how safe they seem. I was there at the college when it fell, and I watched a lot of people die horrible deaths. That was the most secure place I'd been to." She didn't expect him to know anything about the college. She had no idea how long they'd had radio communications.

"You were there at the college?"

"Sure was, uh Sergeant."

"Ha! Please, call me Eric."

"Sergeant Eric?"

"Just…just Eric" he said with a warm smile.

Sarah was feeling something inside she hadn't felt in a long time. Eric had a way of seducing her with his smile. She took a refreshing gulp from the beer, enjoying the cold brew all the way down.

"We heard about the college over the radio. The transmission was cut off. We were pretty sure there weren't any survivors, and that's why we never went there to look."

"It was awful there. I'm not sure how I even got out alive. I don't know if any of my friends made it out alive either." She said to Eric, hoping to hear something about survivors making it to any other posts, primarily David or Jake.

"There haven't been any reports, at least nothing over the radios." He paused for a moment.

"You're right you know, about us needing to get out of here. The old man is stubborn. I think having Cretes and Pearson around remind him of his family. I've done what I can to collect supplies while we're out looking for survivors, but we're running out of food and kerosene. The old man knows it, but I think he's afraid of letting us down or getting somebody killed. We came here with twenty soldiers, and as you know three of us are left. I lost a lot of good men, boys, against those things."

"I'm sorry about your soldiers Eric, I really am. They never signed up for this kind of fight. Staying here doesn't help your odds either though."

"Yeah, Sarah, I know" he was getting frustrated. "We have a better idea of what we are up against now. The situation is only getting worse."

"I know, running out of food."

"Not just that. Come with me Sarah, I'd like to show you something."

Eric took Sarah through the hallways and into the lab. He held her hand tightly to guide her through the darkness. Her tough hands were nothing compared to his giant calloused palms. His hands were warm and comforting despite his rough skin, and she secretly wanted the darkness to last if she could keep her hand in his.

"Oww!" She yelped when her forehead hit a door frame.

"Oh my gosh, I'm sorry Sarah!" Eric said giggling. "I didn't mean for that I swear!"

He came in close to her and with one arm around the small of her back he gently rubbed her forehead with the other. She could smell his skin close to her. His musky smell was sweet, but there was a rugged edge to it also. She wanted to kiss his neck, to feel his soft skin on her lips, but she waited in the dark for his next move.

"Does that feel better? I promise I won't let that happen again. The first pretty girl that comes in here and I run her into a wall."

"It's a little sore but it'll pass" she said real giddy, but she wanted him to continue rubbing her head, as long as he was close. She was a little disappointed when he moved away, but he kept her closer this time, which made her smile. She just wished he could see it.

"Just a little further Sarah. I promise it will be worth it."

She didn't mind the security of him holding her close and leading her, but her anticipation was building.

He led her into a room she could tell was small, and absolutely dark. Every sound they made bounced off the nearby walls, sounding a lot like a storage room. She heard a squeak from the ceiling, and Eric's footsteps up a wooden ladder. Light flooded the small closet when he swung the roof's hatch open, illuminating the wooden shelves and cleaning equipment in the closet.

"I come up here to gather my thoughts sometimes. We have to be careful when looking over the edge so those things don't see us, but it's nice to get some sun."

"I'm right behind you Eric." She tried to keep her voice from sounding too eager, but she couldn't help it.

She didn't notice she put her arm around his back when she stood up beside him on the roof. The sun felt warm on her skin and the moment consumed her. There were birds in the sky; wind blowing through the trees. She could see buildings all around, but it felt like they were in the middle of nowhere. The city was quiet, only nature prevailed.

"Those things are evolving Sarah. We'll have to stay low, but I want you to see this."

Slowly they crept closer to the edge of the roof, blocked from view only by an industrial rain gutter that outlined the clinic. Eric lowered himself onto his stomach, and instructed her to do the same. They low crawled to just an arm's length away from the edge, but could see the streets as close as a block away. There were walkers scattered about, and immediately she noticed the difference. They were no longer staggering, but walking upright like normal living people.

"What are they doing? How?"

"I've noticed them slowly changing. I don't know what this means, but they are slowly changing, improving. There's no telling what they could be capable of now."

"That's not good" she said seriously. "They can still be stopped though right?"

"Destroying the brain still does the job, and I don't think evolution can change that. We just don't know what lengths they will go to now. When the infection was in its early stages the host would normally beat its fists on windows until it was convinced there was nothing left inside. They are starting to get more aggressive, probably from the scarcity of their food source, and they won't hesitate to shatter windows with a single blow. Look across the street there."

He pointed to burger joint across the street called Buns and Beyond. The front windows had been shattered like a spider web, and then pulled out.

"I saw how those things make their way into the store. They chased a group of survivors there, and tried to follow them into the side door. Once they couldn't get in the door, the horde gathered around the windows. One of them punched through the glass with a single blow. His arm shattered, sending bone fragments bursting through his skin. His arm ripped off when he tried to pull it out. He never flinched. The others around him grabbed the hole and pulled. They were in the store in no time. That was tempered glass Sarah. There's no way they should've been able to break through so fast."

"I guess that's why we're on the roof eh?"
She rolled onto her side, looking at him, smiling. She'd had enough doomsday talk. She wanted to feel his touch again. Her fingers slowly started tracing the outlines through his sleeves.

"Eric what do you miss most about the old world?"
He grinned, thinking about it. He rolled onto his back, putting his hands behind his head for comfort. Sarah noticed his shirt slide up, exposing his sculpted abs.

"I miss Sunday afternoons."

"Sunday afternoons? What's so special about Sunday afternoons? There's an afternoon everyday Eric."

"Not like Sundays. I take the day off from all work, the sun shines brighter, and the air is fresher. Best of all, the grill is hotter."

"So you cook out?"

"Every Sunday. Football on the TV, bratwursts on the grill, cold beer on ice. I used to turn my phone off because all the people I cared about where at my house. There were no rules. Everyone could be themselves with each other. You can't find freedom like that anywhere else."

Sarah rolled closer to him, sliding her hand up his shirt. Her fingers ran across his smooth skin, sending a tingling sensation through their bodies.

"No freedom quite like it huh?" She said before leaning in for a kiss.

He embraced her as their lips touched. He ran his fingers through her soft blonde hair as the sun blanketed them with the midday warmth.

"What are they saying?" A troubled Doris asks.

"There's a lot of static. I think I understand, but that's impossible. Ahhh these headphones are shot!" yelled Pearson as he threw them off his head.

"Put it through the speakers Pearson!" Dr. Benson ordered.

"Atlanta are you sure?...That's three total correct?...Okay thank you Atlanta, that confirms our reports from the North. Dallas out."

"They don't....really mean that do they? They can't do that! There are survivors out there!" yelled Pearson. Dr. Benson was the first to respond.

"Cretes find Sergeant Mason and Sarah and get them down here."

Eric and Sarah were holding each other on the roof when Cretes startled them bursting through the roof's hatch.

"Sarge you and Sarah need to get down here fast!"

"What's up Cretes?!" Eric said, snapping back into leader mode.

"It's the radio Sarge, all hell is breaking loose!"

"Sarah we need to go. Let me help you up."

She had completely forgotten her leg was still bandaged and sore. The moment her bliss with Eric was broken, she began to feel the pain again. Eric helped her move far enough away from the edge and out of view from below, where they could stand. They moved quickly down the ladder, Sarah stumbling over the last step. Her eyes weren't adjusted to the darkness that consumed the room when the roof hatch closed. Cretes led them down the hall with a kerosene lantern, and into the radio room.

Dr. Benson and Doris were having a quiet conversation when they walked in. Pearson was sitting in front of the radios holding his head in his hands on the folding table. Eric was the first to ask about the emergency.

"What's going on here? What have you heard?"

"This is bad Sergeant. Apparently the President is cleaning up the major cities with nuclear weapons. I didn't vote for him. Now we'll have to leave here soon, we're too close to the city. We'll burn alive."

It was amazing how subtle Doris could be, but scare the hell out of Sarah at the same time.

"What?! Are you telling me we are going to get nuked?!"

"Well we don't know for sure dear, but it could happen." Doris finished with a smile.

Eric immediately pulled Cretes and Pearson into the hallway and began telling them something as they walked to the forward waiting room. They were quiet enough Sarah couldn't hear, but that was the least of her worries.

"What is the other post going to do? Are they leaving the city?"

"We don't know dear, that was the last transmission.

"The old man and his nurse wife are like parents here. They won't let us do anything and we know it's not safe. Get us out of here Sarge." Cretes begged.

"We've got to be very careful with our planning boys. Don't start thinking irrationally because you want to leave."

Sarah came out of the radio room and put herself into the soldiers' conversation.

"I want to take one of those trucks, and drive to the superstore with all the ammo we can carry."

"Which truck do you want to take?" Eric chuckled.

"I had my eye on that armored bus there." pointing out the front window to a large military vehicle.

"Oh the MRAP? Yeah that'll get us anywhere we need to

go safely" he said with a smile.

"Is there any ammo left on the trucks?" Cretes chimed in, knowing the full load of the MRAP.

"The truck has two thousand rounds of linked ammo, a full tank of diesel, and a box of MRE's behind the seats. Unfortunately the Ma Deuce is dismounted from the truck and at the machine gun pit."

"The Ma Deuce?" Sarah had to ask, she wasn't familiar with the soldier lingo.

"The fifty caliber machine gun. We definitely want that."

"Oh yeah!" She exclaimed.

"Cretes and Pearson get the guns ready, Sarah come with me. Let's brief the others."

CHAPTER TWENTY TWO

The break room was empty when we walked in. In the middle of the room was a round table, where Ray and I sat down, Jake beside me with a map, and Peter had a notepad and pen.

"We are going to need armored transport, and there are a lot of people here." I started.

Peter spoke next with his findings.

"I've talked to everyone, and most are onboard with the plan. The others will follow I'm sure. Two men and woman know how to drive big rigs, giving us three total. We should be able to fit everybody in three trucks, but we'll need another for supplies. It's going to be a long convoy, so we'll need security from the trucks. We have four bay doors to pull the trucks in for loading."

Ray was next with his input.

"Security won't be that easy. We have a handful of rifles, some handguns, and a decent amount of ammo. However, getting through a horde could be disastrous. I'm sure it will be a long drive, and we will be on thin ice the whole way. I say we need another truck in front to help clear the way. Jake do you have a route?"

"We can take I-45 all the way down to Galveston. It's a five hour drive without any stops, so we can assume an eight hour drive in the least. However, the highway will lead us straight through downtown Houston. There are sure to be hundreds, if not thousands of walkers there. We can take a main road around the city, which will set us back another two hours minimum. We don't know if Houston is on the nuke list, or when it might get hit. The sooner we are out of the city the better, so it's a risk either way."

Peter finished with a list of everything we said.

"There are some pretty big requests here gentlemen. You're asking for five trucks, all with guns. That will stretch our convoy to a quarter mile easy. Then we'll have an eight to twelve hour drive with everything from a horde of thousands to nuclear weapons in the way. The rubber band is stretching thin boys. We have two rig trucks parked behind the store backed up to the bay doors. It's safe to assume one truck can and should be filled with supplies. I agree with Ray, about a blocker up front with guns."

We each had very good points about the mission. Our previous adventures had risks, but this was very large scale. We knew what our plan was going to be, I just didn't know how much we were capable of.

"Let's start with the two trucks in the back. Once they are in the bay doors we'll fill one with supplies and check the other for passenger room. It could be a bumpy ride, and we don't need people bouncing around in the back."

"Who's going to get the trucks?" Peter asked.

We looked at each other, waiting for a volunteer. I knew when Jake mentioned Robin he was no longer interested in the risky stuff. I didn't blame him. He had something worth saving now.

"I'll do it."

"I'll do it."

Ray and I spoke at the same time.

"Okay sounds good. I'll let you do what you need to do, and we'll make arrangements to get supplies moved to the shop. The keys to the trucks are in the bay."

Peter trusted us for the job. We were now on a timeline so we couldn't wait for nightfall.

"Peter can you arrange a team to be at the bay doors for security? We're going to get the trucks now."

"I'll do that David."

Ray and I stepped out of the room to find the truck drivers. They weren't far away; the two men were sitting at the picnic tables enjoying a sandwich. We discussed the plan with them, gave them each a handgun. When they were done eating, we would meet them by the back door. Jake said he would take a couple guns on the roof for overhead support. Everything was going smoothly.

Ray and I got ready at the back door with John and

213

Chuck, our two drivers. Ray and I loaded our shotguns, they had their handguns ready. Peter met us at the door with a radio.

"Jake said there are about twenty over a hundred yards away. We are using Ray's method at the front of the store; we've got a group keeping their attention focused on them. Jake is ready when you are."

Ray and I nodded at each other, ready to go. Peter pulled the chain from the door.

"From here you'll have about thirty yards to the trucks. Good luck."

I pushed down the lever and the sunlight flooded in. We could easily outrun the walkers, and maybe get to the trucks without them seeing us.

It took a moment for our eyes to adjust to the light. We moved down the stairs and jogged to the trucks.

"Those suckers don't even stand a chance. I bet I could hit one from here." Chuck said, aiming his pistol towards one.

"Don't do it Chuck" Ray quickly replied, but it was too late.

Chuck fired a round at the nearest walker, about sixty yards from us. His shot missed, and now every walker was facing us. We continued moving quickly towards the trucks, but we didn't anticipate the next move. The walkers broke into a dead sprint towards us, moving much faster than we were. *I thought they couldn't fucking run!*

"What the hell is going on Dave?! I thought they couldn't run!" John screamed.

"I don't know! But don't stop running!"

My chest was burning when I reached the truck. I heard shots firing from the roof, but the corpses were still running hard and fast at us. The drivers were still behind us, they were struggling to keep up. John was first to the nearest truck, panting for air when he got there.

"Get in! Get in!" Ray screamed at him, as he sprayed buckshot into the nearest undead. It's head snapped back as it's skull sprayed into the air. Chuck could barely move around the truck so I had to pull him by his arm to the door. I shoved his fat ass in the door, shooting a dead woman just feet away, her headless body falling at my feet. *Too close for comfort.* John's truck roared to life, and I knew that meant only more creatures would come. Ray and John were locked in the other truck, now I had to get to the other side. It would be quicker than crawling over Chuck, but I had to hurry. Chuck started the truck as I ran around the front. I shot another man but only clipped his chest, giving me time to reload and take another careful shot. There were dozens more moving towards me, too many to handle myself. The shooters on the roof were hitting them, but not in the head, only slowing them down.

"Unlock the fucking door!"
As soon as I heard the lock move I jerked the door open and lunged inside, slamming the door behind me. An older man's face smashed into the window, gnawing at it as if he could chew through the glass.

"Get us out of here Chuck!"
The truck lurched forward, spewing black smoke from the pipes. Chuck pushed the truck through the small horde, the truck bouncing as the tires rolled over them. The men outside the bay doors were shooting as fast as they could as we drove by. The truck barely fit but once we were in, the doors slammed behind us with the security boys barely making it in. Fists and bodies slammed into the door when it closed shut. Bullets were flying down from the roof. I could hear them hitting flesh, sending chunks of skull into the other side of the door. *They can hit them when they're twenty feet away.* Peter met us in the garage, greeted by a furious Ray.

"What was that all about mon?! They aren't supposed to fucking run!"

"I don't know ray! Whatever is keeping them moving must be repairing muscle tissue!"
A group of men came running through the garage towards us. Peter gasped before he could yell.

"Oh Jesus Eddie's hurt!" Peter yelled.

They were carrying a man in his forties, bleeding severely from the shoulder. He was barely conscious, struggling to say something. They set him down near the entrance to the inside, not wanting to expose him to the community.

"Just kill me. Just kill me." He kept repeating, his mouth now sputtering blood.

"He's bitten Peter, we can't keep him here."

"You just want to throw him outside?! You bastard!"

"Damn it Peter listen! He's not going to make it. We can keep him in here, but he's going to die soon."

"Don't let me become one of them!"

"Okay. Just....keep him here and when he goes...he goes. Keep an eye on him."

"Yeah. I got it Peter."

John and Chuck didn't pay much attention to the wounded man's status; they stayed back talking about the trucks. I met Ray coming around the truck.

"What the hell are we up against David? They didn't move like that before. They can outrun some of us now."

"I don't know Ray. Let's go inside, I'll tell Peter to meet us in the conference room."

The room was quiet. I couldn't think of anything to say, thankfully Peter coming in broke the silence. He sat at the table, running his hands through his hair. I didn't know how to approach the conversation I wanted to have, so I just blurted something out.

"Peter you said something about muscle tissues rebuilding. Dead bodies cannot do what they just did. How do you think this happened?"

Peter took a long sigh. Ray was leaning forward in his chair, waiting for any explanation.

"I'm not an expert on human muscle tissue David, but I know that muscle needs protein to rebuild. Obviously these soulless bastards are getting protein from the flesh they eat. Now whatever the virus is, it's reanimating dead cells. We can assume it's capable of rebuilding muscle tissue as well."

"Are you telling me they're getting stronger?"

"Maybe, but unlikely.... I don't know."

"You think or you know Peter?"

"Damn it David I don't know! They were slow before, now they're fast! I don't know if they are getting stronger, I don't know if they are getting smarter."

"Smarter? They're dead!"

"David the man's not a doctor. Leave him be." Ray interrupted; he could tell I was getting aggravated. I backed off the questioning; it wouldn't do any good yelling at each other. The silence now was somewhat relaxing, until the door burst open, Jake moving quickly in.

"What was that all about?! The walkers are running now?!"

"Nobody's a doctor here Jake, we can't say anything for sure."

"That's fine David, but you better get on the radio and warn people about their speed now."

CHAPTER TWENTY THREE

The soldiers had their rifles loaded and positioned themselves by the front door. Sarah was using a pistol one of the soldiers was issued that was found after the initial attack. They were staged in the waiting room, ready to run for the truck. Virginia came running into the room yelling for Sarah.

"Wait! Don't go out there! Sarah Wait!"

"Virginia please! Lower your voice!"

This time she whispered.

"Sarah you need to come back to the office, Dr. Benson needs to talk to you. Please."

"Okay, Virginia. I'm right behind you."

Dr. Benson was sitting in his comfortable office chair when Sarah walked in. The single kerosene lantern provided a mellow glow in the dark office.

"Sarah I understand you want to leave here, and I know I can't talk you out of it. Before you step out that door, I should tell you about the radio transmission I just received. Sarah could hear the soldiers in the waiting room, excited about going outside. Eric was doing an ammo check and inspecting weapons.

"I'm listening Doctor."

"The superstore post across town has taken a casualty. They have a plan of escape now that requires trucks, and while trying to bring two semi trucks into the garage a man was bitten."

"That can happen Doc. It's the nature of risk." Sarah rudely interrupted, but the Doctor remained calm.

"That's not what I wanted to tell you Sarah. It seems they are evolving."

"Evolving? Evolving how?"

"They are no longer walking after their prey Sarah. They are capable of long sprints, and at the fullest speed their body's will allow."

"That's impossible."

"Not quite impossible, maybe improbable. You see Sarah,

the virus is capable of animating the dead cells, and rebuilding new ones. The diet for these creatures is purely protein, giving them everything the virus needs to feed. The virus takes over the body, eventually killing the host. To keep itself alive it continues to animate and rebuild dead cells, thus growing muscle tissue. Medically speaking, these creatures won't get smarter, but they will get stronger. I suspected this when Pearson told me about his platoon leader getting pulled apart. That would take an amazing amount of strength. The brighter side of this is that the creatures are in fact just that, creatures. There is nothing human about them anymore. They carry the natural instincts of the human, because that is something programmed in the brain. We are dealing with an enemy we've never experienced before Sarah. If you are going to carry out your adventure with the lives of those three boys and God bless her, that sassy Virginia, you're going to need to know your enemy."

"If what you're saying is true Doc, then you have every reason to come with us. They will break into this clinic faster than you think and you will not survive the attack Doctor."

"That's something Doris and I are prepared to face it when it happens Sarah. I just want to know you are also prepared to face it."

"Dr. Benson it is ridiculous to stay here! We have room for you and Doris in the truck; we will make it to the superstore!"

"That reminds me Sarah, I need to tell you their plan. Those semi trucks are going to take them to Galveston, where they will board a ferry that will take them to an oil rig in the Gulf of Mexico."

"Oil rig?"

Oh my God David is alive!

"Who is leading this mission?!"

"I don't know Sarah. I just know they could use your help and some of those big guns outside the clinic."

"Come with us Dr. Benson!"

"No, Sarah. Doris and I have talked about this. We have

lived a long and wonderful life. We don't want our last remaining days to be spent in Hell. This is non negotiable. Take care of them Sarah. Be good to Eric, he's taken quite a liking to you."

She knew he wasn't going to change his mind. She did the only humane action she could think of. With her right hand she pulled the pistol out of her belt and set it on the desk in front of him.

"Keep it. This too, is non negotiable."

"God bless you Sarah. I wish you the best."

Sarah walked out of his office with a new perspective of war. Casualties didn't mean losing someone to the undead. In the little time she had spent with Dr. Benson and Doris, she was convinced the world would soon be losing two great people.

Sergeant First Class Mason began briefing the crew.

"Make sure your rifles are chambered, and you know exactly what you're role is. Cretes you are driving the MRAP. I'll be security for Pearson. Pearson you'll get that fifty cal off the tripod and into the truck. Virginia you'll be in the truck with Cretes. Sarah you'll be in the back hatch of the truck watching our asses when we load the gun in. Nobody drag ass because these things are fast now. Everybody clear?"

"Hooah!" Pearson exclaimed. The others nodded.

They staged at the front door, ready to burst out. Eric was in front to lead Pearson, right on his tail, to the big gun. Cretes and Virginia were next, and Sarah would cover the rear. Before bursting through the door, Sarah looked back to see Doris and Dr. Benson standing together in the hallway. A tear welled up in each eye as the Doctor waved them goodbye. She waved back, and then wiped her eyes, focusing on the issue at hand. They burst through the door, Eric with his rifle tucked into his shoulder and looking down his sights. He and Pearson dashed to the machine gun. Cretes and Virginia sprinted to the rear hatch of the MRAP, pulling the door open. Sarah took a last glimpse of Doris and Dr. Benson, with enough time to catch a tear rolling down the Doctor's face. She hurried out the door to the rear hatch. Several undead down the street heard the commotion and began running full speed towards the group. Eric was first to fire, the loud crack from the muzzle echoing off the building. He was a true shot, and one by one the creatures fell, but their numbers only increased with the sound of each shot. The MRAP was loud when the cold diesel engine turned; the valves were clattering as the engine warmed. Virginia took a seat up front in the buckets with Cretes. Sarah stayed by the rear hatch, waiting and yelling for the other two to hurry. Pearson yanked up on the machine gun, but its eighty four pounds proved tough.

"Hurry I gotta reload!" Eric yelled to Pearson.

Pearson with all his might, and some grunting, pulled the weapon off the tripod and carried it on his shoulder. Eric fired his magazine's last round, but was already moving towards the hatch and wasn't concerned with reloading yet. Pearson moved as fast as he could with the heavy gun on his shoulder, Eric encouraged him with his aggressive tone to run faster. Sarah was now in the truck, weapon facing out, ready for any undead. Eric grabbed one end of the gun to help Pearson with the load, moving up the stairs first. He was at the top step when Pearson's end fell to the ground. He and Sarah saw the corpse smash into Pearson's body like a linebacker sacking the quarterback. Pearson screamed as it sank it's teeth into his flesh, then pulling away the skin that covered his collar bone. More of them piled on top of Pearson, quickly covering him like lions. Eric brought his rifle up, but it only clicked when he squeezed the trigger. Sarah fired into the mass of attackers, not stopping until her thirty round magazine was empty.

"Go! Go! Go!" Sarah screamed to Cretes.

The hatch was still open when the giant truck rolled forward. Eric was denying what he just saw with pleas of no's, but he knew it was real. Sarah looked back to see the attackers smashing the doors of the clinic in, flowing inside like a lethal wave. She heard a single gun shot, followed by another, and the clinic fell silent.

Sarah moved through the cab to the front where Cretes and Virginia were sitting.

"Cretes get us on the highway and don't stop until we get to the superstore."

CHAPTER TWENTY FOUR

The sun was setting now, slowly sinking below the horizon. The dull orange glow matched the mood in the community. I had never met Eddie, but it was always painful to watch someone go. There were several bags of soil loaded onto the truck now, and more bags stacked outside ready for packing. A few people had taken some TV's out of the box and filled it with seed packets, ready to be loaded after the soil. The facility was slowly being taken apart, even the kitchen was getting torn down, but the cooks kept some gas stoves out for one last hot meal. Peter made an announcement that he wanted everyone in the community to have dinner together, in celebration of the times they'd had here. Many of the picnic tables were pushed together, making four long rows long enough for the sixty or so of us here. The cooks wanted to use most of the meat, because it wouldn't keep all the way to the docks, and they couldn't fit any more in the coolers. There was plenty of fresh food here I know we couldn't take, so I imagine the dinner tonight would be quite plentiful. I tried to find Jake for conversation, but I was told he was on the roof with Robin. They were probably watching the sunset. There were a few people getting together for a last night campfire on the roof, and when I heard Ray would be there I left my position after I brought the last bag of tools to the garage for loading.

On the far side of the roof I saw two folding chairs facing towards the sunset. I recognized the wild hair in the left one to be Jake's, Robin beside him holding his hand and a bottle of wine. The sky west of us was lit brilliantly with bright orange radiating from the sinking sun. Not a cloud in the sky. The orange faded to red as nightfall chased the light out of the sky. Behind me was a black endless sky filled with stars, while the fading glow from the sun still illuminated my face. The warm summer night's air brushed across the roof, whistling through my hair, tickling the long stubble on my cheeks. Tonight was different than the nights before, since Day Zero at least. I had never appreciated the beauty of the sun as it gave it's last attempt to shine on us for the day. *I wish Sarah was here to appreciate this with me.* I missed her more than ever now. I thought back to that last night at the college, trying to play different scenarios in my head, each one involving her survival. *There's no way she's not alive. It's not supposed to be this way. I never got to tell her how I felt.* I stood at the edge of the roof, watching the sun as it slowly slipped out of sight. Only a dull red haze lit the western skies now, and nightfall was getting closer. I heard footsteps behind me, coupled with some cheerful laughter.

Ray and three others I'd not been introduced with yet came with folding chairs towards me; Ray was carrying two chairs. I assumed and hoped the second chair was for me.

"Lovely night for fire, isn't it?" Ray asked me as he handed me the chair.

"David, this is Randy, Sharon, and Elizabeth. Everybody this is David."

We said our hello's and shook hands. Randy was a skinny guy in blue jeans and a red plaid button up shirt with a trucker hat. He looked like he'd been smoking cigarettes since he was twelve years old. Sharon wore jeans and a dressy button up, but she still looked out of place. I could tell she was a business woman that was strictly by the rules and was never seen in anything but a suit. Her Northeastern accent completed the image. Elizabeth had a homely look to her, like the soccer mom that drove the kids around all day.

We arranged our chairs around a starter log and some wood scraps they'd gathered lying around after piling them on some potting soil so the roof wouldn't burn. Ray got the fire started with a flip open windproof lighter before he assuredly put it back in his right pants pocket.

"Who brought the marshmallows?" Randy asked

jokingly.

"I've got everything I need." Sharon said as she uncorked a cheap bottle of champagne.

Elizabeth didn't say anything, and wasn't amused by the fireside comforts the others talked about. The fire warmed up quickly, and soon we had a legit campfire. The three of them were friendly enough with each other I assumed they'd been here together for a while.

"Nobody's going to take that bottle from you Sharon; you don't have to put it all back just yet." Randy said.

"When did you become my daddy? I can take care of myself. Besides if you were my daddy you'd be gone already."
Certified crazy woman. She's using her daddy issues to fuel her career and avoid settling down. I don't want to hear about her issues so I better start before the booze does.

"How long have y'all been here?"

"Too damn long. Everything's been shit since it happened." Randy replied.

"You got that right." Sharon said as she took another drink.

"I lost everything I had after that day. Everything I'd worked my whole life for, just gone. How could God let that happen?" Randy said tearfully.

"What happened?" I asked.

He took a deep breath, and a big gulp from the champagne bottle after Sharon offered it to him.

"It was a day like any other day. I worked as a civilian contractor on a military installation installing radio equipment in tactical vehicles. I had been working there for close to three years, and I was very happy with my job despite the tight security and endless paperwork. I remember the day it happened like it was yesterday. I kissed my wife goodbye before I left the house, and my favorite song was on the radio when I started my truck. Traffic was lighter than usual on the way to the base, and I knew today had potential to be a great day. From the current situations in the Middle East, the base was at a higher level of alert and so the security was beefed up, checking more cars at random at the gates. The military showed an armed presence with soldiers, establishing the M16 toting soldiers were the first you'd see as you rounded the hill coming up to the gate. Driving through the gate and passing many troop formations, I arrived to the warehouse about 30 minutes early. My boss wasn't there and wouldn't be for another 45 minutes (because he was prone to being 15 minutes late). I took advantage of the time by going through the drive thru of Burger King. I ordered the biggest egg sandwich I could get with a large coffee. Today was going to be a good day. I paid at the window, enjoying the tantalizing aroma from the bag. As I began to drive off, I noticed several soldiers hunched over in the lobby and it appeared as though they were throwing up. A sour feeling turned my stomach over, and the smell from the bag no longer appealed to me. *Were they sick from the food? The food I just ordered?* I didn't want to let it bother me, but there were a lot of sick people inside."

He took another sip of champagne.

"Back at the warehouse now, I forced the breakfast sandwich down, trying to enjoy it but couldn't. The office should have been open by now, but no one was there. The warehouse was dark and quiet as the steel door screeched open, the orange glow from the rising sun flooded the floor. I wanted to look productive when the boss walked in so I grabbed my tool bag and the clipboard with the day's tasks and opened the humvee's doors. I lost myself in my work, not noticing that I had 7 missed calls from my boss, or that time had flown by and I almost missed lunch. The clock hanging over the tool box read 12:37. I checked the voicemails my boss had left me, and he had been turned away from the gate. Nobody was allowed on post. *What is going on now?* It was probably a threat someone had called in, or the cops were looking for somebody, but most likely it was nothing. After all, the threat level had been raised and the soldiers were quick to react on the minimalists of threats. I didn't hear the last message he'd left, a fire truck came screaming by with it's sirens on. I got in my truck to do the usual lunch run; drive by the fast food chains to find the shortest drive thru line. Traffic was beyond insanity down every street. A black four door sedan almost slammed into the side of my truck when it blew through a red light. I passed a sandwich shop that was always busy at lunch time, but my jaw dropped when I saw the front door. There were people running out of the building, being chased by others covered in blood. Screams filled the air as the mass of people turned to fighting and mists of blood spraying the concrete. Soldiers were attacking each other. Not with weapons, not with fists, but biting into each other ripping flesh from bone, like animals. A truck jumped the curb and plowed into the drive thru line, sending glass and painted fiberglass across the grass as smoked filled the air. My head slammed into the steering wheel with the sound of metal crunching and my seat belt almost ripping into me. I felt the warm liquid trickle down my forehead and down my nose when I lifted my head up to see the car I just rear ended. *So much for driving an old pickup. An airbag could have saved the bump on my forehead.* A young female soldier stepped out of the car holding her neck, not giving a hint of notice to the chaos across the street. She had hit the car in front of her as a result of me not paying attention, and now we've added to the insanity. An older male soldier crawled out of his crumpled BMW and staggered towards the girl. I reached into the glove box for my insurance card, always kept near the 20 year old instruction manual for the truck. When I looked up over the smoking grill, the man had his arms wrapped around the girl, viciously tearing at her throat with his teeth. Blood poured down her uniform, collecting in a puddle beneath her. I threw the shifter in reverse and mashed the gas pedal with no regard for anyone behind me, and luckily there wasn't. I had to get out of here. Not only was there bloodshed all around me, but I was involved in a wreck and leaving. My mind was made up to go home until this hell was resolved and deal with the consequences later. The truck struggled to accelerate towards the intersection, where an idle line of brake lights filled the way out.   Behind me crowds were gathering and running towards the busy streets. I cute through a parking lot to get closer to the gate, and it worked getting me closer to the front of the traffic jam, but the guards had administered the steel walls that blocked the exit. They were going to do whatever they could to keep the madness behind those walls. The engine groaned as I mashed the accelerator again, this time jumping a curb and moving across an open field towards the high chain link fence that separated this base from the outside world. I heard pops coming from the gate, they sounded like tires popping. Bullets riddled the side of my truck, one coming close and shattering the window beside me. In my rear view I saw more cars following me, silver suburban following close on my bumper. There was aggressive terrain on the opposite side of the fence, the side I needed on. I drove along the fence looking for a safe passing point, when I noticed the suburban turn into the fence and smash through. It bounced over the bumps and drops in a dusty flurry, but it was making progress. I slowed down and took a wide turn through the grassy field. Cars were already following the suburban through the fence, quickly creating a bottleneck. There was a demolition derby in front of me now, and there was no way I could make it through. Military Police cars screamed across the field towards us, lights and sirens on. The four cop cars stopped 100 yards away from the cars, and each front door opened with a man holding a high powered rifle. Like a handful of firecrackers, pops and flashes filled the air as a wall of lead shredded through the wrecked cars. I didn't hesitate to slow down, just jerked the steering wheel right and slid around in another 180. My truck was on it's last run when I smashed through another section of fence, and kept the gas pedal down as I bounced over the hills and bushes. All I could think about was getting home to my wife. We'd been married three weeks now. I promised her the best life a man could give her. I moved her here. Hell opened it's gates today. The city was in a state of worry as I flew out of the trees and skidded onto the highway. Whatever was happening on the base hadn't made it's way to the city yet. My faithful truck of 20 years died just a block from my house. I didn't care; I left the truck beside a curb and took the keys with me. I ran as fast as I could in my heavy work boots, finally making it to our home's front door. I fiddled with the key trying to ram it in the lock, but finally turned the lock and exploded inside. My lovely wife was standing there, confused, holding a glass of tea. I locked the door behind me and frantically turned on the news channel. She was beginning to worry, and started asking questions quicker than I could answer them. I calmed her down, she breathed, and I rubbed her shoulders. "Something has happened baby." We looked in awe as the details emerged from the television. That is how Day Zero started for us."

"Where's your wife now?" I regretting asking the moment I said it.

"She passed away in the quarantine zone at the football stadium. I was the last man out of that place alive. I know because her hand was ripped out of mine when the horde grabbed her and pulled her inside."

"I'm sorry to hear that. She's at a better place now."

"Is she? She's walking around as a corpse now. She's lifeless, soulless. Maybe by the grace of God he took her soul to heaven, and she's not suffering inside that lifeless shell."

I didn't have any answers for him. I wish there was something I could say, but there's nothing to say that he hadn't already thought or tried to drink away.

"I was at fuckin' ground zero." Sharon spoke out.

I knew she was trying to one-up his story; and I knew she was lying when she said she was at ground zero. *I* was at ground zero.

"I was in a fuckin' airport. I was waiting on a flight home to Jersey. The airport here is so damn big and confusing."

"Why were you here?"

"I was here for a new client we were trying to bring in. I worked for Trinergy. We did experimental work for new energy solutions. Our science branch was working on a way to maximize the output of fossil fuels. We really had something to. What we were about to introduce was going to dominate the market. I flew to Texas to work a deal with a coal shipping company here that brought coal in from Mexico. By combining coal and gasoline we'd figured out a way to produce three times the normal output, and we already had a great sponsor with gasoline, now we were working on the coal distributor. I pulled out all the stops with this company. I gave my best speeches, presented the best numbers, and damn it my slide shows were the best. Those arrogant pricks told me they would think about it. I flew to this shit hole and sweat through some of my best suits so they could tell me they would consider it. I hope they're all dead."

She lit up a cigarette, and exhaled a deep breath of smoke slowly.

"I was sitting in the boarding area watching the televisions and thinking about the last week. My bosses didn't spend $10,000 to send me to Texas for me to come back empty handed. I was solid gold. No one could touch my sales. Talking to me meant you would end up doing things my way."

She took another long drag, proud of saying that about herself.

"As the news kept talking about a widespread epidemic of the flu, I looked around at all the sick people around me. People were coughing and blowing their noses around me. It felt like the waiting room at a hospital. The airport staff was coming around with thermometers and passing out over the counter flu medicine that was nothing more than hot tea and lemon. What a joke. Against my better judgment I left my seat in the waiting area to get a hot dog from a vender deeper into the airport. I spent fifteen fucking dollars on a hot dog and coffee. I was waiting behind some fat bastard at the condiment counter when the announcement for my flight came over the loudspeakers. I saw some sick old woman had taken my seat, and it seemed like every other person in that area was sick. I decided to wait by the vendor while the others boarded after the plane unloaded. It was bad enough I'd be on the plane with them; there was no point in being around them longer."

She took another long gulp of the champagne, followed by a deep drag from her cigarette.

"Words can't describe the situation when things go from routine to absolute fucking crazy. The doors to the boarding ramp burst open, and the pilot came running out screaming. Everyone that was sick and focused on their own problems quickly directed their attention to the pilot. Panic starts as a queasy feeling in your stomach before it pours from your body as a scream. My adrenaline started pumping as I watched the pilot continue running away. Everyone looked at each with a horrified expression on their faces, and then the horde came. The whole damn plane was infected. The pilot had landed the plane and was able to escape, but everyone else was dead. They poured from the ramp like a dam had burst. They attacked everyone around them; moving along the line of people waiting to board, like a buffet. The air filled with screams and panic. There were two types of screams. Those that were scared shitless, and those that felt the life being bled out of them. The difference was usually the gurgling and bloody air bubbles. Within minutes the entire boarding area looked like the aftermath of a medieval battle. There was blood everywhere. My god was there blood. I stood there frozen in shock as the people were getting ripped apart and eaten. I saw what mankind is truly capable of when there are no limits. I had no longer paid attention to what I was doing, and the hot coffee that spilled down my skirt was the only thing that broke my frozen state. All at once, the questions and scenarios of how I was going to escape this flooded my mind. Do I grab my stuff or do I just run? The dead kept multiplying and the screams were dying out. Sorry, no pun intended."

She used her cigarette to light another, then threw the old butt into the fire.

"The stampede of living sounded like bulls parading through the terminal, all in the same direction. They were like rats in a maze. The hallways and escalators bottlenecked the herd, slowing them down so those in the rear and those that had been trampled were getting eaten like the weakest of the herd. I'm 43 years old, and there's no way I could compete in that crowd of panicked people. I saw an exit door that led to the tarmac, and it was like a beacon of light that pulled me to it. I stood a better chance running away across an open field than trying to go through the front of the airport where the stampede would just get bigger. I managed to escape through door without getting seen by the horde, but there were six or seven of them feeding on bodies when I ran by. I guess they saw me as fresh meat and they took chase. I wasn't sure when I lost my $700 heels, but they were gone by the time I reached the doors. I pushed through the doors into a quiet staircase down. When the doors shut, the screams and violence seemed to stop. I jumped two steps at a time, thinking to myself I hadn't moved like that since high school cheerleading. The doors at the top burst open again, the screams became audible again. The doors shut and the screams went away, but now there were growls coming from the stairs. I made it to the bottom doors and pushed through, to a bewildered man in an orange vest standing there. He had no idea what was happening upstairs. He told me I couldn't be on the tarmac, but I kept running. I yelled at him to run, not having the air or time to explain. They tore him apart like a paper doll. I didn't have to see his death to know what happened. His screams gave me enough detail. I ran as fast as I could. I could taste that hot dog as it started coming up again. I puked up hot dog chunks and hot coffee, but I kept running. A plane was taxiing by; it's engines were deafening. What a mess I must have been, vomit on my chin and my hands cupped over my ears. I bet I looked just like the dead. I ran until I found safety in a shed filled with grounds keeping equipment. I sat in that grass clipping and gasoline smelling shed for almost twenty four hours before I decided to look out the door. I guess what really motivated me to look outside was the hunger and lack of tears. I'd literally cried every drop I could."

She took another long swig of champagne, finishing the bottle.

She put her cigarette out without lighting another.

"When I opened the door it was nighttime. The airport was dark and empty. Parts of it were still burning. I was inside that shed, trapped in my own world so deeply that I didn't even hear the jetliner that had crashed into the airport itself. I was so hungry and thirsty that death didn't even matter. I barely had the energy to run again if I was chased. I wandered around the empty airport looking for food and water. I stayed away from the main terminals, and luckily I found a crate of water outside on a loading dock. I felt like a rat that had crawled out of the sewers and was scavenging for food. I snuck my way across the parking lot and found a taxi that was unattended and left running. I got in and started driving before I realized I had no idea where I was going. I tried following military vehicles, ambulances, police cars, but never any luck finding a safe place. One day I stumbled into this place, and I've been here ever since."

She rolled the empty champagne bottle around in her hands, unsure of what to make of the silence. I knew each of us was thinking that somebody should say something, but we kept to ourselves, thinking of our own survival days.

"That's quite a story." Randy said humbly.

"You've been quiet this whole time Elizabeth. Would you like to share your Day Zero with us?" I asked.

The group got silent. I don't know if they already knew her story, but it was like I asked her to tell me about her first sexual experience. She shuffled in her chair a bit, like getting comfortable would make her story easier to tell. I knew it wouldn't.

"I thought we were safe. I thought help was on it's way. I had picked my kids up from school that day. I remember it so well. My youngest had gotten an A on his English test, and my daughter landed the lead female role in the school play. She'd rehearsed in her room every night. She was so proud, and so was I. I brought them home and helped them with their homework so we could have the rest of the night to celebrate. Celebrating meant watching their favorite movies, with a bag of popcorn and a plate of Oreos with a glass of milk. Their father was still at work, like every other night. The three of us sat on the couch, but before we switched over to the DVD player the news told us how bad the epidemic had gotten. There were shelters setting up everywhere for the healthy. My phone rang. My friend Janet was on the other end, telling me the PTA was telling everyone to bring their families to the school's gym. Water and food would be provided. We packed a few things in the minivan and drove over to Janet's house to get her and her two kids. It was a tight fit, but the school wasn't far."

She asked Sharon for a cigarette shyly.

"I haven't smoked one of these since high school. When we got to the gym, there were people everywhere. The principle was showing people the way in, and once inside the teachers were assigning us cots. I knew one of the teachers well, so she gave us beds near the restrooms. I told my kids to make their beds right away. I didn't want them to have to do it before bedtime, but more importantly I wanted people to know those cots were taken. The night went on, and it was getting late and I'd swear the whole community was there. The bleachers were those retractable kinds, pulled up to the walls. Some of the fathers stayed at the top of them so they could watch out the windows. It felt like we were trapped inside the Alamo, and the enemy was all around us. All of this was happening, but none of us had even seen the so called infected! I kept assuring my kids it was like a big communal sleepover. Trucks began showing up with bottles of water and cases of food rations. It was all so unreal. They had made all these preparations to keep us here with food and water, and we hadn't even seen the police or military even. I grabbed a box of Oreos for my kids, and some crackers for myself."

She began crying.

"I told them they could eat the whole box. They were so happy with a box of cookies and no bedtime. A few of the fathers at the top of the bleachers were gathering around a window, looking out and pointing. The principle stood below them, talking to one of them. He hurried to the doors, but didn't run. Running would have caused a panic. He told the teachers at the doors to get everyone inside and lock the doors behind them. Some of us parents began getting worried. Do you know how hard it is to keep something hidden from your children while you try to plan a way of defending yourself against something you know nothing about in front of them? A man at another window began screaming "Here they come!". That was all it took. Sharon you were talking about that atmosphere when it changes from calm to insanity; I know what you felt. People began running to their children; pulling them away from others and clutching them tightly. The kids began screaming. The teachers locked the doors, even with other families still outside. The principle ran through the gym telling everyone to be quiet. Remarkably everyone listened and the whole gym went silent. I kept my children close to me, tight in my arms. We began hearing the growls outside. They started out just a few; then they grew louder and more of them. Those that were locked outside began screaming as they ran to the gym doors. Fathers, mothers, and children were pounding against the gym doors, screaming to let them in. The principle began wrapping chains around the push bars on the doors, locking them with a padlock. We could have saved those people. The dead weren't that close yet! We left those families there to die. The horde smashed into them. We saw the steel doors push in as those families were devoured. No one should ever have to hear a child scream like that. I hear those screams in my head every night. I don't know what's worse, hearing those screams, or the silence when the screams stopped."

She was sobbing now, wiping her eyes with her sleeves.

"Everyone inside was crying now. The children were scared to death; the mothers did a better job of not showing it. The men tried taking charge, but that was the problem. Too many of them tried to take charge and they all began arguing, which frightened the children more. They were too proud to listen to each other. Some of them wanted to barricade ourselves in the gym. The others wanted to lock the whole school down so we'd have access to all the facilities. I can't tell you which would be the smarter choice, and I can't tell you which was wrong. We never made it that far. The school was known as a safety refuge for everyone, and everyone was invited. The trouble is trying to keep everyone's eyes shielded from the truth."

"What do you mean?" I asked.

"Nobody wants to know that what they are really doing is coming to a fortress because there's something out there that wants to kill them. I know, I was guilty of it. If someone told me to leave my house and come to the school so we could prepare for war, I'd have told them they were out of their mind. No, they needed to keep the school as warm and cozy as could be so people would leave *their* warm and cozy houses. To better answer your question, we didn't fortify the school. We didn't prepare to defend ourselves. The doors to the main halls of the school were unlocked. I'm not saying every time there's a disaster we need to fortify the school, but god damn it when the dead start walking, the time for amenities and conveniences are over. As everyone argued with each other, now the mothers were defending their husbands' theories, nobody noticed the growling outside began to leave the area. The dead quickly filled the hallways. The few teachers and parents in the hallways came running towards the gym, with a horde not too far behind. The living run with such grace compared to the dead, even when frantic. This time we let them come into the gym before we closed the doors. The men pulled the doors shut behind them, and held on to the push handles with everything they had. We were now trapped. The principle was out of chains to lock the doors with, and they couldn't hold on forever. The dead gathered at every entrance, constantly pushing and pulling at the doors. I think the feel of defeat is worse than feeling helpless. Feeling helpless still gives you the option to fight. Defeat means it's over. When I thought for a moment that me and my kids had reached the end; I cannot explain what that feels like. I never wanted to let them go. The thought of losing them made me angry. I was mad at everyone that wanted to argue. I was mad at their pride."

She paused for a moment to pull out pictures of her kids. She kept them with her at all times. The boy was about three in the photos, and the girl six.

"I stood up with my children, and we casually walked to the adjoined concession stand at the back of the gym. I heard some of the guys holding the doors say that the dead were too strong, and they were losing grip. I pushed my kids through the concession window first, then I climbed over the counter. The door to the hallway was standing wide open, and I could hear the dead outside. I hurried to it and shut it as quietly as I could. It was only wooden and wouldn't hold up against the weight of the horde. As soon as I closed it, I heard the doors to the gym burst open. The basketball court became a killing field. I moved to the window to pull the steel curtain down, but just before I got there I was tackled to the ground by a large man. He had blood coming from his mouth and lifeless eyes. He thrashed at me, trying to bite me anywhere. I pushed at his throat, trying to keep his mouth away but he was much stronger than me. I held him away with one hand and felt around with my other. Of all things to find, my hand wrapped around the handle of an industrial ice machine scoop, you know, the metal kind. I hit him as hard as I could over and over again in the face, until it was just a bloody pulp. He didn't go down until I shoved the sharp bladed edge into the side of his skull. I pushed his heavy corpse off of me, and saw people and zombies running by the window. My kids were nowhere to be found. People were getting massacred on the other side of that counter, and my scoop wouldn't kill them all. I screamed for my children over the other screams, praying they would hear me and come running. I knew they came across that countertop with me, but now they were gone. A group of zombies heard me and began running my way. I didn't want to give up looking, but I had to close the steel roll down curtain. I pulled it down just it time, locking the lever into place. Fists pounded against it, but it never gave. I was the only person in the room other than corpse lying on the floor. I tucked myself into the small staff bathroom and cried for my children. The screaming in the gym didn't take long to stop; it was the changing and growling of the dead to leave that took hours. I was through crying and I wanted to find my children. I opened the door to the stench of death. Everyone was dead."

I didn't know what to say. I couldn't imagine losing a child, especially two and a husband. What would she have left to live for?

"I'm so sorry for your family Elizabeth. I can't even begin to imagine…"

"Why? Jacob and Catherine are asleep downstairs."
She smiled. *Are you kidding me lady?!*

"When I came out of the bathroom, I was startled by a noise coming from the cabinets. When I was tackled by that zombie, my two smart and beautiful children hid inside the cabinet and remained quiet. At first I was afraid to open the cabinet, but when my Catherine opened the door with her hand over Jacob's mouth, I burst into tears. We must have spent ten minutes on the floor of that concession room holding each other. The shuffling of feet in the gym broke up our reunion. This time however, it wasn't the dead. There were people loading the cases of food and water onto pick up trucks. We startled *them* when I opened the rolled curtain, but they were happy to find survivors, especially children. They brought us here. To this day we still haven't seen their father. His work or his mistress kept him away."

Her story made us feel a little better about our situation. Not everyone was at a total loss. I wish we had more champagne to pass around as a toast. We were out of wood and the fire was dying out also. I guess it was time to wrap this campfire up. We all silently agreed, as Randy and Sharon stood up.

"I'm going to go downstairs to. I want to hug my children." Elizabeth said.

"I need more champagne." Sharon slurred.

Ray began walking towards the edge of the roof, digging in his pocket for the lighter. I wasn't ready to go downstairs yet, and talking about loved ones had me missing somebody. I followed Ray for more conversation to keep my mind off of her.

"Texas has the biggest skies I have ever seen."

"That's the truth Ray. Big enough they weren't meant to be enjoyed alone."

"Well here I am David." He laughed as he said it.

"You know what I mean Ray! Asshole. I guess you'll have to do though."

He handed me a cigar from the tobacco shelves downstairs and the lighter.

"I brought the finest cigars labor could buy. Cheers to our last night here. This place has been good to me."

"Thanks for the smoke Ray, but you reminded me of something I always wanted to ask you."

He puffed on his cigar once the ember lit. The breeze carried the sweet smell across the roof, I was sure Jake and Robin could smell it.

"Go ahead and ask, friend."

"Work for food was created from signs the homeless held up right? Great tasting cigars by the way. What was your life like before all this happened?"

"Ah the question that has perplexed everyone here since I arrived. You're alright David. I have been in the States for a year now." he took another long draw from his cigar.

"As you know I came here from Jamaica, for work. My life on the islands wasn't a hard one, but I wasn't a king. I sold many items to tourists, a lot of them like yourself."

"You mean clueless white folk?"

"Ha ha yes like I said. I didn't like that I was nothing to those that lived there, because I sold my items and essentially myself to the foreigners, and I was nothing to the tourists but the man on the corner with the Rastafarian hats and beaded jewelry. I had a steady income to support myself, and put it all back into the island, but I was still in purgatory. I didn't know which side I wanted to be a part of, but I knew I was trapped between the two. I saved enough money, and I listened to the tourists for information on America to decide where I would like to move to. Every man and woman I sold my jewelry to loved Jamaica, but only the Texans compared it to the beauty of their state. There was a sense of pride there I couldn't ignore. When I moved here I kept to myself at first, worried about not fitting in, but that's where I was surprised. The people here let me be to myself. My greatest regret is that I didn't allow myself to flourish once I lived here. I know that feeling of belonging still exists here, and that is why I can't get on that oil rig with all of you. Steel is such a cold skeleton, and I'm afraid I will be changing one empty life for another. I have chosen to stay here and fight after I have made sure everyone here is on that boat."

He took a long puff from his cigar now, trying to light the embers again. I couldn't argue with him over his choice either. In a way I agreed with him.

"I don't blame you for your choice Ray. I can't get on that boat either."

"You have your place in society David, so who is she?"
I couldn't help but laugh at him now. He was a smart man and he knew how to think on his feet, and I was proud to have fought beside him.

"Her name is Sarah. She could be dead, but I feel like she's still alive. She was in the college with us when the dead flooded the halls. I've heard many rumors of her both survival and death. I understand your frustrations Ray. However I know which side I want, it's just a matter of what God gives me."

"Oh brotha, it's not a matter of what God gives you. It's a matter of understanding why he gives you what he does."

"You mean like fate?"

"Fate is such a powerful word, and yet for no reason. Can you tell me your fate?"

"That's impossible Ray, the future hasn't happened yet."

"That is where the word gets it's true power David. When looked at as a future tense, it cannot be defined."

He stopped to take a puff, but I could tell he was waiting on me to rebuttal.

"Fate is having a path set out before you that you always instinctively follow."

"How can something be established if it has not been made yet David?"

I knew he was building up to something. I took a long drag from the cigar, filling my lungs with the sweet aroma.

"Fate is understanding why certain things happened to you at the time they did. For instance, you chose to come here from the college. That is a significant step. It's up to you to decide the pros and cons of why that decision was made. Unfortunately you cannot know the truth about that fateful decision until you are completely happy with the outcome. That is the glory of fate. It doesn't hold the key to your future; it reveals the secrets of your past. Knowing yourself is the only true key to your happiness."

"Okay well what about Sarah then? She could be lying under rubble right now and I'm not there to help her. She is what I want Ray. Are you saying my 'fate' isn't complete yet for the decisions I made to come here? What if I made the wrong decisions?"

"David calm down. I know you want me to say it's all going to work out, but I'm not going to say it. I will just say this to you. Fate is a hungry monster David, and it feeds on patience. Don't let it starve."

I was a little taken back from his comment. I wanted assurance I'd made the right decision. I wanted to hear something that would help me find Sarah. I couldn't think anymore about it. Whether or not I made the right decisions would drive me mad if

I constantly argued for both sides. *Was I being impatient? Was I letting fate starve?*

"I thought I smelled a couple of rusty Cubans over here!" Jake bellowed, holding hands with Robin. "Did you fellas enjoy the sunset?"

"We were just talking about throwing you off the roof Jake!"

He always knew how to cheer me up, without knowing it.

"Yeah, yeah, we'll leave you two love birds up here, Robin and I are going to enjoy some steaks unless y'all want to come to?"

Ray knocked the cherry ember off his cigar and flicked the butt over the edge. I took one last, long drag and did the same. *Cigars and steaks. It's time to enjoy the simpler, finer things in life. Maybe Ray was right. Maybe relaxing and not worrying about every little thing is exactly what I need.* With the exception of some few late packers, everyone was gathered around the tables ready to eat. The atmosphere was different tonight. Aside from the loss of Eddie, everyone was in good spirits. I was seeing more smiles tonight than I had seen in a long time.

Cheers roared throughout the building when plates were brought out from the kitchen. Fists full of plastic spoons pounded each table, but when the table received plates piled with food the pounding stopped and only chewing could be heard. Music from a CD player was playing hit songs from the 90's, which strangely pepped up the mood. Once the pounding and cheering stopped, once everyone had a plate, the rapping of a wooden spoon against an empty pan got everyone's attention. Peter was ready to give us an announcement.

"Ladies and gentlemen, if I could have your attention! Tonight is our last night in what most of us have called home for quite some time. Evil has been both outside and inside our beloved haven, and some of those we cherished were taken from us. Tonight we remember those we have lost. Tomorrow, we leave for the safety of our new home, where we will be free to do what is best for all of us. To start over. To grow as a family!"

Cheers erupted from the crowd. Fists were again pounding on tables accompanied by whistles made of tin. Peter raised his hands to bring the commotion down once again.

"We still have a dangerous journey ahead. I have briefed you all on what to expect on the way to the coast and that it will take many hours. Some of you will be providing navigation. Some of you will be security for the convoy. I want each of you to enjoy your dinner tonight, but remember to stay focused and prepared for the journey tomorrow. Now that we have the formalities out of the way, let's have a round of applause for our chefs....and then let's party!"

The crowd erupted again, beers pushed into the air as a toast to the community. When the beers lowered, the plastic spoons returned to scraping the Styrofoam plates. The steaks were quite tasty, especially for being cooked in such large amounts. One by one the community stood up and returned their plates to the kitchen, then filed into a large area set up for a post dinner movie. Peter went to a lot of trouble to make the last night here a real memorable time for the community. I finished my steak, but I wasn't sure if I wanted to join the others for the movie or spend some time on the roof to gather my thoughts. I saw Jake and Robin dancing and swinging into the movie area, and they made me think of Sarah. *If I stay for the movie, the couples will remind me of Sarah, but if I'm alone with my thoughts on the roof I'll more than likely do the same.* Ray snuck up behind be and threw his arm around my neck pretending to choke me, breaking my concentration on the Sarah dilemma.

"David you're going to have to be faster than that if you want to survive these days! I could have taken a bite out of you!"

"Maybe but I would've kicked your ass!"

"Ha ha but in this game the first strike determines the winner!"

"All right you got me there. I don't want to watch the movie. What will you be doing?"

He thought about my question for a moment, like he hadn't made plans either.

"We could do a check on the trucks; make sure they are ready for the trip tomorrow?"

"That sounds good, let's go. Are you worried about tomorrow?"

"No more than another day we spend here David. I think it's better than staying here waiting for a bomb to hit us."

"Good point. Remember what you said about getting on the rig? It feels like we are quitting. I want to fight back and regain this world for the living."

"I know exactly what you mean. I came here for a better life, and I refuse to run from what I fought so hard for to achieve."

The final boxes were being loaded by five men when we came into the garage bay. Two men were standing by with shotguns, I assumed the door guards.

"You're too late. We're done with the boxes." One of them called out.

"We didn't have any popcorn for the movie so we decided to come here. We won't get in the way." It was all I could say to the stranger.

"Have it your way chief."

There was a rack of ammo by the garage office, both Ray and I instinctively moved towards it to refill our magazines. Ray always carried his assault rifle with him, and luckily this time a few extra mags to fill up. I packed the magazines for my pistol as tight as they would hold, and put a handful of bullets in my pocket. Like Ray I normally carried my rifle with me, but tonight

I left it by my sleeping pad.

"You know David, we're not going to have much of an opportunity to find a vehicle if those trucks are on the ferry. I assume there will be a horde chasing behind us all the way to the docks."

"You're absolutely right, and I don't want to gamble on luck either. Do you know how to hotwire a car?"

"I don't know anything about hotwiring cars mon c'mon! I told you I was a legitimate businessman!"

"I figured I'd ask. So what are we going to do?"

Pop! Pop! Pop! Pop! Pop! Gunshots rang out from the rooftop! Ray and I looked at each other, waiting for the other to react.

"Should we go to the roof?!" He asked.

"They have gunners up there already; we can stay here in the garage to help out if needed." I responded, trying to keep ourselves from panicking.

"We got a truck coming in!" yelled one of the men with a shotgun.

I heard more gunshots from the roof, and the growling was getting closer. The clatter of the diesel motor grew louder than the growls as it got closer. The only garage bay left was number four, so Ray and I got ready beside the shot gunners poised at the door. One of the men grabbed the bottom of the door to thrust it open. Light quickly filled the floor of the garage as the truck was speeding towards us. The nearby walkers dropped their attention from the truck and quickly raced towards the open door in a sprint. The shotguns went off almost simultaneously, each removing the head of a nearby walker. Ray could reach out further with his assault rifle, and was hitting walkers just outside the range of the shotguns and my pistol. With the truck closer I could make out what it looked like, but it was nothing I had ever seen before. There was a large solid bumper on the front higher than my beltline, and the whole truck was painted flat tan. It looked like an armored school bus. The truck barely fit through the garage doors, and once it was in we were quick to shut the door behind it. I needed to reload soon, and there were more walkers moving towards us outside.

I quickly reloaded and squeezed off a couple shots before the garage door came slamming down. I think I hit a walker in the legs before I had to pull my hand inside, but will all my frustration it felt good to hear bullets hitting the dead flesh. The large armored bus stopped abruptly inside, like they needed medical attention fast. I ran across the garage to the office, where a medical kit was stored. I heard the electric motor of the truck come on as it lowered the rear door. The first aid kit was normally kept on a shelf in the office, but someone had moved it, probably to be packed. I frantically looked around the office, but couldn't find it anywhere. Leaving the office, I saw the bag sitting outside the office beside the door that led into the main building. I slung it over my shoulder and ran back to the truck. I saw the first of the survivors, a short haired woman and a large soldier stepping down the ramp when I recognized her and lost my breath. *There's Sarah! She's alive!* Excitement shot through me and I couldn't get to her fast enough. My heart stopped when a man behind her threw his arms around her and they embraced in a victorious kiss.

CHAPTER TWENTY FIVE

Denying my urges to both embrace her with a passionate kiss, and beat the hell out of this strange man, I approached her slowly after the other strangers gave her their informal welcome to the center. Her eyes lit up when she saw me, and she initiated the tight hug with warm, open arms.

"Oh my god David I thought I'd never see you again!"

"I can't tell you how glad I am to see you Sarah. I've missed you."

Gripping her tightly I remembered the lovely smell of her hair, this time there was a slight burnt smell.

"David I want you to meet somebody. This is Eric. He saved my life when I left the college."

Despite not wanting to initiate any conversation with the man at all, I shook his hand and thanked him for helping Sarah.

"I see your wearing fatigues. Is there anything left of the Army?"

"Maybe here, maybe there, but not as a whole. I haven't seen anything that resembles a structured America in several weeks."

I couldn't tell if he saw my dislike in him, and I wondered if he even cared.

"Well you're just in time. We are about to leave this place for greener grass."

"David what do you mean?" Sarah asked.

"Come with me, I'll brief you on our plan."

Eric was helping others get equipment out of the truck, and I was glad to see he was busy.

"Sarah I'm going to stay here and help Cretes get the truck ready to roll again."

"Oh.... Ok Eric. I'll be right back."

I led Sarah to our usual conference room; neither of us said anything during the short walk. I had a lot that I wanted to tell her, but nothing I could say unless behind closed doors. I thought I was convincing when I told Sarah I would brief her about our plans, but nobody followed us to the room. Ray disappeared when he kept Peter from following us and Peter couldn't hide it that Ray told him not to follow us. Once in the room, I lit a few kerosene lamps that hadn't been packed in the trucks yet, illuminating the room with the mellow glow I needed to calm down.

"That truck you drove here, what is it?"

"That's the MRAP." she said sitting down across the table from me.

"It's armored, powerful, and full of ammo for the biggest damn gun I've ever seen." she continued.

"That truck is perfect to lead our convoy to the Gulf. We are going to the docks to.."

"What's this really about David? You know I don't like bullshit."

She knew my intentions.

"Who's the guy?"

"His name is Eric. He pulled me from a wrecked car that was about to get overrun by a horde. Thank you for asking how I'm doing by the way."

Her tone was so sharp; the only thing it couldn't cut was the tension in the room.

"I'm sorry Sarah. So much has happened lately. I thought you were gone. I did a lot of thinking about you while you were gone. I missed us."

She sat back in her chair, running her fingers through her now short hair and letting a deep breath out.

"Us? There was never really an *Us* David. You never made any advances towards me and I thought you had no interest…"

"I do have interest in you Sarah. I, I want to be with you." I interrupted her.

"David you can't get upset about what has happened. Whatever I felt about you before, I put away. We were a team David, and I didn't want to ruin it. I'm with Eric now, and he's a

248

great man. I'm not in the wrong here, despite what you might think."

She was right. If I'd only told her how I felt before, this could've been avoided. *Or could it? We each thought the other was dead.* She sat in silence, at peace with what she'd said. I knew she was loyal, and there was no talking her out of seeing Eric. When I looked up from the table she was looking at me, and I knew she saw my acceptance of the situation. She stood up and leaned over the table to give me a hug.

"Only time will tell David."

"Yeah. I guess I've got to feed the fate monster."

"What?" She asked confused.

As if everyone was listening outside the door, it burst open and people came piling in like they'd been chatting the whole time, but we knew they were listening. Peter, Ray, Eric, Jake, Robin, and the truck drivers sat down at the table, and Peter began immediately.

"I've talked with Eric about utilizing the MRAP as the lead truck in the convoy and he is on board. As the plan sits, we are prepared to leave tomorrow around noon. Eric, you and Sarah are more than welcome to come with us to the oil rig and the same for Cretes and Virginia."

Eric looked at Sarah; I could tell they were exchanging thoughts.

"I can't speak for Sarah, but I will help you get to the shore. From there, I have to stay and fight for the cause. I have fought and bled for this country, and I'm not stopping now. I will take the MRAP when everyone is safely on the ship."

Peter looked surprised at Eric's decision, but even more surprised when I spoke up.

"I'm going with him."

The silence in the room was as loud as stadium on Friday night. Everyone looked at each other, but Eric and I just nodded at each other.

"I'm going to." Ray said.

"Me to." said Sarah.

"This is insane! You've all risked your lives and survived, why do you want to risk it all by staying?" Peter exclaimed frantically.

Jake and Robin were whispering in each other's ear, then Jake spoke.

"We're going to."

Peter glared at them.

"I get seasick." Robin said with a smile, in her twangy voice.

Peter paused for a moment, thinking.

"Ok, I'm not going to force you into anything. You are invited to come to the rig and stay at any time for as long as you would like. I appreciate your help and everything you've done for us. Eric is that truck ready to go?"

"For the most part, yes. However I've seen trucks of all sizes get bogged down by a horde, so if we are going to lead, I want a plow style bumper put on the front to push the horde out of the way. The Ma Deuce will take care of the rest."

"Good idea Eric. Some of the shelving systems can by put together and make a durable guard, but it won't be strong enough to push cars out of the way. How long will it take to assemble the plow?" Peter added.

"With some help I can have it done by morning."

"Right, so the time for noon still stands. We should arrive at the coast sometime around midnight, God willing there are no major setbacks. That's all I have, if anyone else has anything to say?"

There was a silent agreement that we were done, so we stood up at the same time. Sarah mouthed a 'thank you' to me as she followed Eric out the door. Ray came behind me to heckle me a bit.

"David my goodness! Your fate is a hungry little devil! Ha! Ha! Ha!"

"Ray get us more cigars!" I responded, smiling.

I was able to catch up to Shelby and Sarah on their way to the garage.

"Hey Eric, if we're going to ride in your armored bus I'd like to help getting it ready. I'll grab some metal shelf backings and bring them to you in the garage."

"Sounds great David, thank you.'

Sarah was a little surprised at my offer, but regardless of how much I hated seeing them together, I needed to earn my right to stay with my friends in his truck. I grabbed a shopping cart and moved directly to the kitchen. I had seen some heavy shelf structures near the freezers, if they could hold up several pounds of meat; they should be able to block several pounds of meat. Beyond the double doors the room was quiet. All the food we were capable of packing was already loaded, there was nothing left here for anybody to need a reason to be near the freezers. It was spooky quiet. The squeaking wheels of the cart seemed to echo off the walls, reminding me how scary silence had become. I reached back and felt the grip of my .45 in my pocket, for reassurance. As I squeaked past the freezers, I remembered the frozen zombie Ray and I smashed up inside. However something wasn't right. The freezer beside that freezer had a window covered in bright red blood. *That's not dead blood* I thought to myself. My adrenaline spiked as I pulled the pistol and grabbed the freezer latch. I took a deep breath and yanked the door open, pointing the pistol into the cold fog. Nothing jumped out at me. Nothing yelled or growled. When the fog cleared, I saw a woman's body lying on the floor, a shotgun cradled in her arms. The top half of her skull was missing, most of it in pieces and stuck on the walls and ceiling near collected drops of blood. She was lifeless as a mannequin; only one eye remained in its socket and wide open, staring at me. The freezer had preserved the scene; it was as fresh as when it happened. Inside her skull was a bloody, empty space, with frost forming on the surface. I didn't realize I'd been staring at her for a moment, frozen in shock. Seeing a dead corpse blown apart by bullets was one thing, but she was living when this happened. I didn't close the freezer door when I broke into a sprint towards the double doors into the store.

251

The first person I saw was an older woman and man carrying small boxes.

"Hey I need your help! Someone committed suicide in there!"

The woman's mouth dropped, along with the boxes, and they both followed me to the freezers. The door was slightly open when we walked up to it, and immediately the woman reacted in tears.

"Oh my god that's Wanda! Oh my god why would she do that?!"

Tears streaming down her face, she grabbed the man and pushed her face into his chest. He kept a somber look as he held her, and then looked to me.

"My wife and I knew her and her husband. We used to tend to the plants together on the roof. I don't know how many times Eddie and I would talk about fishing."

"Her husband was Eddie? The man who was bitten?"

"That's right son. They were like two peas in a pod. Next year would've been their thirtieth anniversary."

The woman was screaming into the man's chest now, her tears soaking his shirt. He rubbed his hands up and down her back, trying to calm her, but she kept screaming. This got me thinking of Sarah, and how I felt when I thought she was gone. I told the man I needed to finish getting what I came for, and I apologized for leaving, but he understood.

I found the shelves I was looking for, but they would still need to be disassembled. I wasn't sure how long they would require be to take apart, but for the moment I liked being alone with my thoughts. Seeing Sarah with him wouldn't be healthy right now, and I didn't want to talk about what I'd seen with others because I was trying to erase it from memory. I spent nearly forty five minutes disassembling the shelves, by myself in the light of the lantern. I was ready to leave this damn place, this damn fight, this damn war.

The cart groaned under the weight of the shelves. I thought the groaning was louder than the movie everyone was watching, but until someone said something I wasn't going to change my path to the garage. Squeaking past the moviegoers I felt their eyes burn into me. I knew Peter told others about us not going with them to the rig, and word must have gotten around. I saw looks of disgust, looks of anger. I heard someone comment to another *they came here and ate our food, and what have they done to help?* and that attitude just pissed me off. I finally pushed the cart to the garage, cussing quietly as I shoved it through the door. Eric was mounting some light metal to the truck, but nowhere near as tough as what I had.

"You lookin' to push over grass, or push over the damned?"

"I didn't think you were coming back David, haven't seen you in a while."

"I had an issue in the freezer."

I wasn't sure if I should tell him about Wanda. He had never met either of them, and I didn't want to have to explain what I knew of them to him, just to end with that horrible scene. I was pleased when the matter didn't concern him.

"Well I'm glad you could make it, and it looks like you've got the heavy duty gear."

I nodded and grabbed a wrench. Another soldier named Cretes was helping out, holding up one end of the panel while Eric drilled it in. I struggled getting the heavy shelves out of the cart, but when I sized them up to the truck they would fit almost perfect. As I pulled the last panel out Eric blind sighted me with his question.

"David what's the deal with you and Sarah?"

I nearly dropped the heavy panel on my toes, but my expression hid how much I didn't want to talk about this, especially now.

"Where is she right now?"

"She's in the truck with Ray packing gear we'll need when we leave the convoy. I assure you she can't hear us."

I hesitated a moment, hoping he was right, but I still wasn't going

253

to say anything that I wouldn't want her to hear.

"We've had a colorful history, and we learned to work great together. Listen Eric I don't want this to get weird, and Sarah has taken quite a liking to you, so let's just see what happens. After we leave the docks, maybe you can drop me off somewhere."

"I appreciate your willingness to sacrifice, David, but this isn't my show. If we even consider wanting to fight these things, it's going to take every one of us, and I want to know how far you're willing to go. I like her a lot, and I don't plan on giving her up."

"She's happy Eric. That's all I ask."

We gave each other a mental handshake, which was all the progress we were going to make for the time being.

"You're the commando, what are we going to do to fight back? Where do we start?"

"Believe it or not David, my suggestion is something I learned from you. Like you helped that college with supplies and what not, I think we should help little outposts get established. Very similar to what we are doing here. In a way, we are a very important contributor to this community and getting them to safety."

"I agree with you, and that sounds fine, but these people don't appreciate what we are doing. I walked by the movie room, and if looks could kill, I'd be on the other side of the walls."

We both chuckled, easing the tension between us.

"That's funny David. I know what you mean though. I've been a soldier for several years now, and I've noticed people will go out of their way to avoid or offend me, separated by the occasional grateful handshake. Most people don't understand it's the congressmen and women *they* voted into office that send us to an unpopular war, and we do it because we took an oath. They are frustrated and they don't know where to point the finger at. That's just life. I have a feeling this oil rig is going to be an island of high school drama."

"Ain't that the damn truth."

The more I talked to Eric the more I realized he wasn't a bad guy. He was very down to Earth, and it's possible he could bring happiness to Sarah. I wasn't going to stop my feelings for Sarah; I was going to feed the fate monster. I just hoped I hadn't run out of patience. We mounted the last shelf on the bumper in a 'V' pattern, and it was tougher than we had anticipated. Ray and Sarah joined us marveling at our creation, Ray providing cigars for us to puff on as we talked about everything and nothing at all.

"What I would do for a greasy hamburger right now." Ray started.

"Good luck bud, I think the last burger joint employees were eaten by those fuckers." Eric commented, remembering the burger stand he saw survivors get eaten alive in.

"I think that's the worst part about it all." Eric finished.

"What do you mean?"
Now he had my curiosity.

"Economic collapse is essentially what brought the country to her knees and delivered the final blow, not the walking dead. As apocalyptic as the dead walking the earth sounds, what drove human progression into the ground was panic."

"You're talking about convenience?" Sarah asked.

"Partly, yes. Think about this, a soccer mom evades a group of hungry, dead soccer team of twelve year olds, and hides in her house. Her husband is nowhere around, and she knows nothing of survival. She never leaves the house. Eventually the food runs out, and she starves to death. Now let's say instead of the dead walking, we experienced just an economic collapse. She would be threatened to have her home and car taken from her. Imagine if the first of the month came and nobody could afford to pay bills. It's a chain reaction. Suddenly a few take from the masses. The walking dead could've actually saved her from creditors and realtors coming to take what she could no longer afford. In the case of the dead walking, the economy stops in it's tracks, and many die out of the inexperience to survive on their own, without convince."

Ray, amused by this conversation, pursued further.

"Okay, let's say the dead never started walking. Let's say there was just an economic collapse."

"You mean like the government ran out of money?" Sarah instigated.

"Yeah just like that."
Eric went military intel on us.

"I know where you're going with this Ray; I know how it ends because I've seen it in foreign countries. Let's say a family of two parents, and two kids get the news at the end of the month that they will not be getting paid. Neither parent got fired, but the business cannot pay them for a month because there's no money to pay them with. There's ten days left in the month. They do what they can with the last paychecks they earned, but its burning fast with two children. The first of the month comes, and they have no money saved up. The landlord is demanding payment, along with the utility companies. The only way of persuasion the agencies have is with eviction and utility shut off. The family has eaten the last of the groceries they had, and it's now the middle of the month. The landlord changes the locks one day. The electric company shuts off the power. In one day they've gone from a struggling family to a third world family. In that day they have no food, no shelter, and no safety. The family is going to seek help, and they find it with others in the same situation they are in. They group together; they establish security in an abandoned building. They seek food with the protection of primitive weapons and firearms. By the end of the month an aggressive tribe is born. The tribe's spring up everywhere the depression is felt. In one month, centuries of building and creating is recycled back to the beginning."

He spoke to Ray as if he was expecting to hear everything he said, and then Ray added on.

"It sounds like the same thing that's happening now, only there are dead people walking around trying to eat us. So we can expect the same hostility from survival communities?"

"I expect us to. Unless we are planning to settle down in a community, we need to keep our numbers low, but well trained so as not to come off as hostiles. When I ran with Special Forces in Afghanistan we operated like that essentially for that reason. Numbers are intimidating because they show value of strength. A few, well trained individuals keep their cards close to their chest, metaphorically speaking."

Sarah coughed on her cigar, remembering the situation we'd already had with Eric's examples.

"The apartment complex. The Pit Bulls. They were pirates, but maybe there was more to them. They carried guns, attacked us, but maybe they were trying to find food."

I understood what she was saying, but I had to interject and remind her of who they were.

"Sarah, remember those savages raped and killed people here. They were not survivors looking for food. They were always pirates. We are about to ride around with guns and big trucks, but we don't look to hurt people, that's what makes us different."

"David's right Sarah. We're not savages. That's what will keep us alive."

I was glad Eric agreed with me. I liked the company I was in and I felt confident with this group. We shared some laughs, had a few somber stories, and when the last cigar went out we decided to go to bed. We have a long drive ahead of us.

CHAPTER TWENTY SIX

The sun was especially hot this morning. The thermometer in the garage read 97 degrees by 9:30 a.m. and would only get hotter as the day passed. From the activity of the night before, many walkers heard the banging and drilling in the garage and a horde of a couple hundred collected outside the bay doors. The smell of death loomed in the air, and most of the community woke up because the smell. The store was hot inside; all the means of creating electricity had been removed and packed up. Mosquitoes buzzed in every room, attracted to the sweat of the living. Although they carried blood, the blood of the dead was too thick for the mosquitoes to suck, and the virus couldn't sustain long enough in the bug, so there was no threat from them other than the nuisance. The trucks were full of diesel and supplies, and once the last man was boarded, they would be ready.

"God damn mosquitoes. It's hot and it fuckin' stinks in here."

It was different to hear Jake wake up next to a woman and be in a pissy mood. I agreed with him though, the bugs kept me up all night and it stunk in here. I didn't get much sleep anyway, the thought of what we had to do today kept me tossing all night, and I couldn't get the visions out of my head. I was tired of seeing death. *When this is over, I'm going to get so sloppy drunk I'll forget my own name.*

"Wake up everyone, today is the day!"

Peter was way too awake for a morning like this. I sat up, wishing I hadn't seen Eric and Sarah sleeping under the same blanket. Peter wouldn't let us sleep anymore; he started again with his up and at 'em routine.

"Let's go, it's almost ten and everyone is almost ready to leave. We want to hit the road in thirty minutes."

My grumpiness kicked in.

"All right damn it we're getting up. Eric's used to this

258

wake up yelling shit but you told us we weren't leaving until noon."

I laughed a little inside when Eric flipped me his middle finger as he crawled out of bed.

"Yes I did, but things have changed. More walkers are collecting outside, and there's no reason to wait for more. We're leaving in thirty minutes."

We exchanged a few grunts getting up, but in a few minutes we were on our way to the garage. The store seemed so empty now. Everyone was in the garage waiting for the signal. On the way to the garage, Cretes and Virginia caught up with us.

"Excuse me, Sarge?"

"What's up Cretes?"

"Me and Virginia were going to stay on the rig. I've done a lot for this country and we'd like to start something with this community. Like a retirement you know?"

"Okay that's fine Cretes. You don't need my permission."

"So I won't be considered AWOL? I don't want to get in trouble."

"Ha! You're fine Cretes. I wouldn't worry about getting in trouble."

"Awesome! Thanks Sarge. Oh and by the way, after you went to bed last night I installed a loud speaker system on the MRAP. Now you can blare loud music while you travel!"

"Great. Just what we need."

Eric smiled for Cretes' satisfaction.

Once everyone knew we were in the garage, they began boarding the trucks. I reminded everyone in our group to load fresh magazines and keep their weapons on safe.

"Good move David. I like your style." Eric commended me.

Eric sat in the driver's seat of the MRAP, and I sat in the bucket seat across him to navigate. Sarah stood up in the turret behind the Ma Deuce. I hadn't noticed how large the gun was, but compared to her it was huge. Large rounds the length of my hand were linked together and fed into the fire breather's mouth. The bullets are the size of my thumb. Jake, Robin, and Ray sat in the back of the MRAP, sheltered by inches of armor. We kept the crew of 'Nomads' as we were labeled together, so we wouldn't have to stop and get out once we were at the docks. The trucks were running, but at the last minute Peter sent a group to the roof to throw propane tanks with lit flares taped to them into the horde. Sitting in the MRAP, I couldn't hear much outside through the armor. I saw the group frantically running into the garage and jumping into one of the semi trucks. Three men with hunting rifles lay at the foot of the garage door, as another lifted the door a foot off the ground. The men fired their rifles in unison. The crack of the shots were followed by three deafening booms that shook the building, folding the garage doors inward and shattering the tiny windows after the black blood painted them. The riflemen leapt in the truck and the garage doors opened at once.

Before us lay a mess of pale body parts and black sludge, arrayed out from the ground zero of each explosion. Some of the walkers that were just blown down from the blasts stood up and ran at the MRAP. *It's time to test the push guard.* Eric was thinking the same.

"Fuck it."

He floored the pedal and the diesel roared as the truck lunged out of the garage. The truck punched into the first wave of zombies, having no effect on the truck's performance. The sound of skulls hitting the truck could be heard in the cab, only motivating Eric more. It sounded like pumpkins smashing into the grill, doing nothing to the armor. A smile spread across my face as we paved a path for the trucks behind us.

"Everyone's behind us with no problems!" Sarah yelled down from the turret.

Following the map, I guided Eric to the highway. The MRAP rolled down the road at 70 mph, liquefying any walkers we hit at that speed. Ever so often Sarah would yell, or kick Eric in the shoulder for hitting a walker, spraying the turret with a black sticky mess. The city around us hadn't changed much since we arrived at the superstore, with the exception of the absence of the living. The dead seemed to be everywhere, always searching for someone to eat. The excitement of the trip was wearing off after about thirty minutes of driving. We were on the edges of the metroplex now, getting into the more rural areas. The little towns were empty. If there were any survivors here, hopefully they collected somewhere safe and had a plan to rebuild. Eric and I quickly made a game of identifying the places that had been ransacked of supplies, and the buildings that had been attacked by a horde. We passed a fencing business that had the windows boarded up, with no trespassing signs painted everywhere.

"It's things like that we need to look out for. I bet they are hostile towards outsiders."

It was an advantage to have someone so tactically savvy with us. He would be an asset to keep us out of any unneeded trouble. The structures lining the highway gradually turned to long, open fields. We were finally away from what used to be civilization, and there were no zombies in sight. *It feels weird calling them zombies. They used to be legends of cinema, and nothing more. Maybe it was our fascination with them that led us to their creation. Maybe it's because the risks we face to our chase of immortality could only lead to a side effect of disastrous proportions. Nevertheless, this isn't a movie. What we viewed as horror is now real life.* I looked at my watch.

"It's now noon. I'm glad Peter woke us up earlier, otherwise we wouldn't be an hour and a half away from that hell hole."

Eric nodded in agreement.

"Hey look at that falling star!" Sarah yelled to us.

Eric and I both looked around for it; he saw it before I did.

"Oh shit! Everyone close your eyes!"

The fiery star struck the city behind us, filling the sky with an intense white hot light, overpowering the sun. I winced as I folded my head into my lap, squeezing my eyelids as tight as I could. Behind my eyelids the world turned bright red, and then began fading. I looked in the rear view mirror on my side of the truck, where a monstrous gray mushroom cloud filled my view. Our hand held radios buzzed to life with chatter. Eric barked commands into the radio of first aid for those that looked into the light. The cloud loomed over the sky, filling the horizon behind us with ash. It took a moment for me to realize we'd just witnessed a nuclear missile striking Dallas. Reality came rushing back as my head filled with questions for Eric.

"Are we going to be okay?! Is the radiation going to kill us?! Did that really just happen?!"

"Calm down David! Yes we are going to be okay, yes it just happened, and no the radiation will not affect us."

"How do you know that?"

"Our electronics are still working. We were far enough away we'll be okay, especially if we keep moving away from the blast. The winds will take the fallout east of us."

"I hope you're right Eric."

"Me to."

The radio chatter didn't stop, and Eric went back to aiding those behind us.

"This is truck two, we have to stop. Our driver can't see anything and he says his eyes are burning!"

Of course we would have to stop in this tiny town. I bet this city looked like a chainsaw massacre village before the dead came to life. Eric slowed the MRAP down, staying in the middle of the road. Once we stopped rolling, he jumped down from the driver's seat and ran to the truck behind us. Once there, he saw the driver rubbing his eyes violently, like he had bee stings on his retinas. *That's probably what it feels like* Eric thought. He helped the man move over to the passenger's seat, and another man into the driver's seat.

"I've never driven a big rig! I don't know what I'm doing!'

"It's alright; he's going to help you. He might be blind, but he's still conscious. Sir, do you know what you have to do?" Eric said to the blind truck driver.

"Yeah I'll try, but I'm fucking blind!'"

"You have temporary blindness sir; you should get it back within the hour. For right now I need you to focus on instructing this man how to drive your truck. Can you do that for me?"

"Yeah I'll try. You say I'll get my vision back?"

"Yes sir, but right now I need you to do this."

"Alright I'll do what I can."

Eric could see the nervousness in the man's hands as he sat behind the large steering wheel.

"Sir you're going to do fine, just listen to what he tells you. Describe to him any abnormalities in the road, like hard turns, steep inclines, etc. Okay?"

"Yeah."

As Eric got out of the cab, short cracks pierced the air from the boarded up windows nearby.

"Get back here! You're getting shot at!" I yelled to Eric. He sprinted back to the MRAP, while Sarah turned the turret and pointed at the house.

"Sarah don't shoot! They're just defending their town!" She understood his demand, but she wanted to defend him from the incoming fire also. She yelled at them from behind the large gun, and the shooting from the house stopped. Eric leapt into the driver's seat and slammed the armored door behind him. He was breathing heavily, and he took a moment to relax behind the safety of the armor.

"I think the look of that machine gun scared 'em off." I said jokingly.

"They are just defending their town, like we talked about. That gun would have killed everyone inside and brought the

263

building down to the ground."
"It's that powerful huh?"
"You better believe it."

Over the radio everyone called they were ready to move again, and the convoy moved forward, no more shots were fired from the town. The cab was quiet now. We just witnessed our hometown get vaporized. The streets we grew up on, the stores we met strangers in, the schools we played sports in and had our first love. We would never be able to visit those places again. Only memories remain.

Devastation brings the loudest silence. We were scared. We were angry. There was no need to destroy an entire city. I wondered how many other cities were destroyed. I wondered if in every one of those cities, a group of survivors like us witnessed our homes being destroyed. We may never find those that did this, but I hope vengeance seeks them. Endless fields of grass alongside the highway reminded me of the emptiness around us. Although most of the population was walking around looking to eat the rest, all this space would provide room for hope.
"It's nice to be somewhere away from any hordes." I said to Eric.
He had sat so long with his jaw clenched, no wonder he had to stretch his mouth open before he could respond.
"Yes it is. Unfortunately the only places they aren't at provide no shelter but distance, and that's no way to live. From what we saw earlier, the major cities are only going to become wastelands. We'll need to avoid those at all costs. We've witnessed the dead get stronger and more resilient, now they'll have radiation, and god knows what that will do to them."
"You think it could change them?"
"Maybe a little. Not like in the movies though. They're not going to grow tentacles or anything, or start flying. Radiation will just evolve them differently. Hell, maybe they'll have flippers."

"Great then we'll have swimming zombies. Do you think sharks will eat them?"

"I don't know, they couldn't be that tasty, or filling for that matter. They'd be like beef jerky for a shark. What if they bit the shark, then we had zombie sharks?"

"I wonder if their rows of teeth would keep growing? Would they mutate again?"

"Land shark."

"Yup. Land shark."

All we could do was laugh at this point. Nowadays anything cost bullets or a soul, except for laughter.

The tires of the MRAP hummed down the road. We were about halfway there now; the prison on the map marked the halfway point. As we passed the prison, Eric slowed down to see the macabre scene. The fences stood as they always did, but behind them hundreds of walkers milled around the yards. There were bodies everywhere on the ground, mostly half eaten. Several walkers were in the yard, but I wonder how many living people were there, locked in their cells. They were safe from the dead, but were trapped from survival. That seems more like purgatory than anything else. You don't want to die, but you don't have the option to live. Either starve to death or be eaten. Chills ran down my spine. For the first time, I felt sorry for the inmates, the guards, anyone trapped inside. They thought prison was a cage before, now it was a tomb.

"How about some target practice?" Sarah asked from the turret.

"No, save the ammo. Don't worry baby, you'll get your chance." Eric replied.
It slightly stung me when he called her baby.

"That prison's a ticking time bomb. When that fence comes down, there'll be a flood of dead leaving there."

"Imagine what it's like inside. Dark tunnels of death, the living trapped inside cages. I couldn't imagine life worse than that." I said, cringing.

"I don't want to imagine. A good buddy of mine is in prison right now. I wonder everyday if he's still alive."

"Eric you have a buddy in prison? Do you mind asking what he's doing there?"

"It's not for anything you might imagine. We went through selection for Special Forces together. We became good friends during our time there, and after graduation we were assigned to the same unit. We deployed to Afghanistan together, and we fought together. I can't count how many times we nearly died there. After our tour we were invited to selection for Delta Forces, but I blew a knee out on a HALO jump, and I was ordered to a regular line unit. He was practically twice my age and he made it. Last I heard he was assigned to some top secret weapons project, but somehow ended up in prison shortly after. He wasn't the type of guy that would steal or leak information, so I don't know what happened. That's the last I ever heard of Ben Oslo."

"Government secrets huh? Conspiracy theories?"

"That Cloak and Dagger shit ended after the Cold War. Nobody fights like that anymore."

"You're saying your friend was trustworthy, I'm just saying big brother can be shady. Our government did just nuke my hometown."

"Yeah I haven't been able to figure that out. I've met our president, and he's not that kind of guy."

"Well who would have control of nuclear missiles if not the president?"

"I don't know."

We could see the skyline of Houston in the distance. The skyscrapers stood tall, no smoke coming from them and no mushroom cloud. The sight was slightly relieving, because we didn't want to go through the city after dark. The sun would be down in about an hour, hopefully by the time we were on the other side. As we got closer, the conversations in the truck got quieter. Eric told Sarah to be ready on the gun, looking for any threats. The buildings along the outskirts of the city were empty, both looted and burned out. The traffic was always terrible, now the cars would never move. Roads everywhere were littered with burned car shells and wreckage. It was like time was accelerated here. The grass was tall and growing through every crack in the empty streets. The buildings had already begun falling apart, most windows were smashed out. I joked with Eric about the sight.

"Looks like everything's normal here."

"Yep. Just like it's always been."

Our humor was silenced when we both saw the cluttered road ahead. As we got closer to downtown, more cars filled the road and it was getting harder to maneuver through the wrecks. The skyscrapers loomed over us, casting dark shadows across the wide highway. As the skies grew darker, Eric turned on the truck's lights. The skyscrapers that lined the highway had boards over the bottom two floor's windows, and several of the windows all the way to the roof had been smashed out. Inside I saw a few offices illuminated with lanterns, and people standing beside them, watching us.

"There are survivors in those buildings." I said.

"Yeah, but nobody's trying to flag us down. I don't like this." Eric replied, in a worried tone.

Making a tight turn around a burned out bus turned sideways on the highways, we saw the road ahead was completely blocked by wrecked cars. There was no squeezing through. Just before the pile up began, there was an open path to an off ramp, leading into downtown.

"Well that's convenient." I said, trying to bring light to the situation.

"This is a god damn ambush." Eric replied, quickly darkening the situation.

"Why do you say that?"

"The wrecked cars we've been passing made S-curves, like a serpentine to slow down traffic. Now our only path is to an off ramp that leads into downtown, where there are people watching us from a high vantage point. It's an ambush if I've ever seen one."

"What do you recommend? We have to go through here, at least while there's still some sunlight."

"I agree. Just be ready. Sarah get ready girl, this could get interesting."

We crept down the off ramp, doing about 30 mph. Eric got on the radio to notify the trucks behind us to be cautious, with rounds loaded in every rifle. The streets below the highway were dark; we could only see a few blocks even with the lights on. At the intersection at the end of the ramp, more wrecked cars guided us to turn right, taking us further from the highway. I was starting to suspect Eric was right. Another block down the wreckage guided us to a left turn, between towering office buildings. The moment we turned left our jaws dropped. A horde of dead filled the road as far as we could see. Hundreds, no, thousands of walkers filled the streets, all turning towards us as our headlight struck them.

"Sarah it's time to rock 'n roll!" Eric shouted to her.

"Fuck it; they know we're here now!" He said as he pressed play on the sound system Cretes installed. An adrenaline fueled scream of heavy metal blasted through the speakers.

I heard the 'Ka-shunk' of the Ma Deuce as she chambered the first round.

BLAP!BLAP!BLAP!BLAP!BLAP!BLAP!BLAP!   The   gun boomed above us, echoing off the buildings around us, deafening the inside of the truck. Brass casings were falling to the floor. In front of us a path was being cleared, as arms and torsos were getting ripped apart by the monstrous bullets. Shredded corpses fell to the ground, leaving a bloody mist where they once stood. Eric mashed the accelerator and we began rolling over soupy bodies. The MRAP bounced up and down as we drove through the horde. Beside us were hungry faces, running into the side of the truck. I could hear their fingertips ripping on the side of the armor as they tried to claw their way in. We made it two blocks into the horde when the final round on the belt fired, and the weapon stopped. Our path quickly filled with walking dead, moving towards us with arms outstretched.

"Reload! Hurry!"

"I'm trying! The ammo weighs a fucking ton!"

Our homemade plow began pushing the initial wave back, but another twenty feet in the horde the truck began to bog down. Ray and Jake popped up through the rear roof hatches, shooting their assault rifles into the crowd. They were dropping bodies with each shot, but where one fell another filled in.

"We don't have enough bullets for all of them!" I yelled to Eric.

"It's too late now!" He returned.

I saw flashes of light from the windows above, but instead of seeing blood splatter, I heard the bullets tinking against the armor. The rear hatches slammed shut, Ray and Jake falling to the floor.

"They're fucking shooting at us!" Jake yelled to us.

"Why are they shooting us?! Sarah shoot the windows!"

I couldn't tell who was yelling anymore, there were gunshots all around us, and the engine roared, struggling to keep us moving. Sarah loaded the Ma Deuce again, then thundered rounds into the nearby buildings. The bullets were tearing away at the walls, I thought they would stop shooting as us, but they didn't.

"Sarah clear us a path or we're going to stall out!" Eric ordered.

Despite getting shot at, she did as told and cleared us another block of movement. The engine opened up as the truck rolled forward again, bouncing over the bodies. The trucks behind us stayed close to our back end, hoping to get out of this soon. With room left to move, Eric slammed on the brakes.

"What are you doing?!" I yelled.

Before he could answer I saw it. A bright flash sent a fireball towards the front of the truck, slamming into the bumper and splintering our push guard with a deafening explosion, sending Sarah falling to the floor of the MRAP.

"That was an RPG!" Eric yelled.

"Why are they trying to kill us?!"

"They want the truck! If we don't get out of here we are all dead!"

"I'm hit!" Sarah yelled.

"Oh shit are you okay?!" I screamed as I sprung out of the chair to help her.

I saw blood spreading across her shirt near her right shoulder. I pressed my hands as hard as I could on the wound to slow the bleeding.

"How bad is she?" Eric yelled over the gunfire.

"She took shrapnel to the shoulder. I think it just grazed her!"

"Keep pressure on it! Use your shirt if you have to!"

When Sarah's gun stopped firing, the path filled in. The streets were now dark with the exception of headlights and sporadic burn barrels in the offices beside us. Flashes from muzzles in every window lit up the sides of the buildings, with fires and explosions sounding off next to us. We were in a war zone. The MRAP wouldn't go any further, and the dead began rocking it back and forth.

This is it. This is where we die. Bullets were whizzing in through the open turret, preventing us from shooting back. Jake slammed the secondary turret door shut, hearing the lead slap the armor. He moved back and took a seat next to Robin, dropping his rifle and clutching her. Eric got out of the driver's seat and came to Sarah's side. Everyone knew this was the end, but nobody wanted to say it. I looked out the front window, praying for a sign of hope. All I saw was more fire. Fireballs from the sky came screaming down.

BOOM! BOOM! BOOM! BOOM! The bottom floors of

the buildings that surrounded us exploded when the fireballs hit, sending bricks and melted glass into the horde, chopping them apart. The fireballs continued hitting the street, destroying everything made of flesh that was in the open. The MRAP vibrated as the ground rumbled around us. The first floor of the buildings were being blown from the inside out. The fireballs stopped, but what looked like a long stream of fire sprayed the upstairs of the buildings, sending a shower of brick and concrete down on the streets. The armed attackers that didn't retreat inside exploded when the stream hit them.

"What the hell is going on?" I asked, looking at Eric.

"Cannons and artillery fire? There's a Spectre Gunship above us!"

"A what?"

He didn't answer, he jumped into the driver's seat and floored the pedal. I grabbed the radio and told the convoy to hammer the pedal and don't let off. The trucks bounced over the bodies and broken bricks that covered the street. We made it almost two blocks when a thunderous roar shook the trucks. The flash from the explosion lit the interior of the cab as it reflected in the side mirrors. I looked back to see one of the skyscrapers crumbling from the bottom floors and crashing to the ground. Another monstrous explosion followed, toppling the building across the street. Dust came roaring past our convoy, the smell of ash and death carried with it.

"What the hell is going on?" I asked Eric, my only input from the military world.

"I don't know David, but I'm not touching the brakes until we reach the coast."

The dead continued moving towards the convoy. Hordes were rushing in from alleys and side streets, filling the avenues ahead of us with flesh hungry attackers. The hordes moved like fluid. The moment a group of corpses were disintegrated another group would fill their spot. There was no end of the dead. With the light push bumper now gone, Eric used the forty ton MRAP's front bumper to push burning cars out of the way, keeping the convoy's momentum. The side streets were blocked with rubble, enough to prevent vehicles from leaving this path of death. The towering skyscrapers that loomed all around us came crashing down as we passed them, the large fireballs coming from the sky continued bringing the structures down. The ground shook around us from explosions, rocking the MRAP back and forth as we pushed towards the end of the ambush. Several times I wriggled my fingers in my ears to check my hearing. I thought my ears were bleeding. The convoy snaked through the wreckages that were meant to slow us down, but if we slowed we'd be crushed from the gunship's cannons. The shooting from the office buildings ceased, but the mutli-barreled cannon from the gunship continued cutting through walls, killing all inside. I stared at the side mirrors, watching the carnage behind us. The city was crumbling behind us, nipping the rear bumper of the last truck. I jumped back in my seat as a semi tractor door screamed past the MRAP, ripping my mirror off.

"The last truck just exploded!" A terrified voice in the radio screamed.

"Say again?!" Eric called back, trying to remain calm.

"The last truck exploded! There's nothing left! They're all dead! Get us out of here Eric!"

There were almost thirty people on that truck. In an instant, they were vaporized. I hope they were dead before their bodies felt the shattering of eardrums and organs liquefying.

Eric maintained the same speed, guiding the MRAP through the wrecked cars and walking dead with precision.

"You heard him Eric, get us out of here!" I yelled.

"And then what?! The moment we leave the safety of the skyscrapers that gunship will crush us!"

"What do we do?! The on ramp is coming up soon! Will the Ma Deuce reach the gunship?!"

"No! We need a fucking miracle!"

A beacon of hope shined a mile down the road in the form

of two trails of smoke from the ground into the sky. The first rocket screamed towards the gunship, but the gunship's flares sent the rocket off course, exploding in open air. The second rocket screamed into the side of the gunship, filling the sky with a hot ball of fire. The explosions behind us stopped. The clatter from the diesel engine was the only rumble now, smoking and sputtering as Eric pushed the engine's limits getting on the highway.

"Did that really just happen?" I asked him.

"I don't know, but we owe somebody a great debt." Eric answered.

I thought there was no better time than the present.

"Ray how about a round of cigars?" I yelled into the cab.

"Are we safe mon?"

"Safe enough. Give me one of those." I heard Jake say.

Exhausted cheers filled the cab of the armored truck. Jake somehow bandaged up Sarah while the bombs were bouncing the truck side to side. She was in pain, but she'd be okay. She was the first to light her cigar.

Our headlights lit the way ahead of us, the wrecked cars getting fewer and fewer. The city had been destroyed by fighting and looting. Many buildings had boarded up windows over broken glass, but there were no signs of life inside. It's not that anybody was hiding, there were no living souls inside. I honestly believe after seeing downtown minimized to rubble, there were no living souls remaining in Houston. The truck behind us reported that two of them had been killed by bullets ripping through the trailer, and three people had minor gunshot wounds. I couldn't stop thinking about the people in the third truck. They took a direct hit through the roof of the trailer, the round was powerful enough to leave a crater under the truck. *We were almost to the coast. Soon these people would be safe. I had no idea where to start once everyone was sailing off and we were still on the docks. Maybe we would travel around, helping out those that needed us. If they needed us. What can we do that they can't...*

"We got company." Eric said, breaking my thoughts.

"Where? What's up?" I looked out the windows, forgetting my mirror had been ripped off.

"There are four trucks behind us about a half mile back. They're not speeding up to our convoy, they're just following from a distance."

I picked up the radio, but the driver behind us came over the net before I could.

"We're being followed! What do we do?!"

"Tell him to calm down." Eric requested.

"Calm down. Are they shooting at you?" I asked.

"No, not shooting at us, but why are they following us?"

"I don't know, but we don't know their intentions yet, so don't do anything drastic. Follow us, and we'll get you to the pier. Once there, look for a ferry with enough room for your truck. We'll stay back and provide security while you're loading up. We're almost there. Hang tight."

I remembered the multitude of ferries around the bay that would take people to the islands that littered the coast. They kept enough fuel in them to run all day, and surely they would have enough to make it to the nearest rig.

"I see water!" Eric observed.

"We're almost there, about three more miles and you'll see a sign with palm trees on it. Turn left at the sign, and we'll be near the docks." I called over the radio.

"Do you think they're hostile?" I asked Eric.

"I don't think so, but because they're not shooting now doesn't mean they won't later. It doesn't make sense to follow us this far if we just passed through their turf. Jake why don't you get on the gun just in case, but don't fire unless they do!" Eric instructed.

Jake kissed Robin and stood up in the turret, facing the gun to the rear. The headlights hit the sign I was looking for, and I pointed out a turn around spot to Eric once we made the left turn into the parking lot. The semi trailer behind us continued to a nearby docked ferry, stopping just short of the chain running across the drive. The passenger got out and dropped the chain, then guided the truck onto the boat. Eric turned the truck sideways to block the road into the harbor, and to protect the others from gunfire. Once the truck stopped on the boat, the deck filled with activity as people exited the truck. The headlights that had been following us stopped side by side fifty feet from us.

"Hurry up!" I yelled to the boat.

The boat's motors fired up moments after I yelled, Eric and me sighing in relief at the sound. We heard doors open and guns chambering rounds towards us now. The headlights and flashlights blinded us from seeing anyone. A stern voice broadcasted over a bullhorn.

"Get down from the turret, do not fire! You will safety your weapons, stay inside your truck, and you will follow us, or you will be fired upon. Do you understand?"

What the hell is going on now?

Jake was quick to get out of the turret. Eric honked the horn and flashed his lights in agreement. Their doors shut quickly and they left in a file, just like they arrived.

"That was pretty organized." I commented to Eric.

"Yes it was, just like we trained in Special Forces."

The trucks used their headlights to instruct us to file in the middle of the convoy. We did as they told, and followed the trucks. Three of them were black suburbans, but the rear truck was an extended cab truck, with a large machine gun mounted in the rear. They guided us through a few small streets between abandoned factories, snaking through the industrial district. Finally we drove through an open garage door into a well lit open warehouse. The windows were blacked out, and the only light emitted through the open bay door. We were guided by a man with an assault rifle to the middle of the warehouse floor. The convoy circled around us, more men with assault rifles stepped out and trained their sights on us the moment their truck stopped. The man with the bullhorn gave us instructions again.

"Open all of your doors and step out of the MRAP without your weapons and move to the back of the MRAP."

We did as we were instructed.

"Lie down on the ground, with your hands behind your back. Remain still as someone comes by and pats you down. Do not speak. Do not move or you will be fired upon."

Two men walked behind the MRAP and cleared the inside with their muzzles.

"Truck is clear."

Three different men pat us down from head to toe, leaving no pocket unchecked.

"They're clear sir."

The man with the bullhorn spoke again.

"Stand up, with your hands down your sides. Do not place your hands in your pockets."

We stood still, but growing impatient with the procedures. The man with the bullhorn waved to someone out of sight, then stood stiff as a board. A man followed by two others approached from an office. Eric stiffened tight as a board, snapping his right hand to his forehead.

"Hello, Mr. President."

CHAPTER TWENTY SEVEN

I couldn't believe it. The leader of the free world stood ten feet from us.

"At ease soldier."

Eric lowered his salute and put his hands behind the small of his back.

"Sergeant First Class Mason is it?"

"Roger Mr. President."

"You were assigned to Special Forces Group Eagle correct?"

"Roger Mr. President."

"Who are they?" The president pointed to us.

"They have helped me lead many people to safety, and they are a great asset to our cause."

The President paused for a moment.

"Do you mean that truck of people that left on the ferry?"

"Yes Mr. President."

"We tried to stop you, but you did a good job of blocking the road. Let's hope the pirates don't get them. What exactly is your cause Sergeant?"

"We have tried to help all those we can, Mr. President."

"Perfect. All of you follow me please."

The President and the two armed men led us into the office with two armed men standing at attention beside the door. Once inside, the riflemen closed the door and stood at attention. There were two gray haired men in fatigues sitting at the large round table, instructing us to sit down as well. We gave our names and birthplace to the men, along with any city in the states we'd spent more than three months working in. The man in fatigues at the President's right side wore four stars on his collar, and began speaking.

"Ladies and Gentlemen you are aware of the threats that surround us."

"Yeah like the nuclear missiles you used to destroy our

cities!" Sarah interrupted.

"Ma'am please, I'll explain everything. We are not responsible for the nuclear strikes that have occurred."
Eric put his hand on Sarah's leg to calm her down, then addressed the General.

"Sir what is going on? The missiles that took down the Spectre Gunship, was that your operation?"

"Yes Sergeant that was us. We picked up a half dozen stinger missiles in Mexico. We were monitoring airwaves while you were in the planning phase of bringing those people to the oil rig. We knew the quickest route would be through the city, but we had no way of contacting you about the ambush. Our radios are not equipped to broadcast over civilian channels."

"Ok Sir, so who was in the gunship?"

"That gunship belonged to the PRAC, the People's Revolutionary Army Command."

"Who are they sir?"
The General took a drink of water, motioning to one of the guards to bring us water also. He finished the glass, and then began.

"During the wars in the Middle East, our government grew divided about the future of the United States and Arab relations. Most of what you have seen in the media represented the mainstream ideology of our government's intentions. However, there were a small few that felt differently about the outcome of the wars and felt we should take all the power from the Middle East and control the oil production there. Their intentions were fueled by fears of retaliation from the Middle East, mimicking the World Trade Center attack. These people held high security positions in our government and worked in every branch. They proposed an idea to Congress, and were approved to design a system that could control some of America's greatest military assets, from unmanned aerial bombers to nuclear missiles, all from a mobile, bombproof computer."

"Sir why in God's name would they create that?" I asked.

"David right? WAHBL was created to defend our nation against any attack, foreign or domestic. That little incident off the coast of Iceland just spun the world out of control. At the first sign of infection in the major cities, priority for specialized Delta Teams was to secure WAHBL and take it deep inside a mountain at a location known to only a few. The team was led by General Stinson. We believe he's the leader of the rogue faction."

"Wobble sir? And General Stinson?" Eric asked, confused.

"When All Hell Breaks Loose, Sergeant. PRAC emerged from the shadows, and the Delta operators tied with this organization took WAHBL to the secure site, and have been controlling military assets from there. Not even the president knows where they are located. That Gunship that brought the city down around you was controlled by them. General Stinson is in command of his own army, many of which are specially trained soldiers that have gone rogue as well. Our intelligence says they believed you to be a part of us, the remaining few of the U.S. Government, because you were in a military vehicle."

"Why are you telling us about this?" I asked the General.

"Yes sir, and why are you in Houston?" Eric continued.
The soldier brought us each bottled water. This was the first real clean water we'd had in weeks. I was glad to see he didn't offer us that cheap Genesis water.

"With the initial infection reaching Washington D.C., the President boarded Air Force One with most of the people you see here. We were flying to NORAD when the pilot reported seeing a predator drone following us. The two fighter pilots escorting us engaged the target, one of them destroyed by the missile from the drone that was locked on to Air Force One. God bless him for his sacrifice. The other pilot blew up the drone, but was destroyed over Kansas from a Surface to Air Missile site controlled by WAHBL. The President ordered the pilot to fly to an undisclosed airstrip in Mexico. We've been carefully maneuvering from city to city to get back into the states, building our numbers and planning an attack against PRAC to retrieve WAHBL."

We were at a loss. Speechless. Hope is the most important aspect of survival, and it was lost. The living dead consumed most of the world, and the only living souls left were determined to destroy the rest. I looked at the others, remembering the conversations we'd had about changing the world for the better. Ray stared at the table inches in front of him. Jake and Robin were holding hands, unsure of what to do. Sarah was biting her lip like she always does when she's nervous. Eric was looking at me, no fear in his eyes. Fuck it.

"What's your plan General?" I asked.

"We must get WAHBL back, or destroy it. Keep in mind you will be going up against the most advanced military weaponry in the world. Reports are coming in from around the nation of the country's status. The infection has spread from coast to coast and there is no safe quarantine zone that we are aware of. The state governments and state lines no longer exist. The country has gone tribal. Small factions are establishing outposts everywhere. Whether their intentions are hostile or friendly, we will not know. You will join a highly trained group of individuals to find WAHBL, and eliminate all those involved with it's attacks."

Eric started the questioning.

"Sir how are we supposed to find WAHBL?"

"We believe its location is deep in the Virginia hills. The east coast remains as baron, blackened wastelands from the nuclear attacks, which further leads us to believe General Stinson's location is underground. By eliminating the society above, he's provided security for the compound. Scout teams have reported several sightings of hordes that survived the nuclear fallout, but we aren't sure yet how the radiation has affected them. We know of a man that used to work with WAHBL, and he knows of the secret location, if he's still alive."

Everyone was alert now. I could see the interest in their faces. Robin was a little uneasy about the idea, but she had

280

nowhere to go, and she wanted to stay with Jake. Ray wasn't as excited about joining an army, he just wanted to help rebuild. I knew Sarah would go if Eric was involved, and there was no way he wasn't going to leave this operation. I wanted to stop General Stinson before he was in complete control of the apocalypse, and I wasn't letting Sarah out of my sight.

"General you said you know a man that could help us find WAHBL?" I asked.

"Yes, but it's a long shot. He's confined in a prison at Fort Leavenworth, Kansas. He was invited to be a part of the rogue unit, but when he turned down General Stinson, The General had him put in Administrative Segregation as a security risk. He's probably hidden in a spider hole somewhere deep in the prison. We'll need to find him and break him out so he can lead us to WAHBL, that's where we are going after this briefing. His name is Benjamin Oslo. We have a safe facility in Oklahoma that we will gather at and train our army. The President himself will be there to watch over and advise. I won't lie to you, this mission will be the most difficult that any of us have faced. General Stinson is determined to be the next leader of the global superpower and he must be stopped. He stands in the way of the next evolution of mankind."

We looked at each other in agreement. This was insane. We were being asked to play a part in the most important era of human history. There was nothing behind us, so the only thing we could do was move forward.

"When are we going to Oklahoma General?" Mason asked.

"Now."

EPILOGUE

Everyone was gathered in the dining hall for Ted's announcement. Voices filled the air, along with the clattering of trays hitting tables from tired arms. Tommy was more excited about the meatloaf and skillet potatoes than anything Ted would have to say. It had been a long day, and the meatloaf was the first step to relaxation for Tommy. He smiled as he prepared himself with fork and knife to dig into the hot aromatic plate of deliciousness. Just as he made his first cut into the meat, Ted entered the hall.

The noise quieted down to just below the usual chatter, but every face was turned towards Ted as he made his way to the microphone and speaker that was set up minutes prior for his announcement. Everyone was ready to leave this rig. Tired of working nonstop, and tired of being here. The next rotation was due last week, but the ship never came. They wanted to see their families. They wanted to see their friends. They wanted to be home. Ted thumped the microphone to check it's volume.

"Hello? Hello? Can everybody hear me?"

After a few thumbs up from the back he continued.

"Good evening everyone! How is everybody doing tonight? As you all know we should have been on a boat home last week, but our replacements never got here. I have some unfortunate news. I talked on the phone with my boss this afternoon, and he has informed me that things have gotten a little wild back home. For reasons unknown, there have been power outages nationwide. These outages have knocked out much of the communications through the nation and overseas, thus why none of us have been able to call home lately. We are sending the small ship we have here over to Iceland to get us as many of the supplies we can get that were supposed to be on the ship that didn't come. The primary crew and some strong hands are requested to load the ship from the mainland, but that can be addressed later. I don't want anybody to panic about the situation at home; I've been informed there is no reason for alarm. Until the situation is resolved however, I'm sorry to tell you that we will be the working force on this rig."

Ted took a moment to let the news sink in, and then to allow everyone to exhale.

"Now who's ready for the good news?" he didn't get the cheers he was looking for.

"Aquafex has agreed to pay everyone overtime pay until the next crew arrives!"

The solemn faces turned to smiles when the room heard the news. A few cheers and whistles sounded off as a few people clapped.

Ted turned off the microphone as he made his 'open door policy' statement again, then left the dining facility. Tommy took another heaping bite of his meatloaf, the meat cooling off from sitting. He hadn't even noticed how slow he was eating as he listened to Ted. A young white man beside him leaned over to share his sunny outlook.

"Overtime pay man! How awesome is that! Keep me here for another month I don't care!"

Tommy smiled to please the man's motivated spirits, but he couldn't get excited. He wanted to go home.

I should have gone home with David and Jake when I had the chance.

He tapped his fork on the plate beside the half eaten meatloaf, trying to encourage himself to finish it.

Maybe it won't be long. Maybe the next crew will get here next week. On a good note I'll be making a ton of money while I'm here. Maybe it won't be so bad. It's just like working on a rig back home; I just can't...go....home. Sigh.

The man spoke again to Tommy, trying to get a rise out of him to match his own excitement.

"I hope that ship doesn't come for another month!"

Made in the USA
Lexington, KY
01 May 2018